Linda Turner

The Lady In Red

Silhouette®

INTIMATE MOMENTS®

Published by Silhouette Books

America's Publisher of Contemporary Romance

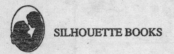 SILHOUETTE BOOKS

ISBN 0-373-07763-7

THE LADY IN RED

Chapter 1

"What do you mean you don't want me to cover sports?" Blake Nickels demanded in surprise. "I'm a sports reporter, Tom. And a damn good one, too."

"And at one time you were a hell of a news reporter, too," Tom Edwards reminded him as he searched his desk drawers for a stick of gum. He was in the process of giving up smoking after twenty years, and he scowled when he could find nothing but a eucalyptus cough drop to fight his craving. "In fact," he continued as he popped the foul tasting candy into his mouth, "the way I remember it, you won several national awards."

"That was before," he growled.

He didn't have to explain before what—they both knew. Once Blake had been one of the hottest crime reporters in New York City. Then an informant had given him some information that had ended up costing the snitch his life. Devastated, he'd packed up his toys and gotten out of the game, moving from the notoriety he'd earned in New York to the obscurity of covering sports in a town in New Mexico that was no bigger than a pimple on the map. That had been eight years ago. As far as Tom knew, Blake hadn't gone within a hundred miles of a police scanner since.

Which made what he had to ask him all the more difficult. Wishing he had a cigarette, Tom pushed himself to his feet to restlessly prowl the confines of his office. "Lynn Phillips took maternity leave four months early this morning on the advice of her doctor," he said grimly. "If she doesn't get complete bed rest, she could lose the baby."

· On the job for only two days, Blake racked his brain for a face to put with the name. "Phillips. The crime beat, right? Oh, no, you don't!"

"Now, Blake, don't go flying off the handle. Just give me a chance to explain—"

"You crafty son of a bitch, there's nothing to explain. I can read you like a book. I know you, remember?"

They'd been best friends since grade school—there wasn't anything that one didn't know about the other, including how the other's mind worked. "You called me up offering my own column on the sports page just to get me over here, didn't you?" Blake demanded, jumping to his feet to glare at Tom. "It was all just a trick."

"You were thinking about leaving Lordsburg anyway. You said so yourself. Ever since Trina ran off with that truck driver and married him when you weren't looking—"

"Leave Trina the hell out of this," he growled. "The woman's name is no longer in my vocabulary."

"Fine," Tom agreed. "Then what about Pop? With your parents going off to France for a year, you know you were worried sick about him being here in San Antonio all by himself. By accepting my job offer, you killed two birds with one stone—you got away from *that woman* in Lordsburg and you could come home to watch over your grandfather until your parents get back. Instead of yelling at me, you ought to be thanking me, you old goat. I did you a favor."

"Favor?" Blake choked. If he hadn't been so irritated, he would have laughed. Leave it to Tom to twist things so he looked like a choirboy. "You call manipulating me to get me on the payroll, then assigning me to the crime beat a *favor*? If you'd mentioned what you were planning at the beginning, I never would have left New Mexico."

"I wasn't planning anything. I wasn't," he insisted when Blake merely lifted a dark brow at him. "Oh, I knew Lynn was pregnant, of course, and that she'd be leaving eventually, but I expected to have another four months to fill the position if I couldn't talk you into it. Dammit, Blake, take it, will you? At least for a little while until I can hire somebody else? You're the only one I've got on staff who can give Sabrina Jones some competition."

Blake might not have known Lynn Phillips and most of the rest of the *Times* staff, but he'd only been in town one day when he'd read Sabrina Jones's bylined story on the front page of the San Antonio *Daily Record*, the other major paper in town. She was good, dammit. Good enough to be writing for any major newspaper in the country, which was, no doubt, why Tom was worried. The *Times* and *Daily Record* were in a knock-down-drag-out, no-holds-barred subscription war right now, and the *Times* was going to get its butt kicked without someone who could give the Jones woman a run for her money.

"I'm out of practice," he hedged. "It's been eight years since I've done that beat."

"I don't care if it's been a hundred. You're the best damn reporter I've ever known. That includes sports, crime—hell, even the obits. The second you catch the scent of a story, you'll be off and running, just like old times. It'll be great."

His expression shuttered, Blake couldn't share his enthusiasm. He wanted to tell him that he didn't care how many murders and sex crimes he covered, it would never be like old times again, but he was afraid Tom was right. He'd really enjoyed covering sports, but nothing had ever challenged him like crime. It was like an addiction that had called to something in his blood—he'd thrived on it. And in the process, he'd lost his objectivity and become obsessed with getting the story. Nothing else had mattered. And because of that single-mindedness, a man had lost his life.

A man who had trusted him, Blake remembered grimly. A man who had seen something he shouldn't have and who should have gone to the police for protection. Blake had sworn not to reveal his identity and he'd stuck by that, but it hadn't done any good. The day after the story hit the paper, the informant had turned up dead, supposedly killed from asphyxiation due to running his car in a closed garage. The police had ruled it a suicide and let it go. Blake had known better. The prominent businessman the informant had exposed as the brains behind an extensive money-laundering and drug-smuggling operation had obviously gotten to him and shut him up for good.

Almost a decade had passed since then, but just thinking about it brought it all back like it was yesterday. He couldn't go through that again. He couldn't put someone at risk just because of a damn story. It wasn't worth it.

So what are you going to do, Nickels? You quit the job in Lordsburg. Remember? You can go back, of course. But what about Pop?

His grandfather, eighty-three and forgetful at times, had no business living alone. Blake could try to convince him to go to New Mexico with him, but the old man could be as stubborn as a mule when he wanted to be. And if he wouldn't go to Paris for a year with Blake's parents, he sure wasn't going to leave his home and everything familiar in San Antonio for Lordsburg.

Stuck between a rock and a hard place, Blake had no

choice but to accept the inevitable. "All right." He sighed. "I'll take over for Lynn. For *now*," he stressed when his friend grinned broadly. "So don't go getting any ideas that this is permanent. As soon as you can hire someone to replace Lynn, I'm going back to sports. I mean it, Tom. I see that gleam in your eye—I know what you're up to. You're hoping that once I get a taste of hard news again, you won't be able to pry me away from it with a crowbar, but that's not going to happen. I'm a sports writer, dammit."

Not sure if he was trying to convince him or himself, Tom only grinned. Blake might think he could walk away from investigative reporting twice in a lifetime, but Tom knew better. One good story. That's all it would take for Blake to be hooked.

The woman was young—mid-twenties—pretty, and dead.

Arriving at the murder scene only seconds after the cops themselves, Sabrina got her first look at the victim at the same time that the two officers did. Her eyes wide open, a look of horror etched in her pale, stone-cold face, the dead woman lay just inside the open front door of her house and appeared to have been there all night. Dressed in a lacy white nightgown and negligee stained with her own blood, she'd been shot in the heart, probably seconds after she'd opened the door.

"Jesus," Andy Thompson, the younger of the two cops and a rookie, muttered. "She looks like she was waiting for a lover."

"If that's who popped her, then she was a lousy judge of men," his partner, Victor Rodriguez, said flatly. "I'll call the ME and Detective Kelly. This one's got his name written all over it."

He turned and only just then became aware of Sabrina's presence. An old friend, he scowled disapprovingly.

"What the heck do you think you're doing in here, Sabrina? This is a crime scene."

Not the least bit intimidated, she flashed her dimples at him. "No kidding? Then I guess that's why I'm here. C'mon, Vic, gimme a break. Let me look around. I'll be out of here before Kelly arrives, I swear."

"That's what you said the last time, and I got a royal chewing out for it." Blocking her path, he refused to let her peer around his broad shoulders and shooed her outside instead. "You know the rules, Sabrina. You want the particulars, you wait till the detective gets here. He'll tell you everything he thinks you need to know."

"You're all heart, Rodriguez," she grumbled as he escorted her well out into the yard, then blockaded the crime scene with yellow police tape to keep her and the curious out. "Kelly won't tell me squat until he's good and ready, and you know it."

"Wah, wah!" he said, grinning as he mimicked a baby's cry. "Quit your crying, Jones. You'll get your story. You always do."

"That's because I'm good at what I do," she called after him as he turned and disappeared back inside. And because she didn't stand around and wait for someone to hand her a story on a platter.

Her hands on her hips, she surveyed the neighborhood. Quiet and moderately affluent, with neatly trimmed yards and houses that would easily sell for a hundred grand or more, it wasn't the type of place where you expected a shooting, let alone a murder. From the small, unobtrusive signs in the front yards, it was obvious that most of the homes had security systems, including the victim's. Yet a woman had been killed—shot, no less—and no one had noticed anything unusual during the night.

Wondering how that could have happened, she headed for the house next door. When Kelly got there, he wouldn't like it that she'd snooped around before his men had a chance to question possible witnesses. But then again, she thought, mischief flashing in her brown eyes, it wouldn't be the first time she'd skirted the rules to get a story. Kelly had to be used to it by now.

Her chances of finding anyone at home at eleven o'clock in the morning on a weekday were slim to none, so she wasn't surprised when no one answered at the first four doors she knocked on. On the fifth, she got lucky.

The man who opened the door to the house directly across the street from the victim's was thin and balding, with a face full of wrinkles and piercing blue eyes that were as sharp as a hawk's. Peering over the top of his bifocals at her, he scowled in annoyance. "If you're selling something door-to-door, lady, you didn't pick a very good day for it. There's been a murder across the street, and any second now this whole block's going to be crawling with police."

"I know, sir. I'm a reporter. Sabrina Jones, with the *Daily Record.* I was wondering if I might ask you a few questions?"

"I didn't see jack squat," he retorted. "Just her body lying in the doorway when I came outside to get my paper this morning. I take the *Times.*"

Sabrina bit back a smile. Readers, as loyal as fans to their favorite pro team, always seemed to be under the mistaken impression that they couldn't talk to her if they didn't read the *Record.* "It's a good paper," she said easily, her brown eyes twinkling. "But so is the *Daily Record.* Did you know the victim?"

His gaze drifting back to the still figure now draped in a yellow plastic sheet, he nodded somberly. "Her name was Tanya Bishop. She was a sweet girl. And smart. A legal secretary. From what I heard, she made good money, but she didn't blow it. She socked it away and bought that house, and she wasn't even thirty yet."

His loyalty to the *Times* forgotten in his need to talk

about the victim, he reminisced about her at length while Sabrina jotted down notes and an image of Tanya Bishop formed in her mind. A young professional woman who was responsible and hardworking, she wasn't the type to make enemies. She didn't drink or smoke or party till all hours of the night. And she was dead…just like Charlene McClintock.

Barely two weeks ago, Charlene had also been found dead. Like Tanya, she'd been young, pretty and professional. Everyone who had known her had loved her. Yet someone had shot her in the heart…just like Tanya Bishop. The similarities between the two murders was not lost on her.

"Were you home all night, Mr.—?"

"Dexter," he replied automatically. "Monroe Dexter. Yeah, I was home. And let me tell you, nobody sleeps lighter than I do. A shift in the wind will wake me up, but I didn't hear anything last night." Emotion suddenly clogging his throat, he swallowed. "What I want to know is how the hell somebody could kill that poor girl without making a sound."

Sabrina was wondering the same thing. After thanking Mr. Dexter for his help, she questioned the two other neighbors that were home, but apparently no one had heard anything during the night, not even a dog barking, or noticed any visitors at the Bishop house. Which was damn odd, Sabrina thought, on a street where the homeowners had formed a neighborhood watch to watch over each other.

Questions buzzing like bees in her brain, she headed back to the crime scene to see if the police had found any more answers than she had. As she crossed Tanya Bishop's front yard, she saw that Detective Kelly and the medical examiner had arrived and were in deep conversation as they examined the body. Anxious to catch what they were saying, she hurried forward and never saw the man who deliberately stepped in front of her until she plowed into him.

"Oh! I'm sorry. I didn't see you—"

"I didn't mean to knock you out of your shoes, ma'am, but you don't want to go in there. It's a pretty gory scene—"

They both spoke at once, each rushing to apologize as they broke apart. Feeling like she'd just run full tilt into a brick wall, Sabrina laughed shakily, intending to take all the blame for not watching where she was going. But the second her eyes lifted to the man in front of her, her mind just seemed to go blank and she couldn't do anything but stare.

He towered over her own five-foot-four frame by a good eight inches and wore a black cowboy hat that only added to his impressive height. In spite of that, he didn't appear to be the type of man who would draw a second glance in passing. His face was too ordinary, too lived-in, like the boy next door who grew up into just an average Joe. But looks, she decided, studying him, were deceptive when it came to this man. His mouth seemed to quirk with perpetual good humor, but his angular jaw looked as unyielding as granite, and deep in the depths of his green eyes was a sharpness that missed little. It was, to say the least, an interesting combination.

Intrigued, Sabrina reminded herself she was there to investigate the city's latest murder, not to drool over a tall, dark stranger who seemed to think she was a little woman who'd faint at the sight of blood. Amused, she said dryly, "I've already been in there, and you're right, it is gory. Now if you'll excuse me, I need to talk to Detective Kelly."

Before she could step around him, however, he moved, lightning-quick, to block her path again. Her patience quickly reaching its limit, Sabrina stopped just shot of plowing into his broad chest again and frowned up at him in growing irritation. "Look, I don't know who you think you are, but I've got work to do and you're in my way. Do you mind?"

"Not at all," he said easily. But he didn't move. His mouth twitching with the promise of a smile, he stared down at her searchingly. "What do you mean, you've already been in there? Are you a cop?"

"No, I'm not. I'm a reporter. Sabrina Jones, with the *Daily Record*. Now, if you'll excuse me..."

Stunned, Blake stared down at her in disbelief. *This* was Sabrina Jones? The pride of the *Daily Record*? The ruthless, go-for-the-throat investigative reporter who would do anything short of murder for a story? The way Tom had talked about her, Blake had pictured her as some type of Amazon with more guts than a Marine and a hide like leather. A pushy broad with a reputation for being as tenacious as a bulldog, she should have been tough, brash, and hard as nails.

But the woman who stood before him was anything but hard. In fact, dressed in a gauzy summer dress that draped her slender figure in a cloud of pale pink and fell to just below her knees, her black hair a mass of curls that tumbled artlessly down her back, she looked as soft as cotton candy. A very delectable, feminine piece of cotton candy, he thought with a frown as his gaze slid over her with an ease that had his jaw clenching on an oath. She was short, her bones delicate, the curves revealed by the gently clinging material of her dress enticing. And she was wearing sandals.

His eyes lingering on her toes, he found himself fighting a smile. This was his competition? This dainty woman who looked like she'd swoon at the sight of blood? Oh, she was a good writer, he admitted to himself. He'd read her stuff. She had a way with words. But so did he. And the day that he couldn't write circles around this slip of femininity was the day he'd pack up his computer and find something else to do for a living.

His green eyes starting to twinkle, he deliberately stepped in front of her again, blocking her way. "So you're Sabrina Jones," he drawled. "I've got to admit, you're not what I expected."

Brought up short, her nose just inches from his broad chest, Sabrina glared at him in growing exasperation. "Look, cowboy, I don't know who or what you are, but I've got work to do, and you're in my way."

"Get used to it," he said, grinning as he watched temper simmer in her brown eyes. "I plan to be in your way a lot more before all is said and done."

Her gaze narrowing dangerously, she arched a brow at him. "And how do you plan to do that, Mr....?"

"Nickels," he supplied, holding out his hand as he grinned down at her. "Blake Nickels. With the *Times*. Lynn Phillips had to take maternity leave early. I'm her replacement."

Sudden understanding dawning, Sabrina eyed his hand warily, amusement flirting with the edges of her mouth. The man had more than his share of cockiness. And charm. But if he thought he could best her in a war of words, he was sadly mistaken. Placing her hand in his for a perfunctory shake, she purred, "I can't say I've ever read any of your work, Mr. Nickels. Should I be quaking in my shoes?"

"If you know what's good for you."

She laughed; she couldn't help it. He certainly didn't lack confidence. But then again, neither did she. "Sorry," she said with a chuckle, "but I don't scare that easily."

"Maybe you should. I'm good, Ms. Jones. Real good."

"And modest, too," she tossed back, grinning.

Undaunted, he only shrugged, devilment dancing in his eyes. "No brag, just fact. Check me out, sweetheart. You might be impressed."

"Maybe on a slow day when I've got nothing better to do," she agreed sassily. Her gaze moving past him to the crime scene, she watched the ambulance crew that had arrived with the ME load Tanya Bishop's body onto a stretcher and knew that the police were just about finished with their investigation of the crime scene. "Right now, I've got work to do. See you around, cowboy."

She darted around him before he could stop her and quickly ducked under the police tape strung between the trees in the front yard. Swearing, Blake started after her just as a tall, redheaded man in a rumpled suit stepped out of the house and caught sight of Sabrina bearing down on him. "Why did I know you'd be here, Jones?" he groaned. "Every time I turn around, there you are. Are you following me?"

"I got here before you did," she reminded him with a cheeky grin. "So what's going on, Sam? From where I'm standing, this looks an awful lot like the McClintock murder."

His brows snapping together in a fierce glare, he gave her a hard look that had Back Off written all over it. "You start a rumor like that, Jones, and I'm going to hold you personally responsible. There's nothing to indicate that the two murders are in any way connected."

Frowning, stuck in the position of playing catch-up and not liking it one little bit, Blake stepped forward. "Blake Nickels, with the *Times,*" he told the other man. "What's this about another murder, detective? I'm new in town and this is the first I've heard about it."

Sam Kelly introduced himself, then explained, "Charlene McClintock, one of the city's up-and-coming attorneys, was killed two weeks ago, but there's no connection—"

"Was there any sign of forced entry or signs of a struggle?" Sabrina cut in.

"No, but—"

"Does anything appear to be missing?"

"Not that we can tell at this time," he said patiently, "but we won't know for sure until we can find a friend or neighbor to go through the place. You're beating a dead horse here, Jones. Drop it."

Sabrina, well used to holding her own with Kelly, had no intention of doing any such thing. "I got it from one of the neighbors that Tanya Bishop was a legal secretary, Sam. That means two women, young and pretty and both involved in the legal profession, have been shot to death within a two-week period, apparently by someone they knew. Are you really going to stand there and tell me that they're unrelated incidents? C'mon, Sam, get real!"

"I'm not telling you anything more than I already have until the lab results come back and we have time to look into both murders further," he said curtly. "Until then, I suggest you stick to the facts and not jump to any unwarranted conclusions. Now if you'll excuse me, I've got to question the neighbors, then get back to the station." With a nod to both of them, he stepped past the two reporters.

Staring after him, Blake swore under his breath. So much for his first day on the job. He'd stood there flat-footed and listened to Sabrina ask questions he hadn't even known to ask, and there hadn't been a damn thing he could do about it. It wouldn't, he promised himself, happen again.

And the sooner Sabrina Jones knew that, the better. Glancing down at her, he found her watching him with brown eyes that were just a little too smug for his liking. Oh, she was something, he thought, fighting a reluctant grin. She thought she had him right where she wanted him, a distant second to her first place in a race in which she had the head start. She was all but crowing and she hadn't even reached the finish line yet. The darn woman didn't realize that he had her right where he wanted her.

"I wouldn't start celebrating just yet if I were you," he

warned dryly. "Just because I was unprepared this time doesn't mean I will be again."

Not the least bit worried, she only cocked her head at him and teased playfully, "What's the matter, Nickels? You don't like coming in second to a woman? Get used to it, cowboy. I'm just hitting my stride."

That was the wrong thing to say to a man who thrived on a challenge. "Oh, really?" he drawled. "Well, just for the record, sweetheart, the fact that you're a woman has nothing to do with anything. I don't care if you're purple— I don't like eating your dust. Next time I'll be ready for you."

It was an out-and-out warning, one that only a foolish woman would have ignored. And Sabrina was nobody's fool. Blake Nickels might have been a little out of his depth this time, but as she watched him stalk off to his car, she had a feeling that he was going to be a force to be reckoned with. His eyes had held a sharp intelligence, and then there was that jaw of his—as hard and immovable as concrete, it had had determination written all over it. Not that she was worried, she quickly assured herself as she turned to her own car. This was her town, her beat. Blake Nickels was the new kid on the block. She knew her own abilities and could handle anything the man could dish out.

She deliberately pushed him from her thoughts, but hours later, when she was back at her desk at the *Daily Record* working on her story about the city's latest murder, it wasn't poor Tanya Bishop's lifeless body that stirred to life in her mind's eye—it was the memory of Blake Nickels' smile. Wicked, teasing, dangerous. No man had a right to look so good just by curling up the edge of his mouth, she decided, trying to work up a good case of irritation. A frown furrowing her brow, she tried to force her attention back to what was sure to be a front-page story, but just thinking about Blake and that grin of his made her lips twitch.

And that worried her. Blake Nickels was full of charm and devilment, and she wouldn't, couldn't, like him. She didn't care if he was the next best thing to sliced bread, he was the opposition, the competition, a male chauvinist who didn't like standing around with his hands in his pockets while she asked all the questions. Given the chance, he'd snitch a story right out from under her nose if she relaxed her guard for so much as a second.

If that wasn't reason enough to avoid him like the plague, the fact that she found herself thinking about him when she had a hot story to write was. She wasn't looking for a man to distract her, or do anything else with her. The women in her family didn't handle relationships well. Between the two of them, her mother and grandmother had been married eight times, and Sabrina had decided at an early age that she wasn't going to follow in their footsteps. Then, three years ago, she'd met Jeff Harper.

She winced at the memory. All her fine resolves had gone up in smoke the first time he'd kissed her. In spite of the fact that they'd had absolutely nothing in common, she'd fallen for him like a ton of bricks. When he'd asked her to marry him, she'd convinced herself that *she* wasn't like her mother or grandmother—*she* could make a relationship work. She'd then spent the next two years trying to do just that, and they'd both been miserable. When they'd inevitably agreed to divorce last summer, it had been a relief.

In spite of that, she didn't regret her marriage. She'd learned the hard way that she, too, like the rest of the women in her family, had a defective gene when it came to commitment. Unlike her mother and grandmother, however, she didn't have to go through one divorce after another to learn her lesson. Once was enough. She wasn't cut out to be anything but single, and that was just fine with her. As long as she remembered that—and she didn't plan to forget it—she and Blake Nickels would get along just fine.

Caught up in trying to find a possible link between Tanya Bishop and Charlene McClintock's murders, as well as cover the more interesting stories that came across her police scanner, she was actually able to forget that the *Times* even had a new reporter. Then, just as she was about to grab something for lunch the next day, news of a bank robbery in progress had her rushing over to the southside location. It was just the kind of breaking story she loved, and normally, she was the first reporter on the scene. Not this time, though. Blake Nickels was already there, standing in the bank parking lot interviewing a witness, and the rat was obviously watching for her. The second she pulled into the lot, he looked up and waved.

Grinning broadly, he pushed his cowboy hat to the back of his head. "Hey, Jones, what took you so long?" he teased. "You having a slow day, or what?"

Heat flushed her cheeks, the grin that tugged at her mouth impossible to hide. "Put a sock in it, Nickels," she tossed back, trying and failing to maintain a frown. "I know this might come as something of a surprise to you, but some of us actually cover more than one crime a day."

"No kidding? So where were you when I was covering that assault on a nun at Main Plaza this morning?"

"Interviewing a string of restaurant owners who were conned by a homeless lady on the northside. So what have you got to say about that?"

His eyes dancing, he shrugged. "How about I'll show you my notes if you show me yours?"

She wanted the story on the nun, but Fitz, her boss, would have her hide if she so much as shared the time of day with a *Times* reporter. "Not on your life, cowboy," she replied, and turned away to snag a policeman who'd just walked out of the bank.

Turning down Blake's offer, she quickly discovered to her chagrin, proved to be a mistake. Oh, the police were willing to give her the details of the heist and a brief description of the robber, who had escaped with fifty thousand dollars and was last seen racing west on Loop 410 in a white van. But there was only one witness—the teller—and after she'd given the police a statement, the only reporter she'd agree to talk to was Blake.

Unable to believe she'd heard her correctly, Sabrina said, "What do you mean you won't give your story to anyone but Blake Nickels? You talked to the police."

"Oh, I had to tell them," the pretty blonde said airily. "But Blake asked for an exclusive, and I said okay." All innocence, she smiled sweetly. "So you see, I can't go back on my word. It just wouldn't be ethical, now would it?"

Indignant, Sabrina just barely bit back a scathing retort. If the bubblehead of a teller wanted to talk ethics, she never would have let Blake talk her into an exclusive in the first place. And for a darn bank robbery, of all things! She'd never heard of anything so ridiculous in her life. She only wished she'd thought of it.

Frustrated, steam all but coming out of her ears, she forced a smile. "I appreciate your ethics, Ms. Walker, but your boss might not be too pleased when he hears that you're only talking to one reporter. The bank just lost a substantial amount of money that probably won't be recovered—unless word gets out about the robbery and a possible reward." Reaching into her purse, she pulled out a business card and handed it to her. "Think about it. If you change your mind before my deadline, give me a call."

The woman took her card, but Sabrina knew better than to hold out hope that she would use it. You only had to see her staring after Blake like he was the greatest thing since Elvis to know that she was thoroughly smitten. And for some reason she couldn't explain, that irritated Sabrina to no end.

As her gaze followed the teller's to where Blake stood fifty yards away, finishing an interview with one of the first officers on the scene, she told herself he wasn't going to get away with it. He could sweet-talk every woman he saw for all she cared—some people would stoop to any level to get a story—but he wasn't going to stop her from doing her job! Not if she had anything to say about it. Her jaw set, she started toward him.

Thanking the investigating officer, Roger Martinez, for his help, Blake was jotting down notes in the small notebook he never went anywhere without when he looked up to see Sabrina bearing down on him like a ruffled hen with her tail feathers in a twist. So, he thought as a slow grin skimmed his mouth, she'd found out about the exclusive. Now the fur was really going to fly.

"Hey, Jones," he greeted her as she drew near. "You look a little out of sorts. Something wrong?"

Color flying high in her cheeks, she gave him a withering look. "You're damn right something's wrong! You're a yellow-bellied, toad-eating weasel. How dare you!"

Grinning, he chuckled. "Honey, when you get to know me better, you'll find out that I'll dare just about anything. I take it you've been talking to Jennifer Walker."

"If you want to call it that. She wouldn't tell me a darn thing, and you know it. Because *she* promised *you* an exclusive."

Enjoying himself, Blake grinned. "And all I had to do was ask." Leaning closer, his eyes dancing with mischief, he confided, "I think she likes me."

For a moment, he could have sworn he heard her grinding her teeth. "Then the woman has no taste," she snapped in a low voice that didn't carry any further than his ears. "You ought to be ashamed of yourself."

"Why? Because I thought of it before you did? C'mon, Sabrina, admit it. The only reason you're in a snit is because I outfoxed you."

"Don't be ridiculous," she fibbed. "This story is a matter of police record, and I'll get it with or without that blond bimbo teller's cooperation—"

Making no effort to hide his amusement, he cocked a teasing brow at her. "Blond bimbo? Do I detect a little jealousy here? Why, Jones, I didn't know you cared."

Sabrina's lips twitched. Lord, he was outrageous! She'd always liked a man with a quick wit, and if she didn't watch herself with him, she was going to find herself charmed into liking him. And that could be nothing but a disaster.

Somehow managing to look down her nose at him in spite of the fact that he towered over her, she studied him consideringly. "Don't let it go to your head, cowboy. The only thing I care about is the story, and you're throwing up roadblocks. Now, I wonder why that is? You running scared, Nickels, or what?"

"Of you?" He chuckled. "I don't think so. I read your story in this morning's paper, sweetheart." Not batting an eye, he quoted word-for-word from her front-page story on the Bishop murder in the morning edition of the *Daily Record*. "'Tanya Bishop was dressed to meet a lover. A lover who may have killed her.'" Clicking his tongue at her in teasing disapproval, he grinned. "Naughty, naughty, Jones. Of course she was dressed for bed—she was killed during the middle of the night—but that doesn't mean she was expecting a lover. And what's this *may* business? The last I heard, a good reporter stuck to the facts and nothing but the facts, not supposition."

Her cheeks flushed at the gentle criticism. Darn the man, she should have caught that. And when she hadn't, her editor should have! But she'd have eaten worms before admitting it. Instead, she purred silkily, "Why, Nickels, I'm flattered you went to the trouble to memorize my work. Are you one of our new subscribers? You should have told me and I might have been able to get you a discount."

"To the *Record*?" He snorted, amused. "I don't think so. I like my news hard and gritty, and I'll bet your readers do, too. In fact, I'll bet you dinner at the restaurant of your choice that before the month is out, my paper, not yours, is winning the subscription war."

"Watch it, Nickels. I have expensive taste."

"So it's a bet?"

Hesitating, Sabrina reminded herself that he was a man who didn't always play by the rules. And there were some very expensive restaurants in town. If she lost, she'd feel the blow not only in her pride, but in her pocketbook. But she'd never been one to play it safe, and there were some things a woman with daring just couldn't walk away from. And Blake Nickels, she reluctantly admitted, was one of them.

Grinning, she held out her hand and silently prayed she didn't live to regret her impulsiveness. "You're on, Nickels. If I were you, I'd start saving my pennies. This is going to cost you."

Chapter 2

She was running late. Her alarm clock hadn't gone off, and she'd unconsciously taken advantage of it, waking a mere ten minutes before she was due at work. Horrified, Sabrina jumped out of bed and threw on some clothes, but even moving at the speed of sound, it was well after she should have punched in at the paper when she slammed out of her house and dashed to her car. Mumbling reminders to get herself a new clock, she raced down the street, tires squealing, and headed for the freeway three blocks away.

She'd barely shot onto the entrance ramp when she had to hit the brakes. A four-car pileup a half a mile ahead blocked all three lanes, slowing traffic to a virtual crawl. She'd be lucky if she made it in to the paper by noon.

Fitz was not going to be pleased.

Sabrina winced and rubbed at her temples, where a dull pounding started to hammer relentlessly. It was not, she decided, going to be a good morning. As far as bosses went, Fitz was a real gem when it came to letting her run with a story, but he was a real stickler when it came to reporting in in the morning. If you were going to be late, you'd better have a darn good excuse.

Staring up ahead at the whirling lights of at least three patrol cars and two ambulances, Sabrina saw a uniformed officer slap handcuffs on one of the drivers and started to smile. This wasn't evidently one of your average rush-hour fender benders. Things were starting to look up. Fitz wouldn't be nearly as inclined to give her one of his patented speeches about punctuality if she came in with a story. Sending up a silent prayer of thanks for gifts from God, she eased over onto the shoulder of the freeway and raced down it toward the accident scene.

It wasn't noon when she rushed into the *Daily Record,* but it was pretty darn close to it. Glancing at the clock in the lobby, Sabrina winced. Fitz was going to have a hissy. It wouldn't, she thought with an impish grin, be the first one that she'd caused. She seemed to have a talent for it where he was concerned.

"Well, well, well," a familiar, gruff voice drawled sarcastically as she stepped off the elevator and turned to come face-to-face with her boss. "If it isn't our star reporter. And she's actually putting in an appearance at work. Glad you could join us, Ms. Jones. I hope it wasn't too much of an imposition."

Well used to the cutting edge of the old man's tongue, she ignored his sarcasm and gave him a cheeky grin. "Not at all, boss. I'm sorry I'm late, but I knew you wouldn't want me to leave the scene of a story—"

"What story?"

"A four-car pileup on the Loop. It seems that a red van was weaving back and forth between the lanes before it plowed into a car full of college kids from Austin on their way to the coast. The van driver was drunk as a skunk— and you'll never guess who it was."

"Who?" he growled. "And this better be good, Jones. I've been trying to track you down all morning."

"I know it, boss, but I was stuck on the freeway with no way to call you. And it was the mayor's son, Jason Grimes! He'd been out carousing all night in daddy's car."

"What? Why the hell didn't you say so?"

Knowing she was forgiven, Sabrina laughed. "I would have given a hundred bucks to have had a camera. Nobody was hurt, but those kids from Austin were fighting mad when it looked like the cops were going to let Jason off the hook. He's an obnoxious little brat at the best of times, but when he's drunk, he's an arrogant son of a gun. He made the mistake of telling one of the kids from Austin that his daddy would see that he didn't even get a ticket for reckless driving, let alone arrested for a DWI, and the kid took a swing at him. He's not quite as pretty as he used to be."

Fitz's sharp gray eyes started to twinkle. "Now ain't that a shame? And he was such a good-looking boy. Write it up, Jones. Then nose around down at the police station and see if you can find out what the policy has been in the past toward young Jason's drunk driving. If he's gotten special privileges, I want to know about it."

He started to turn away, only to remember her tardiness. Glancing over his shoulder, he warned, "And don't be late again, Jones. Next time, you might not be lucky enough to have a story fall in your lap the way this one did."

"No, sir. I mean yes, sir, it won't happen again." Saluting smartly, she dared to wink at him. "I'll get right on it."

He scowled like an old Scrooge, but Sabrina caught the twitch of his lips before he headed for his office. Chuckling to herself, she turned toward her own desk, her thoughts already jumping ahead to the opening line of her story.

Distracted, she didn't see the note lying right in the middle of her desk until she sat down and started to turn toward her computer monitor. Then she saw it—a single sheet of white, unlined paper folded in half with her name handwritten on the front. Perched precariously on top of some notes from yesterday's bank robbery, it could have been left there by anyone—her co-workers left notes for her all the time. But those were handwritten on little yellow stickies, not typed ones on what looked like fairly expensive textured paper.

Wondering who it was from, she reached for it and had a sudden image of Blake teasing her yesterday about her coverage of the Bishop murder. It would, she thought, unable to hold back a smile, be just like him to take it upon himself to critique another of her stories. Only this time, he'd put it in writing and obviously bribed someone in the lobby to deliver it to her desk, since there was no envelope. She could just imagine what it said.

But when she leaned back in her chair and flipped the note open, her eyes dancing with expectancy, she saw in a single, all-encompassing glance that it wasn't from Blake. Then the typed words registered and a cold chill crept like a winter fog through her bloodstream, chilling her to the bone.

Sabrina,
Tanya Bishop thought she could compete in a man's world, and she was wrong. I tried to tell her differently. Women are the nurturers, the homemakers, the babymakers. They should be home, raising the next generation and saving the world, not having power lunches and taking jobs away from men who can do the work ten times better. It's not right. I told Tanya that, but she wouldn't listen. She laughed at my warning that she was in danger of upsetting the natural order of things. I didn't want to kill her, but what else could I do? She didn't know her place, so she had to be eliminated. She gave me no other choice.

I know how your mind operates, Sabrina. You think I'm some kind of nut case looking for publicity for a murder I didn't commit. But I really did kill her. We were friends. I hoped we could be more, but she couldn't be what I wanted her to be. *Who* I wanted her to be. So I decided to end it and called to tell her I needed to see her. She was dressed in a white gown and negligee and opened the door to me the second I rang the bell. That's when I shot her. She fell right where she stood in the doorway, and I can't feel bad about it. Other professional women might want to take heed while they still can.

Stunned, her heart starting to pound in her ears, Sabrina stared at the cold, unfeeling words and told herself this was a hoax—one of her fellow reporters was probably watching her right now, grinning like an idiot as he waited for her reaction. But even as she cast a quick look around the city room, she knew deep in her gut that this was no practical joke. The note had a ring of truth to it, a sick logic, that sent goose bumps racing over her skin.

Pale, her fingers not quite steady, she dropped the note as if it were a lit firecracker and reached for her phone, quickly pushing the button for the receptionist's desk in the lobby. "Valerie," she said as soon as the other woman came on the line, "this is Sabrina. Did anyone hand-deliver a note for me late yesterday afternoon or this morning?"

"If they did, this is the first I've heard of it," Valerie replied cheerfully. "Lydia Davidson in classifieds got flowers from her latest heartthrob, but other than that, things have been pretty quiet. Why?"

"No reason," Sabrina said quickly. "I was just wondering. If anyone does come in asking for me, let me know, okay? Thanks."

She hung up, frowning, refusing to even consider the

possibility that Tanya Bishop's killer had hand-delivered a note to her. *If* the thing was even legit, she amended silently. Whoever wrote it must have gotten one of the other staff members to drop it off at her desk. It was the only explanation.

But when she asked around, she got nothing but negative answers. No one had passed a message on to her. No one had seen any strangers or visitors loitering around her desk. For all practical purposes, the note had simply appeared there and no one had a clue how.

Not easily scared, Sabrina told herself she wasn't worried. She could take care of herself—she always had. And if there was a threat in the note, it wasn't meant for her. How could it be? She didn't even know the killer. Whoever he was, he obviously wanted his fifteen minutes of fame, just like everybody else. She could give him that. But first she had to talk to Sam Kelly. Picking up her phone, she punched in the number for the police department.

"C'mon, Kelly, I know you've got the coroner's report—I called the ME's office and asked," Blake said with a grin as he lounged in the chair across the desk from the detective. "What's the big secret? Everyone knows Tanya Bishop was shot in the heart. All I want is the time of death."

"You'll get it just like everyone else at the press conference this afternoon at three," Sam said firmly. "That gives you plenty of time to make the morning edition."

In years past, Blake had worked with detectives who hoarded information like misers stockpiling gold, giving it out in beggarly bits and pieces like they were doing the world a favor. Sam Kelly didn't strike him that way. He didn't play games or do anything that might have been considered unethical. He was a strictly by-the-book man, and Blake had to admire that. In a world where whole police departments were as crooked as a dog's hind leg, it was nice to know there were men like Sam Kelly still hanging in there, doing things the right way, fighting the good fight. But it made getting information out of him damn difficult.

"The morning edition's not the problem," he said ruefully, opting for the truth. "It's Sabrina Jones."

His craggy face cracking in a smile, Sam leaned back in his chair and surveyed him knowingly. "So Sabrina's giving you fits already, is she? Somebody should have warned you."

"Somebody did—I just didn't believe him. She's quick, damn quick. And if you tell her I said that, I'll flat out deny it. The woman's already too cocky as it is."

Sam laughed, agreeing. "She never has lacked for confidence. Some men have a hard time handling that. I heard you two have a bet going on—"

Before he could say more, the phone on his desk rang, and with a murmured apology to Blake, he reached over and answered it. Recognizing Sabrina's husky voice, he started to smile. "Well, speak of the devil. I was just talking about you, Sabrina. What's up?"

Snapping to attention at the mention of Sabrina's name, Blake watched Sam's expression turn from teasing to grim in the blink of an eye. All business, the detective reached for a pen and started jotting down notes. "No, don't touch it any more than you already have," he said quickly. "We'll need to test it for fingerprints, then send it to the lab to see what they can make of it. I'll be right over."

Impatient, the one-sided conversation giving him few clues to what was going on, Blake started throwing questions at the other man the second he hung up. "Don't touch what? Is Sabrina in some kind of danger? What are you sending to the lab? Dammit, Sam, what's going on?"

For a moment, he thought the other man wasn't going to tell him anything, but then Sam sighed and said, "I guess there's no reason to keep it a secret—you're going to find out soon enough anyway. Sabrina got to work late today—just a few minutes ago, in fact—and found a note someone had left on her desk. It appears to be from Tanya Bishop's killer.''

"What?!''

"*Appears* is the operative word here,'' he stressed. "At this point, we can't be sure it's from the real killer, but Sabrina's not taking it lightly. In fact, she sounded pretty shaken.''

"Well, I would think she damn well would be. Why would the bastard send her a note?''

"The man's a murderer, Blake. He's already killed once, possibly twice, if he offed Charlene McClintock. Who knows what's going on in his head? And he didn't *send* it. Sabrina thinks he hand-delivered it.''

"Son of a bitch! You mean he just walked right into the *Daily Record*?''

"That's the way it looks. I'm heading over there right now to check it out. I'll see you later at the press conference.''

"The hell you will,'' Blake said, rising to his feet. "I'm going with you.''

Sitting at her desk, her gaze trained unseeingly on her computer monitor, Sabrina tried to focus on her story about the mayor's son and his drunken joyride, but her concentration was shot. She couldn't write a logical sentence to save her life. All she could think about was the series of veiled threats in the note, threats that could have been meant for every professional woman in the city. Including herself.

When the thought had first occurred to her, fear, uncontrollable and unwanted, had surged in her before she could stop it. And she hadn't liked it one little bit. She didn't like being afraid, especially where she worked. This was her desk, her paper, and no murdering wacko was going to waltz in there and scare the bejabbers out of her just because he had a problem with women in power positions!

Giving up any attempt to work, she sat back and glared at the note, a thousand angry questions spinning in her head. Had the writer really killed Tanya? And why had he sent his note to her? Obviously he wanted his message to get out to professional women who were, in his words, "tampering with the world order," but that didn't mean that she was the only reporter who could relay his message for him. Any television station or newspaper in the country would have done the same thing once the note was declared valid by the police. So why her? From the way he sounded, he didn't even like career women, and she'd never claimed to be anything else. What did he want with her, anyway?

Frowning, she was still trying to figure that out when Sam Kelly walked into the city room. And right behind him was Blake Nickels, strolling in as if he was taking a walk in a park!

Stunned, Sabrina couldn't believe her eyes. "What's he doing here?" she asked Sam by way of a greeting.

"Now don't go getting all bent out of shape, Sabrina," he soothed. "He was at the station when you called, sitting right across from me at my desk. What was I supposed to do? Lock him up so he couldn't follow me?"

"It's a thought," she replied, shooting Blake a narrow-eyed look that didn't faze his teasing grin one iota. "You've got a lot of nerve coming here, cowboy. What do you want?"

"A story." Plopping down on a corner of her desk, he tilted his cowboy hat to the back of his head and crossed his arms across his chest as if he planned to stay awhile. "The last I heard, you were it."

Despite the fact that she was still unsettled about the note, she couldn't help but appreciate the vagaries of Fate.

Biting back a smile, she asked, "Have you ever heard that old saying 'what goes around, comes around,' Nickels? Well, it looks like it's your turn to get what's coming to you. Yesterday, you had an exclusive. Today, I do. Isn't life funny?"

"Oh, yeah. It's a regular riot," he drawled.

Captivated by the flash of her quick grin, he wondered if she had any idea how tempting she looked, her gaze level with his for once since he was sitting, satisfaction dancing in those expressive brown eyes of hers. A man could be forgiven for kissing a woman under such circumstances, and the sudden need to do just that stunned the hell out of him. Where the devil had that come from?

You've been too long without a woman, his common sense muttered in his ear. *That's the only explanation. Sure, she's a pretty little thing, but she'd just as soon have you for breakfast as look at you. She's the competition. Remember?*

Brought up short by the reminder—and annoyed at the need for it—he scowled and glanced down at her desk. "So where's the note? At least let me take a quick peek at it before you toss me out of here."

Lightning-quick, she grabbed his hand and tried to tug him to his feet. "Not on your life. You've seen and heard all you're going to, so get. I'm sure Sam has a lot of questions, and I have no intention of answering them in front of you."

"Spoilsport."

Her efforts to move him about as effective as a gnat's, she dropped his hand and squared off in front of him like Sugar Ray Leonard. "Don't make me get tough with you."

"At last she's going to get physical!" he teased, his eyes laughing at her. "Yes, Virginia, there is a Santa Claus."

"Blake—"

When she used that tone, he knew she meant business. "Okay, okay. You win." Though he was left with no choice but to back off, he had no intention of going far. Not until he had some answers. Reluctantly, he pushed himself to his feet. "Enjoy your victory, Jones. The next one may be a long time coming."

Shooting one last, searching look at her desk, he turned away and gave every appearance of leaving as he headed for the exit. But just before he reached it, he glanced back over his shoulder and found Sabrina in a serious discussion with the detective, who was carefully examining a sheet of paper on her desk. That was all the opening Blake needed.

Stopping at the water fountain in the hall to talk to a pretty young copy girl who looked like she was hardly old enough to be out of high school, he shot her his most charming smile, pushed his cowboy hat up off his forehead, and prayed she hadn't heard of him as he introduced himself. "Hi, I'm Blake Nickels. I came with Detective Kelly—"

Her blue eyes bright with shy interest, she said huskily, "I saw you when you came in. Are you a detective, too?"

"Not quite," he hedged, and told himself it wasn't a lie. He hadn't actually misrepresented himself, which would have been unethical—he'd just let her jump to her own conclusions because he had no other choice. If he identified himself as a reporter with the *Times,* she and everyone else in the building would send him packing as fast as Sabrina had. Pulling out his notebook, he said, "I was hoping you could answer some questions for me."

"About the note Sabrina got?"

"You know about it?"

"Oh, sure. The news went through the building like wildfire. The killer just walked in and left the note on her desk."

In the process of reaching for the pen in his shirt pocket, Blake glanced up at her in surprise. "Someone saw him?"

She hesitated, then had the grace to blush. "Well, no, not exactly. But how else could it have gotten there if he didn't deliver it in person? All the employees have been questioned, and no one knows a thing about it."

She had a point, one that Blake didn't like one little bit. Tanya Bishop's killer was no stumbling novice. The man—he'd heard of no evidence that pointed to the sex of the murderer, but his gut was telling him it had to be a man—had been smart and cunning enough to surprise her, then kill her without leaving a single clue. Just the thought of him walking into the *Daily Record* and finding Sabrina's desk without anyone being the wiser turned Blake's blood cold. If the bastard could track her down so easily at work, what was to stop him from following her home?

His expression darkening at the thought, he said tersely, "That must have been a hell of a note, if he was willing to take that kind of risk to deliver it. Any idea what was in it? I haven't seen it yet."

The girl nodded, indignation sparkling in her blue eyes. "It was a bunch of garbage about women not knowing their place and taking jobs away from men. Supposedly, that's why Tanya Bishop was killed. She was warned to stay home where she belonged and she laughed in the jerk's face."

His pen flying over the pages of his notebook in his own brand of shorthand, Blake took down every word and could already see the headlines. But the elation he should have felt at outsmarting Sabrina in her own backyard just wasn't there. Not when she had drawn the attention of a murderer. He tried to tell himself that he would have been disturbed by the thought of any colleague receiving what sounded like a threatening note—it was nothing personal. But this felt distinctly, disturbingly, personal.

"Did I say something wrong? You look awful mad all of a sudden."

Glancing up from his notes, he found the copy girl staring at him with a puzzled frown. "No," he said quietly, forcing a crooked smile that didn't come as easily as it usually did. "You didn't say anything wrong. My mind just wandered for a second. Is that the gist of the note?"

She nodded. "Pretty much. Except that it was a warning to other professional women that the same thing could happen to them if they're not careful."

To Blake, that sounded more like a threat than a warning, one directed right at Sabrina. And if she didn't have the sense to recognize that, she wasn't as smart as he thought she was. Thanking the copy girl for her help, he returned to the city room to find Sabrina pounding out a story on her computer while Detective Kelly questioned the other *Record* staff members.

Crossing the room in four long strides, Blake came up behind her and boldly began to read the opening paragraph on her monitor. "That'd better not be what I think it is, Jones."

Startled, she whirled in her chair, her hand flying to her throat. "Damn you, Nickels! You scared the stuffing out of me! What are you doing here? I thought I told you to leave."

He grinned, but there was little humor in his eyes when he said, "Nobody scares me off a story that easy, honey, especially a shrimp like you." Dropping with lazy grace into the chair positioned across from her desk, he nodded to her computer monitor, where the opening lines of her story were still clearly visible. "You're not really going to print the contents of that note, are you?"

"Not print it?" she choked, swivelling the monitor so he could no longer see the screen. "Are you out of your mind? Of course I'm going to print it!"

"Don't you think that's a mistake? What if it's bogus? You'll come off looking like a fool."

"I'd rather risk that than not let the professional women of this city know that there's a psychopath out there with a vendetta against them. This man, whoever he is, doesn't live in a vacuum, Blake. Somebody out there knows him, and when they read his note in the paper, they just might come forward. Anyway, the note's not bogus. If you don't believe me, ask Sam."

Dammit, he didn't have to ask Sam. He'd heard enough from the copy girl to know that she was right. And that's what worried him. "Then that's just one more reason not to print it," he said stubbornly. "If the killer really wrote it, he didn't send it to you because he wanted to be friends or give you the scoop of the century. It was a threat to you and every other career woman out there, and you'll only encourage him if you print it."

"Don't be ridiculous," she scoffed. "You're just ticked because I've got the inside track on the best story to hit this town in years. You know you're going to lose our bet and it's driving you up the wall." Daring to smile at him, she goaded sweetly, "Better save your pennies, cowboy. You're going to need them, and then some."

Frustrated, his hands curling into fists to keep from reaching across her desk to shake the stuffing out of her, Blake couldn't for the life of him understand why he was so burned. He didn't want to see her or anyone else get hurt, but the lady meant nothing to him. Oh, he liked her well enough, but he'd always been a sap for smart, independent women. He liked bran, too, but he knew better than to overindulge. And Sabrina Jones was definitely an indulgence he wanted no part of, especially after Trina had made a fool out of him. He was concerned, just as he would be for any other woman who was standing on the edge of disaster and didn't know it.

Still, she could obviously take care of herself. She might

look as soft as a powder puff, but underneath that cloud of silky black curls and the soft blouses and skirts that emphasized her femininity was a woman who had a reputation for being tough when it came to her work. If she wasn't worried about developing a tenuous relationship with the killer, why should he be?

Because two other career women had no doubt once thought they could take care of themselves, too. And now they were dead.

"This has nothing to do with the damn bet," he said curtly, pushing to his feet. "I was just concerned for your safety, but I guess that's not my problem, is it?" Not waiting for an answer, he headed for the door.

He walked away from Sabrina because she hadn't given much choice, but there was no way in hell he was walking away from the story, he decided as he pulled out of the *Record*'s parking lot a few minutes later. There was a reason the killer had sent it to Sabrina, and he meant to find out what it was—with or without her cooperation.

And there was no better place to start his investigation than with the lady herself. When she found out about it, she was going to be madder than a wet hen. Grinning at the thought, he stopped at a convenience store and borrowed a phone book to look up her address. Seconds later, he was headed for the near north side.

She lived off St. Mary's Street in an older neighborhood that had once been quite nice but had declined as the city grew. Most of the homes were wood-framed, with wide porches, many of them sagging and sad-looking. More often than not, graffiti marked fences and walls, a by-product of the gangs that had taken over the area and claimed it as their own. It went without saying that crime was high.

There were pockets of hope, though, Blake noted. A cluster of homes here and there, even a whole block where homeowners were trying to reclaim their neighborhood.

Here, the homes were painted and restored, the yards mowed. And it was here that Sabrina lived.

Parking at the curb in front of her house, Blake found himself smiling at the sight of it. Somehow, out of all the houses on the street, he would have known without asking that this one was Sabrina's. The winding walk that led from the curb to her front porch was bracketed with flower beds that were bursting with wildflowers, and on the porch itself were bright pots of geraniums and begonias that were as thick as thieves. Every yard on the street seemed to have flower beds, but while the others were neatly trimmed and organized, Sabrina's were wild and free and bold with color. Just like the woman herself, he thought with a frown. And it was that boldness that was going to get her into trouble if she wasn't careful.

But that wasn't why he was there, he reminded himself grimly. The killer had made Sabrina a part of his story when he'd delivered that note to her. Until the murderer was identified and caught, Sabrina was the only living tie to the man that anyone was aware of, and Blake meant to find out why. What it was about her that attracted the killer's attention?

Studying the homes of her neighbors, he decided to check the one on the left, where there were two cars in the driveway. The old lady who answered the door was round and jolly, with a double chin and inquisitive blue eyes that twinkled behind the lenses of her glasses. Lifting a delicately arched brow at him, she said, "Yes? May I help you?"

"I certainly hope so, ma'am." Introducing himself, he pulled his wallet out of his back pocket and showed her his credentials. "I'm Blake Nickels, with the *Times.* I wonder if I could ask you a few questions about your neighbor, Sabrina Jones?"

Alarmed, her easy smile faltered. "Why? Has something happened to her?"

"No, she's fine," Blake quickly assured her. "In fact, I just left her a few minutes ago at the *Daily Record.*" Knowing there was no way he was going to find anything out about Sabrina without her friends' cooperation, he quickly told the older woman about the note. "The police are aware of the situation and are checking out the note in the hopes that it will lead them to Tanya Bishop's murderer, but I'm more inclined to check out Sabrina. The killer didn't just pick her name out of a hat. He chose her for a reason. I was hoping you or one of the other neighbors might be able to tell me why by giving me some information about her background."

For a moment, Blake thought she was going to turn him down flat. Not committing herself one way or the other, she studied him through the screen door, then nodded as if coming to a silent decision and pushed open the door. "I'm Martha Anderson. Come on in. If Sabrina's in trouble, I want to help."

Blake only meant to ask her a few questions, but the old lady was obviously lonely and hungry for visitors. After settling him at her kitchen table, she fixed them each a glass of iced tea, then settled into the chair across from him, eager to talk.

"Sabrina's such a wonderful girl," she confided. "And everybody around here is just crazy about her. It's such a shame about her husband—"

"Husband?" Blake echoed, sitting up straighter. "I didn't know she was married."

"She's not...now," Martha replied. "How that girl could be so smart and make such a huge mistake, God only knows. Anyone with eyes could see that Jeff Harper was about as wrong for her as a bad case of the flu, but she was infatuated and just threw caution to the wind. She's like that, you know," she added, leaning closer as if she was confiding a secret. "Impulsive. Lord, that girl's impulsive! I swear she doesn't have a self-protective bone in her body, but you won't find a better friend or neighbor in this city. When I broke my hip last year, she was over here just about every evening to cook supper for me. And then when Louis— Louis Vanderbilt, he lives on the other side of Sabrina—had to have his dog put to sleep last summer, Sabrina went out and bought him another one. I cried myself, just seeing how moved he was.''

"What about this Jeff Harper character?'' Blake asked with a frown. "Where's he? And how does he feel about her dating again?''

"Well, that's just it, dear,'' the old lady replied. "She doesn't date. Ever. As far as I've been able to tell, she hasn't been out a single time since she and Jeff split. Not that he would care. He's already remarried and got a baby on the way. As far as I know, Sabrina hasn't seen him in over a year.''

Intrigued, Blake found that hard to believe. Whether he wanted to admit it or not, Sabrina Jones was a beautiful woman with a sassy personality that any man with blood in his veins would find hard to resist. She had a job that took her all over the city and gave her plenty of opportunities to meet people. So what was wrong with the men in San Antonio? Were they blind, or what?

"So she doesn't date and there's no men in her life,'' he said thoughtfully. That ruled out the possibility of the killer being someone she'd been involved with romantically. "What about enemies?''

"Enemies?'' Martha laughed, her blue eyes fairly sparkling behind the lenses of her glasses. "You obviously don't know Sabrina very well or you wouldn't even ask that. She can be as nosy as an old woman when she's after a story, but she's just doing her job. Nobody holds it against her.''

Obviously extremely fond of Sabrina, she drew a tantalizing picture of her that Blake found thoroughly captivating. But she didn't tell him anything that even hinted at why Tanya Bishop's killer had turned his sights on Sabrina. Thanking the old lady for her help, he went looking for more answers from the other neighbors.

Since most of Sabrina's neighbors were retired, he didn't have any trouble finding someone to talk to. Unfortunately, he didn't get the information he was hoping for. All of them knew and liked Sabrina and had their own stories to tell about her, but none could think of a single reason why a killer would send her a threatening note. Except for Louis Vanderbilt.

A quiet, unassuming man who was out walking the now-grown Labrador that Sabrina had given him as a puppy, he paled when he stopped to talk to Blake and was told about the note. "Sabrina did a special series last year about sexual discrimination in the workplace," he said quietly. "It was excellent. In fact, I think she won several awards for it. But one of the editors at her own paper quit over allegations that she stirred up, and from what I heard from Sabrina, he vowed to get even. But that was months ago. Sabrina probably forgot all about him. Do you think he could be the one who sent her the note?"

Blake didn't know, but it was definitely worth checking out and mentioning to the police. Feeling like he was finally getting somewhere, he quickly jotted down notes. "What was the man's name? Do you have any idea what happened to him after he quit the *Record*?"

A thin, balding man with wire-rimmed glasses and the kind of ageless face that didn't show the passage of time, Louis murmured to the Lab, who was impatient to resume his walk, and tried to remember. "It seems like it was Saunders or Sanders or something like that. Carl, I think. Yeah, that was it. Carl Sanders."

Shaking his head, he whistled softly as the facts came rushing back to him. "He was a nasty sort. If I'm remembering correctly, he was arrested for punching his wife about a week after he lost his job. She later dropped the charges and he sort of faded from sight after that. Which isn't surprising considering the fact that all the TV stations in town picked up the story," he added. "After all the negative publicity, he'd have been lucky to get a job as a dogcatcher, which was no more than he deserved."

"Did he ever contact Sabrina? Ever show up here at her home and harass her or send her any kind of threatening letters?"

Shocked, the older man said, "Oh, no! Not that I know of. Sabrina never mentioned any kind of letters, and I know for a fact that he never came around here. This is a very close-knit neighborhood, Mr. Nickels. We're all friends and watch out for each other. Sabrina and only a handful of others work—the rest of us are retired—so there's always someone home on the block. If Carl Sanders or anyone else had tried to get to Sabrina, you can bet one of us would have seen him.

"Of course," he added with a rueful smile, "we can't do much to protect her when she's out on the streets. She does tend to take chances."

Blake snorted at that, his lips twitching into a grin. "She's a regular daredevil, Mr. Vanderbilt." Holding out his hand, he said, "Thanks for the information. You've been a big help. If you remember anything else that might be important, would you give me a call at the *Times*? I'd really appreciate it."

A twinkle glinting in his eye, the older man hesitated, then nodded as he returned the handshake. "Sabrina won't like me helping the competition, but if it'll help keep her safe, I'll be glad to do it." The Lab tugged on her leash again, and with a murmur of apology, the man continued his walk.

Staring after him, Blake grinned. Whether he knew it or not, Louis Vanderbilt hadn't just helped the competition. He'd given him enough information that would—if it proved reliable after further research—blow Sabrina and the *Daily Record* right out of the water. It was, he decided, picturing the huge steak he was going to let her buy him next month, his lucky day.

Chapter 3

An hour later, Blake hung up the phone at his desk at the *Times* with a muttered curse. Louis Vanderbilt's story had checked out—to a point. Carl Sanders *had* lost his job at the *Daily Record* after Sabrina did a series of stories on sexual harassment. And in the single, bitter exclusive interview he'd given the *Times* after his abrupt resignation, he had placed all the blame on Sabrina. There was no question that the man was a chauvinist of the worst kind and that he had the mind-set and motive to at least be considered a suspect. The only problem was that less than a month after he quit the *Record,* he had apparently moved to Billings, Montana. A check with information and a short call to a C. Sanders there had verified that he was still there and wanted nothing to do with anyone from San Antonio.

Considering that, and the fact that he couldn't stroll into his old workplace without being recognized, the odds were slim that he'd threatened Sabrina, let alone killed Tanya

Bishop or Charlene McClintock. So he was back to square one, Blake thought in disgust.

"Problems?"

Looking up from his musings to find Tom grinning at him, he growled, "No, thanks. I've got enough of my own. One, in fact, that you're probably not going to like."

"Let's hear it and I'll let you know," his friend and boss said as pulled up a chair. "Lay it on me."

"Tanya Bishop's killer sent a threatening note to Sabrina Jones." He filled him in on his conversation with the copy girl at the *Record* and his canvasing of Sabrina's neighbors. "This Carl Sanders character sounded like just the type of lowlife who would do something like this, but with him out of the picture, there aren't any other suspects. So the only story I've got is a note I haven't actually seen. I know its general contents, but not any specifics I can quote. And even if I did, I don't like the idea of encouraging the jerk."

Tom frowned. "If you're suggesting we don't print the story at all, I can't go along with that. Two women have died in two weeks, Blake. The whole city's abuzz about it, and just this morning, I heard on the radio that a record number of women are buying guns to protect themselves. Any developments in the case have to be reported—even if it concerns a reporter for the competition."

"But the killer wants recognition," Blake argued. "Why else would he have sent the note to Sabrina? If we give him that recognition, not only do we chance turning this into a media circus, but we'll be giving him what he wants. He could get a real taste for this type of thing."

"And kill more?" Tom asked shrewdly. "I doubt it. He didn't need any encouragement for the first two. I can't see why he would now."

"But—"

"This isn't anything like the situation in New York eight years ago, Blake," he cut in quietly. "You don't have information that's going to get someone killed. If anything, letting everyone know what kind of threats this jerk is making could save lives. Exposure and the knowledge that most of the city is on the lookout for him may be the only things that keep him in check.''

Put that way, Blake had to agree. Still, he didn't like the idea of publicizing the jerk's sudden interest in Sabrina. Who was he? What did he want with her? And why was he—Blake—so concerned about her safety when she could obviously take care of herself? She wasn't his problem. Why did he have such a hard time remembering that?

It was nearly dark when Blake finally left the paper and made his way home. When he'd first moved to town two weeks ago, he'd planned to move in with his grandfather so he could keep an eye on him, but the old man had let him know that first day that he didn't need a baby-sitter, despite what Blake's mother thought. Amused, Blake hadn't pushed the issue. Pop had always been an independent cuss, and arguing with him only made him dig in his heels. So Blake had assured him that he'd moved to San Antonio for a job, not to watch over him, and backed off.

He'd had, however, no intention of leaving the old man to his own devices. Finding himself an apartment several blocks away from the house his grandfather had lived in for over sixty years, Blake had planned to come up with an excuse to check on him every day. So far, that hadn't been necessary. If his grandfather didn't call him around supper time every day, he was invariably waiting for him when he got home. After the first few days of finding him waiting on the landing outside his second-story apartment, Blake had given him a key.

Now, as he climbed the stairs, he caught the scent of chicken frying and had to grin. The rest of the world might be cutting back on cholesterol, but Pop didn't have much use for what he considered a conspiracy dreamed up by a bunch of quack scientists who wanted to control the world. A cook in the navy, he'd been eating bacon and eggs and fried foods all his life, and at eighty-three, he was still going strong. Why the devil would he want to change his diet at this late date?

Letting himself in, Blake followed his nose to the apartment's small kitchen just in time to see the old man slip a pan of homemade biscuits into the oven. Propping a shoulder against the doorjamb, he teased, "You'd make some old woman a great husband, Pop. Want me to place a personal ad for you?"

The old man only snorted, his grin a mirror image of Blake's. "What makes you think I could only get an old one? In case you didn't know it, I'm a damn fine catch. I've got all of my own teeth—"

"And most of your hair," Blake added, chuckling.

"You're damn right," his grandfather agreed, playfully patting the cloud of wavy white hair that was his only vanity. "And you're going to look just like me. If I were you, I'd be thanking my lucky stars you got your looks from the Finnigans, boy. Your daddy's bald head shines in the moonlight."

"Only when he polishes it," Blake retorted, repeating one of his father's favorite jokes about his lack of hair. Pushing away from the doorjamb, he strode over to the stove and started lifting lids. "You making gravy, Pop? I can't remember the last time I had your gravy."

With pretended fierceness, the older man swatted at him, shoving him away from his cooking. "Get out of there before I forget you're my favorite grandson."

"I'm your only grandson." Blake laughed, snatching a green bean before he stepped back. "When do we eat?"

"When you set the table. I can smell those biscuits, son. Get moving."

His stomach grumbling, Blake didn't have to be told

twice. Grabbing plates and silverware, he quickly set the table, then moved to help his grandfather dish up the food. Five minutes later, they sat down to a feast that would have fed a small army.

Filling his plate, the old man, as usual, asked about work. "So how'd it go today? You run into that Jones woman today?"

The question was smoothly, casually added, almost as an afterthought, but Blake wasn't the least bit fooled by his grandfather's attempt at subtlety. He'd made the mistake of telling the old man about Sabrina that day he'd met her at the scene of Tanya Bishop's murder, and ever since then, Pop had been convinced that Blake was interested in her. A day didn't go by that he didn't ask about her.

Shooting him a hard look, he warned, "There's nothing going on between Sabrina and me, Pop, so don't start getting any ideas."

As innocent as a choirboy, he arched a craggy brow. "Did I say there was? All I asked was if you ran into her today. If you read more into that, then it seems to me that you're awfully sensitive where that girl's concerned."

"I'm not sensitive," he began defensively, then caught the gleam in the old coot's eye. "You old rascal, I know what game you're playing and it's not going to work," he warned, grinning. "Just because Sabrina and I run into each other covering the same stories—"

"So you did see her!"

"Yes, but—"

"I knew it!" he cackled gleefully. "You just can't stay away from her. So tell me about her. Is she pretty? How old is she? I know she's got spunk—you can tell it from her writing. I always did like a girl with spunk."

Amused in spite of himself, Blake said patiently, "Yes, she's pretty, but that's got nothing to do with anything. She got a threatening letter from Tanya Bishop's killer, and I went over to the *Daily Record* to cover the story. That's all there was to it.''

The old man snorted, unconvinced. "You went over there to make sure she was okay and you know it. That's good. A man should protect the woman he cares about—even if she can take care of herself. So why haven't you asked her out?" he demanded, pointing a chicken leg at him. "A girl like that won't stay single for long."

"I don't know about that," he said dryly. "According to one of her neighbors, her ex-husband burned her bad and she doesn't even date. Anyway, even if I was interested—which I'm not saying I am—I can't ask her out. She works for the competition."

"So? What's that got to do with anything? Your grandmother's family didn't even talk to mine, but Sadie was the prettiest thing I'd ever seen. And she had just as much spunk as your Sabrina. I'm telling you, boy, you'd better snap her up while you can. Women like her don't come along every day of the week. Believe me, I know. Why do you think I never married again after your grandma died? A good woman is hard to find."

Giving up in defeat, Blake laughed. "Okay, okay! I'll think about it."

Pleased, the old man passed the platter of chicken to him and grinned. "If you're going to get mixed up with a woman like that, you're going to need to keep up your strength. Here. Eat."

Tired, a nagging headache throbbing at her temples, Sabrina pulled into her driveway at twenty minutes to seven and sighed in relief. Finally! It had been a long, disturbing day, and all she wanted to do was collapse into bed, pull the covers over her head, and forget the world. Tomorrow would be soon enough to worry about the two women who had been murdered and the note personally delivered to her from their killer.

But as she cut the engine and stepped from her car, she found herself wondering if the killer who had dared to track her down at work had made it his business to find out where she lived. A first-grader could have done it—she was in the book, under S. Jones. There were three others, but that wouldn't present much of a problem for a man who had committed two murders without leaving behind a single clue that could be used by the police to identify him. All he would have to do was scout out the others or follow her home from work.

A cold chill slithering down her spine in spite of the fact that the heat of the day had yet to ease much, she whirled, her heart thumping, and searched the street in both directions. But the neighborhood was blessedly normal, and there wasn't a stranger in sight. Louis was washing his car next door, and across the street, the Garzas' oldest son, Chris, was mowing the lawn. Other than that, the street was quiet and deserted.

"You're being paranoid, Sabrina," she chided herself as she waved to Louis and Chris, then turned back to unlock the front door. "And that's just what the killer wants. Why else do you think he sent you that damn note? He's trying to scare you and you're letting him. What's the matter with you? You're not the type to jump at your own shadow. Straighten up, for God's sake! No one's been here, so quit looking over your shoulder and get inside. You're perfectly safe."

Her chin up, she hurried inside and did something she rarely did except at night when she went to bed—she shot the dead bolt into place. The click it made was loud in the silence, and she couldn't help but smile sheepishly at her own foolishness. "You're losing it, Jones," she chided herself, and turned toward the kitchen to see about supper.

She'd barely taken two steps when there was a sudden knock at the door. Startled, she jumped, then cursed herself for being so skittish.

It was probably just Chris wanting to know if he could mow her lawn, she decided. He was saving for a car and did chores for her and everyone else in the neighborhood whenever he got a chance.

But when she opened the front door, it was Mrs. Anderson who stood there smiling gaily, a plate of just-baked brownies in her hand. "Hi, sweetie. I saw you drive up and thought I'd bring you some dessert for after supper." Not the kind to stand on ceremony, she didn't wait to be invited in, but simply swept inside and headed straight for the kitchen. "I won't stay long—you look a little tired. Did you have a rough day?"

If she hadn't been so drained, Sabrina might have laughed. "Don't ask." She caught the scent of warm chocolate then and lifted her nose to the air. "Mmm. That smells heavenly. How did you know I needed a chocolate fix, Mrs. A.?" she asked as she followed her down the entrance hall to the kitchen at the back of the house. "I didn't even know it myself."

"That isn't surprising, considering the day you've had," the older woman said as she set the brownies down on the table and waved her into a seat. "Sit down and dig in, honey, while I get you a glass of milk. My mama always said nothing tasted better than something sweet from the oven after a bad day. What do the police say about that nasty note you got? I hope they're doing something about it. Just imagine, a cold-blooded killer waltzing into that paper and leaving you something like that! All I can say is, if I was in charge, I'd string him up by his thumbs the second I got my hands on him."

In the process of bringing a nice thick square of brownie to her mouth, Sabrina stopped halfway. "You know about the note?" she asked in surprise.

Her faded blue eyes dancing, Martha Anderson sank down in the chair across from her and leaned close to confide, "That nice Mr. Nickels came by asking about you earlier and told me the whole story. I tell you, I was shocked, dear!''

"Blake was here? Asking about me?"

"Oh, yes. And he was very concerned." Helping herself to one of her own brownies, she took a healthy bite and frowned. "I think these need a little more sugar. My sister gave me the recipe, and this is the first time I've made them. What do you think? Should they be a little sweeter?"

Struggling for patience, Sabrina assured her they were delicious just the way they were. "But what about Blake? Just what kind of questions was he asking?"

"Oh, the usual thing," she said airily. "I think he thought the killer might be someone you know, so he wanted to know about your background, if you had any enemies or former boyfriends who might have a grudge against you, that sort of thing. I laughed, of course. I just can't imagine you having any enemies. Why, you even managed to stay friends with Jeff after you two split, and how many people can say that?"

"You told him about Jeff?"

She nodded and rattled happily on. "It just came up when I mentioned that you didn't date much. Then Mr. Nickels just naturally assumed that there must be some bad blood between the two of you, so I had to set him straight."

Suddenly realizing for the first time that she might have let her tongue get away with her, she frowned worriedly. "You're not mad because I told him about the divorce, are you? I really didn't mean to tell tales out of turn, but he was so nice. And he seemed genuinely concerned that you were in danger. I just wanted to help. If something happened to you because I kept a vital piece of information to myself, I'd never forgive myself."

Knowing the way Mrs. A dearly loved to gossip, Sabrina knew that was never going to happen, but she only smiled and patted her hand. "Nothing's going to happen to me," she assured her. "And no, I'm not mad." At least not at her. But Blake Nickels was another matter. Temper starting to simmer in her eyes, she said, "You did the right thing, Martha. I'm just surprised that Blake felt the need to question you and the rest of the neighbors. I saw him this afternoon at the paper, and he never said a word about his plans to check me out."

"Well, you work for opposing newspapers," she pointed out with a mischievous grin. "Maybe he wanted to outscoop you on your own turf."

"He wouldn't dare," Sabrina began, only to hear his teasing words ring in her ears as clearly as if he were standing beside her.

Honey, when you get to know me better, you'll find out that I'll dare just about anything.

"Oh, I'd like to see him try," she seethed. "That note was delivered to me, not him, so that makes it my story. He's not going to come in through the back door and snatch it right out from under me. Just wait till I see him again—he's going to get an earful."

Martha laughed gaily at that and rose to her feet. "Just don't be too hard on him, sweetie. He's such a nice-looking young man. And he wasn't wearing a ring," she added with twinkling eyes. "Who knows what might develop if you give him a chance?"

A snowball had a better chance in hell, Sabrina thought with a snort, but there was no use telling Martha that. A hopeless romantic, she had been trying to find Sabrina a man ever since she and Jeff had split. In spite of Sabrina's insistence that she wasn't looking for a man, Martha refused to believe that she was perfectly happy going through life alone.

"The only thing that's going to develop between me and Blake Nickels is an all-out war if he doesn't quit trying to muscle in on my turf," she replied as the older woman turned to leave. "But thanks for the brownies—they were just what I needed."

Wandering back to the kitchen after she'd shown Martha out, Sabrina couldn't shake the image of Blake canvasing her neighborhood, questioning the neighbors about each other and her friends. And the more she thought about it, the more indignant she got. Talk about nerve! The man had it in spades. Who the heck did he think he was, anyway? She wasn't the story here—the note and whoever wrote it were, and if Blake didn't realize that, maybe it was high time she told him.

Steaming, she walked over to the kitchen wall phone, snatched it up, and punched in the number for information. Seconds later, she had his phone number and address. Scowling down at them, she started to call him, only to hang up before she completed the call. No, she thought, her brown eyes narrowing dangerously. Some things were better said in person. Not giving herself time to question the wisdom of her actions, she grabbed her purse and car keys and headed for the door.

Blake and his grandfather were in the middle of watching a baseball game and arguing over which was the better team when the doorbell rang. Seconds later, someone pounded angrily on the front door. The old man arched a brow and said dryly, "Somebody sounds madder than a hornet. You expecting company?"

"Nope. Not that I know of." Pushing to his feet, Blake strode over to the apartment's front door and peeked through the peephole. At the sight of Sabrina standing there, glaring up at him as if she could see him through the door, he started to grin. Evidently, she'd found out that he'd been asking around about her, and she was more than a little ticked about it. He could practically see the steam pouring from her ears.

Pulling open the door, he made no attempt to hide his

grin. "Well, well," he drawled. "If it isn't Ms. Jones. And to what do I owe the honor of this visit?"

Giving him a look that should have turned him to stone where he stood, she didn't wait for an invitation to come inside, but simply stepped around him and whirled to let him have it with both barrels. "All I can say for you, Nickels, is you've got a hell of a nerve. How dare you badger my neighbors and friends about me and pretend to be concerned about my safety when all you were really after was a damn story! Of all the low-down, underhanded, despicable—"

"You tell him, missy," an unfamiliar gravelly voice said encouragingly from behind her. "He ought to be ashamed of himself, and if he wasn't too big to take a switch to, I'd do it for you."

Startled, Sabrina jerked around to find an old man seated in a rocker in front of the television and obviously enjoying her tirade. Mortified, she blushed all the way to her toes. Driving over there, all she'd been able to think about was what she was going to say to Blake when she saw him, and like an idiot, she hadn't even stopped to make sure they were alone.

Wishing she had a hole to climb into, she said stiffly, "I'm sorry. I didn't see you sitting there."

"That's all right." He chuckled, rising to his feet. "It's been a while since I've heard a woman give a man a piece of her mind. I enjoyed it." Offering his hand, he stared down at her with sparkling green eyes that reminded her of Blake's. "I'm Damon Finnigan, Blake's grandfather. Most people call me Pop. You must be Sabrina Jones. I've read your stuff. It's good."

Surprised, Sabrina blinked. "You read the *Daily Record*?"

"He likes to keep up with my competition," Blake confided as he shut the front door and strolled over to join them. "He's one of your biggest cheerleaders."

"You're damn right," the old man agreed, giving Sabrina a playful wink. "If I was just a little bit younger, I'd give this young rascal here a run for his money."

"Pop—"

"A run for his money?" Sabrina echoed in confusion, frowning. "What—"

"Pop likes to tease," Blake said, shooting the old man a hard look that should have shut him up. It didn't.

Unrepentant, his grin daring, his grandfather only laughed. "It's one of my better talents, but I know a pretty woman when I see one. And so does Blake. He told me you were pretty, and he was right."

Swallowing a groan, Blake wanted to strangle him, but Pop had had his say and was obviously content to leave while he was ahead. "Well, I guess I'd better get out of here and let you two talk," he said cheerfully, heading for the door. "I need to get home anyway. I don't like to drive after dark."

"It was nice meeting you, Mr. Finnigan," Sabrina called after him.

"You, too, missy. And it's Pop. Mr. Finnigan's that old man that used to be my granddad."

With a promise to call Blake later, he shut the door on his way out, leaving behind a silence that all but hummed. Her temper now under control, Sabrina let the silence stretch a full minute before she said coolly, "I like your grandfather. He's sweet. Too bad you don't take after him more."

A dimple in his cheek flashing, Blake chuckled. "Actually, I've been told I'm just like him. I guess you'll have to get to know us both better, though, before you see the similarities."

"Fat chance, Nickels," she retorted. "In case you haven't figured it out yet, I didn't come here to be sociable. Especially with a rat like you."

Instead of insulting him, her hostility only seemed to

amuse him. "No kidding? Now why doesn't that surprise me?"

"You are the most aggravating—"

"Guilty as charged."

"Sneaky—"

"I know," he agreed cheerfully. "It's deplorable, isn't it? But my mother swears that once you get used to it, it's one of my more endearing qualities."

Her lips pressed tightly together, Sabrina swore she wasn't going to laugh. Damn the man, how was she supposed to tell him off when he agreed with everything she said? Stiffening her spine, she said through her teeth, "If that's an invitation, thanks but no thanks. I'd just as soon cozy up to a snake. Any man who would go behind my back and grill my neighbors about me and the men in my life is a—"

"Damn good reporter," he finished for her easily. "Of course, I could have come to you for that information, but somehow I don't think you would have told me that you spend your Saturday nights in bed with a good book."

"You're darn right I wouldn't have! Because it's none of your business. And who said that about me, anyway?" she demanded huffily. "I have lots of friends and go somewhere almost every weekend."

"We're not talking about friends here, sweetheart, but boyfriends. You know…men? Those good-looking, superior creatures who take a woman out, wine her and dine her, and sometimes want something more than a peck on the cheek in return? If you had any contact in the past with the pushy sort and offended him, he just might be the kind to hold a grudge and go after you and all the other women who gave him the cold shoulder over the years."

"That's ridiculous! *I* am not the story here."

"Aren't you?" he asked quietly. "Think about it. If any other woman but you had gotten the letter, you would be asking the same questions of her neighbors that I asked of yours. There's got to be a personal link. If all the killer wanted was a forum to express his view, he could have sent the note to the editor for the letters column. But he didn't. As far as we know, he hand-delivered it to you personally. There's got to be a reason for that.''

He had a point, one that made her more than a little nervous and irritated her at one and the same time. Tamping down the uneasiness that stirred in her stomach, she turned away to pace restlessly. "This is all just conjecture. It has to be. Don't you think I would know if someone I knew was capable of murder?''

"Maybe. Maybe not," he said with a shrug. "Psychopaths are damn clever.''

"But I don't know any psychopaths.''

"Not that you know of, anyway.''

"Dammit, Blake, stop that! I know what you're doing, and it's not going to work.''

"Oh, really? And what am I doing?''

"You're trying to distract me from the real issue here, which is *you* poking *your* nose into my life. It's got to stop.''

His eyes searching hers, Blake couldn't believe she was serious, but there was no doubting her sincerity. She actually expected him to walk away from what could be the story of the decade because she asked him to. Roguish humor tugging up the corners of his mouth, he said, "Sorry, sweetheart. No can do.''

"What do you mean...*no can do?* Of course you can! If you really want to find the murderer, go talk to the friends and family of those poor dead girls. That's where the story is.''

"Bull. *You're* the story, Sabrina. We both know it—you just don't want to admit it because it scares you to death.''

"That's not true! I've never been afraid of anything in my life.''

"Well, you'd better be," he growled, stepping toward

her. "Because a little healthy fear keeps people like you and me alive. Whether you want to admit it or not, someone out there means you harm. Until I find out why the killer sent you that note and who he is, everything about you is my business."

"The hell it is!"

"And if you don't like it, that's just too damn bad. Get used to it. I'm a hell of a good investigative reporter, so if you've got a secret, I'll warn you right now that I mean to find out what it is. By the time I get through with checking you out, honey, there won't be a panhandler on the street you've given a dollar to that I won't know about."

She swore at him then, highly imaginative curses that didn't include a single curse word but put him in his place, nonetheless. Against his will, he couldn't help but notice that she was something to see when she had her dander up. Temper blazed in her dark eyes, and twin flags of color burned in her cheeks. Dressed in a red dress that would have looked like a sack on another woman but somehow seemed to emphasize her every curve, she looked soft and feminine and full of fire. And he couldn't remember the last time he had wanted a woman so badly.

The thought caught him off guard, killing the grin that curled his lips. This wasn't the time to even think about getting romantic with a woman. Especially this woman, he told himself firmly. She wasn't in the mood. Hell, she was practically spitting daggers at him and would probably scratch his eyes out if he so much as touched her.

But even as he ordered himself to back away from her, he was eliminating the distance between them, as drawn to her as a moth to the scorching heat of a candle. And something of his intent must have gotten through to her because she faltered suddenly, her eyes wide, as he reached for her. "What are you doing?"

"Giving in to temptation," he said with a devilish grin, and hauled her into his arms. Before she could do anything but stiffen and gasp in outrage, his mouth was hot and hungry on hers.

He'd only meant to catch her by surprise and steal a kiss that would shut her up, but the second his lips touched hers, there was a spark of heat, a flash of desire that caught fire like a gasoline spill, and in the next instant, he felt like he was going up in flames. Burning for more than just a taste of her, he could have no more stepped away from her than he could have cut off his right arm. Her name a prayer, a curse, on his lips, he dragged her closer and gave in to the need that had the blood roaring in his ears.

Stunned, her head spinning and her knees threatening to buckle at any second, Sabrina clutched at him like a drowning woman going under for the last time. Trying to hang on to her common sense, she told herself that they had been headed for this from the second they met. Every time their eyes met, the attraction was there like a tiger hiding in the shadows, waiting to spring. She could handle it. She could handle *him*. Or so she'd tried to tell herself.

But now, caught tight against him, every nerve ending she had throbbing from his closeness, she felt as giddy as a young girl being kissed, *really kissed,* for the first time. All her senses were attuned to him…his hardness, the feel of his heart slamming against hers, the underlying tenderness of his kiss, the rush of his hands over her. And with every slow, intoxicating rub of his tongue against hers, the craving that he stirred in her grew stronger, hotter. Her lungs straining, something deep inside her just seeming to melt, she crowded closer, aching for more.

How long they stood there, lost in each other's arms, she couldn't have said. Magic engulfed them, holding the world at bay, and she was entranced. But it couldn't last. His breathing as hard as hers, he wrenched his mouth from hers, glazed eyes sharpened, and suddenly they were both staring at each other in disbelief as reality returned with a painful jolt.

Dear God, what was she doing? This was Blake Nickels, her adversary, the man who could irritate her faster than anyone else she'd ever known, and she'd kissed him like an old maid who'd been given one shot at Prince Charming.

Stunned, her cheeks on fire, she never remembered moving, but suddenly half the distance of the room was between them and it wasn't nearly enough. She had a horrible feeling that putting the entire state of Texas between them wouldn't have been enough. She could still taste him, still feel him against her, still draw in the spicy male scent of him with every breath she took.

And that frightened her more than a dozen notes from a killer. "I don't know what you think you were doing, but if you ever do that again, you're liable to lose a lip, not to mention a finger or two."

As shaken as she, Blake knew he should have taken the warning to heart and gotten the hell out of there while he still could. But the lady had just thrown down a gauntlet that no man with any blood in his veins could walk away from.

His green eyes alight with wicked laughter, he took a step toward her. "I don't know about you, sweetheart, but that sounds like a dare to me."

"Dammit, Blake, you stay away from me!"

"Make me," he said softly, and reached for her.

Ready for him, she made a break for the front door, but she never made it. On the television, the baseball game was interrupted by a special report, and they both instinctively turned to catch it.

"We interrupt scheduled programming for this breaking news story," the local ABC anchorman announced somberly. "There has been another murder of a young professional woman. The police are still investigating the scene in the four-hundred block of San Pedro, but preliminary reports indicate that the murder appears to be similar to that of Tanya Bishop and Charlene McClintock. We hope to have more details at ten. At this time, we return to regularly scheduled programming.''

Stunned, Blake and Sabrina stared at each other. A split second later, they were running for the door.

Chapter 4

Her name was Elizabeth Reagan. She was a twenty-eight year-old loan officer for one of the city's oldest and most successful banks. She made good money, had a lot of friends, and had a reputation for giving the shirt off her back to anyone in need. And she was dead, killed by a single bullet to the heart in her own living room while "Chicago Hope" played on the TV.

Standing on the edge of the crowd that had gathered in the front yard to watch from a distance as the police investigated the crime scene, Blake questioned shaken neighbors and crying friends, but just as with the other two murders, no one had seen or heard anything. All the neighbors had apparently been home at the time, in their homes on a summer evening with their windows and doors shut and the air-conditioning on, totally oblivious to what was going on at Elizabeth's house. Apparently, someone had walked in and shot her and not even a dog had barked a warning. She might have lain there for hours, staring glassy-eyed at her living-room ceiling, if the elderly woman across the street, a Mrs. Novack, hadn't let her cat out and noticed Elizabeth's front door standing wide open, all the lights on in the house, and her car missing from her driveway. She'd immediately called the police. It was a young rookie who'd been on the job barely a week who had made the grisly discovery and called for backup and Detective Kelly.

Frustrated, unable to believe that three murders could take place in three weeks, apparently by the same killer, without anyone seeing anything, Blake slowly made his way through the crowd, asking the same questions over and over again. Did Ms. Reagan have any known enemies? Any old boyfriends who might hold a grudge? Any acquaintances that she'd recently argued with? And always the answer was the same. No. No. No. She was a sweet girl. Everybody loved her. Her killer couldn't have possibly known her. It all had to be a tragic mistake—she must have surprised a burglar, who killed her and took her car.

Kelly and the rest of the investigative team was still inside, but there was no sign of a break-in or forced entry, and nothing but the car seemed to be missing. Blake had barely finished questioning Mrs. Novack about whether or not the vehicle had been there at all that evening when a pale and drawn teenager pushed his way through the crowd and announced to the police that he was Elizabeth's brother. He'd borrowed her car for a date after she got home from work and was, apparently, the last person who'd seen her alive. He, like everyone else, didn't have a clue as to who could have killed her.

Frowning, Blake searched the crowd of neighbors for Sabrina and finally found her talking to a young mother who was standing in the shadows under a magnolia tree, a curly-haired toddler clutched protectively in her arms. Throwing questions at her, Sabrina obviously wasn't having any better luck than he was. The woman just kept shaking her head and wiping at the tears that trailed down her ashen cheeks. As he watched, Sabrina touched her arm in sympathy, but when she turned away, her jaw was clenched with frustration. He knew just exactly how she felt.

Reading over the few facts he'd been able to gather, he swore. There just wasn't much to go on. And what little he had been able to find out, he didn't like the sound of. It went without saying that the victim was a young, single professional woman. She was also, according to the neighbors, petite and slender, with a cloud of black, curly hair that cascaded down her back. From her physical appearance alone, he could have been describing Sabrina.

His expression grim, he tried to tell himself that he was letting his imagination get the better of him. Just because the killer had left her one damn note didn't mean he'd started picking victims who looked like her. It was just a coincidence. But Blake was a man who didn't believe in coincidence...especially when it came to murder.

His gut knotting at the thought, he was just wondering if Kelly had made the connection when the man himself appeared at the entrance to the cordoned-off house and spoke to the uniformed officer standing guard there. A few seconds later, the man ducked under the yellow crime tape that blocked the doorway and slipped into the crowd. When he returned, he had Sabrina with him.

Pale and shaken, Sabrina stood in the dead woman's kitchen and stared in disbelief at the note found by the evidence team on the kitchen table. It was already stored in an evidence bag, but through the clear plastic, she could see that the handwriting was the same as that on the note she'd found on her desk at the *Daily Record* earlier in the day. And like that one, it was addressed to her.

"I can't believe this is happening," she told Sam. "It has to be some kind of sick joke. Who would do this?"

"I was hoping you could tell me that," Kelly said. "I

don't have to tell you that all kinds of weirdos come out of the woodwork on a case like this—you've covered the police beat long enough to know that some people get a real kick out of the thought of being connected to something like this. We could be dealing with that here, but I don't think so."

"You don't? Then who—"

"This particular weirdo knows you, Sabrina."

"No!" Denial instantly springing to her lips, she took a quick step back. "Don't start with me, Sam. You sound just like Blake—"

She started to say more, but there was a commotion at the front door, and they both turned to see Blake trying to talk his way past the junior officer stationed there. With a nod to the rookie, Sam allowed him access, then said curtly, "Since you were in on this earlier, you might as well hear the latest. I'm going to have to make a statement to the press later, anyway." Holding up the bagged note, he showed him Sabrina's name on the front. "We found this on the kitchen table. I was just telling Sabrina that there's a good likelihood that the killer is someone she knows. Apparently, you agree."

Blake nodded, his eyes on Sabrina. "She doesn't want to believe it. What's in it?"

"Basically, it's pretty much a replay of the other one," Kelly replied. "The perp wanted to make sure that Sabrina got the message this time. *'Learn your place,'*" he quoted. "He doesn't want to see her end up like Elizabeth and all the others."

"So why doesn't he just leave me alone?" she demanded. "That'll solve that problem easily enough."

"Because you're the one he's been trying to kill from the very beginning," Blake said flatly. "Dammit, haven't you noticed?"

Confused, she frowned. "That's ridiculous. He hasn't come anywhere near *me*. Except to leave the notes, of course, and I wasn't anywhere in the vicinity when he did that.''

"But every time he kills, he's striking out at you. Look at the victims. If you put their descriptions and yours in a box and picked one out, they would all be the same. A young, single, professional woman who lives alone and has a slender build and dark, curly hair.''

Kelly, looking more dour than Sabrina had ever seen him, nodded in agreement. "This guy, whoever the hell he is, is too methodical and careful to do anything by chance, Sabrina. He chose his victims for a reason, and considering these damn notes, I've got to agree with Blake. The killer seems to be obsessed with you and is working up the courage to come after you.''

Apprehension clawing at her, she shook her head, immediately rejecting the idea even as it struck a chord deep inside her. "None of this makes any sense. Why me?''

Blake shrugged. "Who knows? You're in the public eye. You're a fighter. You live off the St. Mary's strip and look great in red. There's no telling what's going on in this guy's head. But he knows where you work and there's a good possibility he knows where you live since he's getting closer to your front door with every killing. The McClintock woman lived ten miles away from you, Tanya Bishop only four. And this one's practically right around the corner.''

It was, in fact, a little over a mile and a half from her place to Elizabeth Reagan's, but that was still too close for comfort. "That could just be coincidence,'' she began desperately.

Blake swore in frustration, wanting to shake her. "C'mon, Sabrina, you don't believe that anymore than I do! This crackpot's after you and he's going to get you if you don't do something to protect yourself. Dammit, Kelly, talk to her before she gets herself killed!''

Raising a brow at the sudden tension crackling between

the two reporters, the detective watched them glare at each other and forced back a smile. "I hate to sound like a parrot, but he is right, Sabrina," he told her. "For your own protection, you might consider letting someone else cover the murders until we can catch the jerk. Preferably a man."

"And let that murdering slimeball dictate to me how I can live my life?" she gasped. "Never in a million years! Would you expect a man to do that?"

"You wouldn't be in this fix if you were a man," Blake answered for him. "But that's okay. You go ahead and risk your pretty little neck just to prove a point to a madman. When we plant you six feet under, we'll have it carved on your tombstone that you went to your grave a martyr for women's rights."

"I'm not proving a point—I'm just doing my job." Exasperated, she turned to Sam. "Is there anything else we need to discuss? If not, I need to get to the paper and get this written up so it'll make the morning edition."

He hesitated, obviously wanting to add his two cents to Blake's comments, but he only sighed and gave in in defeat. "No, go on. But I want to see you down at the station first thing in the morning with the names of everyone you ever knew who might have a grudge against you. I don't care if it was some jerk in college who didn't like working with you on the school paper—I want his name. Got it?"

She nodded. "I'll come up with a list tonight." Not sparing Blake a glance, she turned on her heel, stepped outside and headed for her car.

Blake almost let her get away with it. Then he remembered a kiss that just over an hour ago had rocked him back on his heels. The lady might think she could take care of herself, but he'd held her in his arms and knew just how delicate and vulnerable she was. He didn't even want to think about what a bullet shot at point-blank range from the gun of a crazy could do to her. His jaw hard with resolve, he started after her.

He caught up with her just past the outer fringes of the grim-faced, silent crowd that still stood on the perimeter of the front yard. "Wait just a damn minute, Jones," he growled as the shadows of the night swallowed them whole. "I've got a bone to pick with you."

She didn't even slow her pace. "I've already said all I have to say to you, Nickels. Don't even think about getting in my way."

With two quick strides, he was not only in her way, he was blocking it. "You're either crazy as a loon or you've got a death wish—I haven't decided which," he muttered. "Stand still, will you?"

"I'm in a hurry, Blake. Unlike you, I seem to be the only one around here concerned with a deadline."

"Oh, I'm aware of it, all right. It's just that some things are a little bit more important than making the morning edition."

"Like what?"

"Your life."

"We've been all over this, Nickels," she said, letting her breath out in a huff. "There's nothing left to say."

"Maybe not," he agreed, surprising her, "but I'm going to say it anyway. For what it's worth, Jones, I used to be like you, obsessed with a story—"

"I'm not obsessed!"

"Then a snitch got killed because of something he told me," he continued as if she hadn't spoken. "It was my fault."

Stunned, she gasped, her eyes wide with instant sympathy. "Blake, no! You shouldn't blame yourself. You're not responsible."

"I lost my objectivity," he said simply, making no excuses for himself. "I was so determined to get the story that I didn't even realize I was putting that kid in danger. I don't want you to do the same thing.''

"But this is different.''

"Is it?'' he asked sardonically. ''Think about it.''

"It isn't just the story,'' she said earnestly. ''It's the principle of the thing. You wouldn't let a murdering piece of trash scare you off a story and I can't either. Because if I do, the word'll be all over the street that all you have to do is threaten Sabrina Jones when she gets too close to a story and she'll fold like a deck of cards. I might as well go back to obits because they're the only stories I'll be able to dig up.''

He winced at the play on words, but he didn't smile. Not about this. ''You won't dig up any stories with a bullet in your heart, either. Have you thought about that?''

"That's a chance I'll have to take.''

"Dammit, Sabrina, you take chances at the horse races, not with your life. I don't like the idea of you traipsing all over the city with a killer on your tail.''

"I don't like it, either,'' she said. ''But it's not going to stop me from doing what I have to do.'' Suddenly suspicious, she studied him through narrowed eyes. ''You're not getting all bent out of shape over this because of that kiss, are you? It was just a kiss, Blake. Nothing else. It didn't give you any rights where I'm concerned, so don't start getting any ideas.''

Normally, Blake would have agreed with her and thanked God that she was being so levelheaded over what he'd intended as nothing more than an impulsive kiss. But somewhere between his intentions and the execution of the kiss itself, things had gotten out of hand. Her response had nearly blown the top of his head off, and her casual dismissal of that irritated him to no end. If she hadn't wanted him to get any ideas, she damn sure shouldn't have kissed him the way she had!

"That wasn't *just* a kiss and you damn well know it,''

he said huskily, his green eyes dark with temper. "You forgot what planet you were on, and so did I."

"I did not!"

"Little liar," he retorted softly, taking a step toward her. "Shall I prove it to you?"

He would have done it, right then and there, but she never gave him the chance. Lightning-quick, she shied out of reach. "Oh, no, you don't! You stay away from me, Blake Nickels!" she warned, throwing up a hand to hold him at bay as she walked backwards away from him. "Do you hear me? You just keep your distance, and we'll both get along fine. I've got a job to do, and so do you, and we're not going to complicate the situation by getting involved. So just stay away from me."

She reached her car then, and darted around it like the devil himself was after her. Letting her go, Blake watched her climb inside and drive away and didn't know whether to laugh or curse. Didn't she know that he'd tried staying away from her from the very beginning? He wasn't looking for the entanglement of a relationship any more than she apparently was. Fate, however, seemed to have other ideas.

The note left at Sabrina's desk was splashed across the front page of the *Daily Record* the next day, and the phones at the police station were swamped with calls from people who were sure they knew who the murderer was. Two days after that, the report on the note found at the scene of Elizabeth Reagan's murder came back from the lab and confirmed what everyone had already suspected— it was exactly like the one found at the *Record*. Written on paper that could have been bought at any one of a hundred or more office-supply stores in the city, it was wiped clean of fingerprints and any clues that might have led to the identity of its author.

With no murder weapon, no witnesses, and none of the

phone calls to the police panning out, Blake did what he did best—he went looking for leads. And he started with the victims. Figuring there had to be some kind of connection between the three women, he checked out their hobbies, any clubs or associations they belonged to, even their churches. And everywhere he turned, he reached a dead end. Frustrated, he was left with no choice but to hit the streets and start making friends with snitches and other lowlifes that were in a position to know what was going down in the city.

He didn't like it. Even though he knew that the chances that the past would repeat itself were slim to none, he wanted nothing to do with informants. That, unfortunately, was a luxury he didn't have—not if he wanted to keep up with Sabrina.

The lady really was incredible. And as much as he hated to admit it, she kept him on his toes and pushed him to do his best work. She covered the city like a blanket, digging up stories on everything from a drug ring and money-laundering scheme on the west side to embezzlement at city hall. He couldn't go anywhere without running into her or hearing that she'd already been there and gone. He found himself looking for her everywhere he went and reading his own work with a critical eye, comparing it to hers. Their styles were different—who could say whose was better? His was grittier, yet hers was just as compelling. With a simplicity that he couldn't help but admire, she pulled the reader into a story and didn't let him go until he reached the end.

If she hadn't worked for the competition, Blake would have subscribed to the *Daily Record* just to read her stuff. As it was, he couldn't do that without helping her win their bet, and that was something he was determined not to do. So he had to be content with picking up the *Record* in coffee shops whenever he could and sneaking a peak at her work so he could tease her about it when he saw her.

And he did see her, in spite of her best efforts to avoid him. In the week after Elizabeth Reagan died, they ran into each other often, but Sabrina was as wary as a kitten with a thorn in its paw. If she saw him first, she cut a wide swath around him and left just as soon as she could. If he surprised her and approached her before she knew he was anywhere within a ten-mile area, she kept the conversation strictly professional and just dared him to bring up the subject of a certain kiss. He didn't. But the knowledge was there between them every time their eyes met.

Grinning at the memory, Blake dragged his attention back to the grumblings of the snitch who'd insisted on meeting him at an out-of-the-way bar on the east side. The place was a dive and smelled like it. Blake wouldn't have touched a drink there if his life had depended on it, but the bar's other occupants weren't nearly as particular.

Watching Jimmy, his snitch, pour rotgut down his throat, Blake wondered how the man had any lining left in his stomach. "Okay, spill your guts, man. What's the word on the street?"

"Nothing," Jimmy claimed, wiping his mouth with the back of his hand. "Honest. Whoever's knocking off those broads is doing it with a clean piece. I've talked to everybody I know and no one sold a hot shooter to the nut case. He already had it or he bought it legit."

Blake swore. He'd figured as much, but with a serial killer on the loose, you couldn't take anything for granted. Jimmy had connections in most of the hellholes in the city. If someone out there had sold a stolen gun to the killer, he would have heard about it. "That's what I was afraid of, but thanks for asking around. If you hear anything—I mean anything—let me know. And get yourself something to eat. You're skinnier than a fence post."

Taking the bill Blake slid him, he grinned, exposing crooked yellow teeth, and snatched at the money as if he was afraid it was going to disappear any second. "Sure thing, man. Later."

He was gone, slipping away and into the shadows of the bar between one instant and the next. Shaking his head over the man's ability to fade into the woodwork, Blake did a disappearing act of his own and headed outside to his car.

His thoughts still on the gun, he was heading back to the paper when the crackling report on his police scanner finally penetrated his concentration. Someone had called in a mugging at an ATM machine. Normally, he wouldn't have bothered to cover such a minor crime, but it wasn't the crime itself that interested him—it was the location. It was just a couple of miles from where Sabrina lived.

Later, he would have sworn he never made a conscious decision to check it out, but he turned right instead of left at the next intersection and found himself heading for the near northside. It only took him minutes to get there, but the police were already there, blocking the parking lot where the ATM was located, leaving him no choice but to find a spot around the corner to park. Not surprisingly, Sabrina's red Honda was already there.

The minute his gaze landed on the sporty little car, he knew he was in trouble. Because it wasn't, as it should have been, the story that had brought him to that part of town. It was the possibility of seeing Sabrina Jones.

In the process of interviewing the victim, Thelma Walters, an elderly neighbor who was surprised by the mugger when she stopped at the ATM to get money for groceries, Sabrina glanced up and felt her heart constrict at the sight of Blake slowly walking toward her. The smile that usually flirted with his mouth was noticeably absent, and in his eyes was something—a heat, a dark intensity—that was aimed right at her. Her mouth suddenly dry, she couldn't remember what she was going to ask next.

"Is something wrong, sweetie?" Mrs. Walters asked suddenly, reaching out to feel her forehead. "You're awfully flushed all of a sudden. Are you feeling all right? Maybe you've been out in the sun too long."

Her blush deepening, Sabrina blinked her friend back into focus. "Sorry," she said, forcing a laugh. "I guess I just drifted off. It must be this heat. It is awfully hot today." Fanning herself, she struggled to concentrate. "Now, about the mugger. I understand you caught him all by yourself after he took off running with your purse. The police said you threw a rock and hit him in the head?"

Pleased with herself, Thelma Walters laughed gaily. "It was more like a pebble than a rock, but yes, I beaned him one in the noggin. He glanced over his shoulder to see what had hit him and ran right into a security officer from the apartments across the street who heard my cries for help." Grinning, she confided, "I used to be a softball pitcher in high school, but it's been fifty years since I threw a ball. I guess I've still got it, huh?"

"You can be on my team any day of the week," Sabrina said, chuckling. "You did get your money back, didn't you?"

"Every penny," the older woman said proudly. "The next time that young man decides to go after a senior citizen, he'd better think twice about it. We're not all old fogies sitting around waiting to die."

Her lips twitching, Sabrina promised to include that little tidbit of information in the story. "Well, that's a wrap, Thelma. Thanks. You want me to call someone to come and get you? I know you weren't hurt, but finding yourself face-to-face with a mugger would shake up just about anyone. Maybe you shouldn't drive."

Her eyes crinkling, the older woman held out her hand to show her she was steady as a rock. "I'm fine, sweetie," she confided, "but if you don't mind, I'm going to see if I can talk one of those good-looking policemen to take me home. I noticed the blonde wasn't wearing a wedding ring, and my niece, Jenny, is looking for a good man."

"Well, then, hey, don't let me get in your way." Sabrina laughed as she stepped back and motioned for her to proceed her. "Go get him, girl."

She was still grinning when Blake strolled over and joined her. Her heart, remembering a kiss she had tried her damndest to forget, knocked out an irregular rhythm in greeting. Annoyed with herself, she lifted a brow at him and gave him a smile guaranteed to set his teeth on edge. "You having a slow day or what, cowboy? These types of stories are usually beneath a superstar like you."

His eyes glinting in appreciation of the dig, he shoved his hands in his pants pockets and rocked back on his heels. "That's funny. I was just about to say the same thing about you, sweetheart. And the last I heard, you were the only superstar around here. When I first came here, all anyone ever talked about was the great Sabrina Jones. For a while there, you really had me shaking in my shoes."

She might have been pleased if he hadn't begun the admission with a qualifying phrase. "For a while," she repeated, her smile tightening ever so slightly. "But not now?"

Delighted that she'd asked, he grinned. "Do I look like I'm worried?"

No, he didn't, she had to admit, irked. In fact, she'd never seen a man who appeared less worried. Loose-limbed and relaxed in jeans and a polo shirt, his dark hair windswept by the afternoon breeze, he looked as if he didn't have a care in the world. If he was concerned about losing their bet at the end of the month, he certainly didn't show it.

Perversely irritated, she said, "For your information, Nickels, I happen to know the victim. She called me right after she called the police. Now that we know why I'm here, what's *your* excuse?"

Opting for the truth, knowing she wouldn't believe him, he teased, "I figured you'd be here, since it was so close to where you live, and I couldn't pass up the chance to see you again. We haven't talked much the last week. Did you miss me?"

"Like a dog misses a flea," she tossed back, not batting an eye. "Why don't you do us both a favor and go back to sports? This town's not big enough for the two of us to both cover crime."

"Then we've got a problem," he said with a chuckle, "because I'm not going anywhere. Anyway, I kind of like running into you just about everywhere I go." Her words suddenly registering, his grin broadened. "Why, Jones, you had me checked out! I'm touched."

She laughed, she couldn't help it, and cursed her slip of the tongue. Damn the man, did he have to be so charming? Lifting her chin, she said, "Don't go jumping to conclusions. Of course I checked you out. I'm a reporter. That's what I do for a living."

She might as well have saved her breath. "Yeah, yeah," he teased. "That's what they all say. Why don't you just admit it, honey? You're crazy about me."

"Me and half the female population of S.A.," she retorted, going along with him. "I bet you can't go anywhere without beating the women off with a stick."

His green eyes dancing, he shrugged modestly. "It's rough, Jones, but I somehow manage to make time for all of them. Shall I pencil you in for Saturday night? It's the only night I've got free this week."

"And I'm busy. Darn! Isn't that the pits?"

"Yeah," Blake drawled, enjoying himself. "I can see you're real broke up about it."

"Oh, I am," she claimed with mock seriousness that was ruined by the smile that tugged insistently at her lips. "I just don't know how I'll get through the rest of the day."

"Oh, I'm sure you'll manage. You can always bury yourself in your work."

"True," she agreed. "And speaking of work, I guess I'd better get back to it." Reaching up, impish mischief sparkling in her eyes, she dared to pat him on the cheek. "See you around, Nickels."

Letting her go, Blake grinned. Little witch. It would serve her right if he snatched her up and laid a kiss on that beautiful mouth of hers. But the next time he kissed the lady—and there would be a next time; he had no doubts about it—he wanted her all to himself, preferably in a dark, secluded place where he could take his time with her. Then they'd see just who was crazy about whom. But for now, there was work to do.

It didn't take him long to get Thelma Walters's side of the story—thoroughly enjoying the attention, she was only too eager to talk about the mugging. Her attacker, however, was a little more tight-lipped; the arresting officer had to supply the thug's name and the information that he had a long record.

Armed with that, Blake had all he needed. And so, apparently, did Sabrina. He saw her heading for her car, which was parked around the corner near his, and fell into step beside her. "Now that we're through with that," he said easily as they rounded the corner, "why don't we grab something to eat? I know this great little Chinese place right down the street."

"Sorry, Nickels. I can't. I—"

Whatever she was going to say next seemed to stick in her throat. Puzzled, Blake frowned down at her. "You okay, Jones? You're looking a little strange around the gills."

Strangling on a laugh, she said, "I'm sorry. I know I shouldn't laugh. It's really *not* funny—"

"What?"

Unable to manage another word, she only shook her

head and pointed down the street. His eyes following the direction of her finger, Blake didn't see anything at first to explain her amusement. Then his gaze landed on his pickup.

Someone had set it up on blocks and stolen the two rear tires.

"Dammit to hell!"

Sabrina tried, she really did, to summon up some sympathy, but she was fighting a losing battle. Muffled laughter bubbling up inside her like a spring, she bent over at the waist and buried her face in her hands, whooping for all she was worth. "I'm sorry," she choked, giggling as she wiped at the tears that streamed from her eyes. "Really, I am! But if you could just see your face..."

He scowled at her, and that set her off again. "Stop it, Blake. You're killing me!"

"I ought to kill you," he retorted, his lips twitching in spite of his best efforts to appear stern. "What kind of neighborhood is this, anyway? Those were brand-new tires!"

"Well, I should hope so." She laughed. "What's the point of stealing old ones? Dammit, Blake, don't you know better than to drive a new truck into this part of town?"

"Apparently not," he said dryly. "I guess I'll have to get an old clunker like yours."

Smirking, she retorted, "At least I don't get my tires stolen in the middle of the day. C'mon, I'll give you a ride to my place and you can call a wrecker from there. It looks like you're going to need one."

She'd only meant to offer a helping hand to make up for laughing, but the minute Blake followed her inside her house, she knew she'd made a mistake in bringing him there. The small two-bedroom home her grandmother had given her when she'd married husband number five was her personal space, a retreat from work and crime and the senseless violence she made a living from in the streets. As she watched Blake look around the living room with interest, she knew she would see him there long after he left.

Panic hit her then, right in the heart, shaking her. Lord, what was wrong with her? He had kissed her one stinking time—*one time*—and she hadn't been able to get him out of her head since. She had to stop this, dammit! She wasn't the type to moon over a man, especially one like Blake Nickels, and she wasn't going to start now. Still, she couldn't help noticing how right he looked in her house.

You're losing it, Sabrina. Really losing it. Shaking her head over her own fanciful thoughts, she motioned to the old-fashioned, Forties-style rotary on the small table at the far end of the couch. "The phone's right there. It'll probably take a tow truck a while to get here. Would you like some iced tea while you're waiting?"

"Oh, don't go to any bother," Blake began, but he might as well have saved his breath. She was already gone, heading for the kitchen as if the hounds of hell were after her. Staring after her, his lips twitched into a smile. He'd never seen her nervous before, but she was showing definite signs of it now. And he had to ask himself why. If he'd been the conceited type, he might have wondered if it had something to do with him.

Grinning at the thought, he strode over to the phone and called information for the number to the garage down the street from his apartment. Placing the call, it took him only minutes to explain the situation and request a tow truck.

Sabrina was still in the kitchen when he hung up, and he couldn't resist the urge to look around. Reasoning that he wasn't going to go through her drawers or anything, he found himself wandering over to the photographs that covered nearly all of one wall. Most of them were wedding pictures taken over the course of what looked like half a century, if the style of dress of the wedding guests was anything to go by.

"They're something else, aren't they?" Sabrina said as she returned to the living room with a glass of iced tea in each hand. Strolling over to him, she handed him his glass and nodded at the picture of a beaming older couple he was studying. Standing on the deck of a ship before a judge, they were dressed in full scuba gear, complete with masks. "That's Grandma and Grandpa Bill," she said, smiling fondly. "Number four."

"Number four?" Blake repeated, lifting a brow in inquiry. "Number four what?"

"Husband number four," she explained. "Grandma likes to get around."

His brow climbed higher at that. "Your grandmother's been married *four* times?"

"No, actually it was five at last count. Well, six, if you count Grandpa Mason," she amended. "She married him twice."

Amazed, Blake turned back to the wedding pictures and frowned, unconsciously counting them. "But there's more than six wedding pictures here."

"Oh, not all of those are Grandma." She laughed. "The rest are Mama. She favors Grandma a great deal, don't you think? In fact, Grandpa Harry said the two of them looked so much alike that they could have passed for twins if they'd been closer in age. It's a shame he and Grandma didn't stay together. I really liked him. But he had this daughter who couldn't stand Grandma, so that was the end of that."

"He divorced her?"

She nodded. "Six months after they married. Grandma was heartbroken until Chester came along."

"Then why is his picture still with the rest? I would have thought she'd have tossed it out."

"Oh, Grandma doesn't hold grudges. Once your picture goes up on the wall, you're up there for life."

Blake almost laughed. She had to be kidding. But there was no question that the wedding pictures were legit. Frowning, he said, "Just for the record, how many times have your mother and grandmother been married?"

Sabrina didn't even have to count. "Eight and holding—if you don't count Grandpa Mason twice. Of, course, things could change at any time. Mom's in Alaska with Hank right now, and Grandma's touring the country with Grandpa George, and I haven't heard from any of them in a while. If there's a shift in the wind, who knows what can happen?"

It wasn't something to brag about, but Sabrina had learned a long time ago not to apologize for it, either. Her mother and grandmother were what they were, and there was nothing she could do to change that. At this late date, she wouldn't even try, but there were times, like now, when she could use their atrocious number of divorces to make a point.

"The women in my family are very good at saying 'I do,'" she said quietly. "They're just lousy at commitment, and it's not even something they can help. It's a defective gene, and the only cure for it is not to get married."

Her tone was light, amused, almost facetious, but as she watched Blake frown, she knew he'd gotten the message. If he was looking for a relationship, he could look somewhere else. She wasn't interested.

Chapter 5

She should have been pleased that she'd made her point and he didn't give her an argument about it. But long after Blake left with the tow-truck driver who stopped by to give him a ride to the garage where he would take his pickup, Sabrina stood in her front yard, frowning as she stared down the street after him. She felt sure he wouldn't try to kiss her again. Why didn't that bring the relief she'd expected it to?

"Somebody having trouble?" Louis asked as he passed by on the sidewalk with his Lab, Lady. "I thought I saw a tow truck stop here."

Jerking out of her musings, Sabrina summoned a smile. "Oh, hi, Louis. Yeah, there was a wrecker here. Mrs. Walters was mugged at the ATM on McCullough when a mugger tried to rob her. While Blake and I were covering the story, somebody stole the back tires off his pickup."

"In broad daylight?" Louis exclaimed. "And no one saw anything?"

"Well, I don't know about that," Sabrina said dryly.

"A mockingbird can't land on the back fence without old lady Charleston seeing it two blocks over, so I thought I'd ask around and see what I could find out. If you happen to see two slightly used Michelins lying around while you're walking Lady, let me know, will you?"

"I'll keep my eyes open," he promised. "But if I were you, I'd check first with that Gomez kid down on the corner. From what I've seen, he's a little thug. The police have already questioned him a number of times about several robberies in the area. Stealing tires sounds like something that'd be right up his alley."

Sabrina nodded. She'd been thinking the same thing herself. "You might be right. I think I'll check him out right now."

"Be careful," he warned as Lady grew impatient and started to tug him farther down the street. "With someone like that, you never can be sure of what he's capable of."

That might have been true of someone else, but Sabrina had known Joe Gomez since he'd been in grade school. Despite the fact that he was a gang member with a reputation for stealing just for the heck of it, he had a twisted code of ethics when it came to robbing his own neighbors. He just didn't do it. But that didn't mean he wouldn't know who did.

Heading up the street, she approached the Gomez house cautiously, more out of respect for Killer, the Rottweiler that was usually chained to the tree in the front yard, than because of any fear of Joe. The dog, however, was nowhere in sight. Relieved, she strode boldly up onto the front porch and knocked on the weathered siding next to the wrought-iron grillwork that covered the front door.

Deep in the bowels of the old wood-frame house, she heard Killer's fierce growl and a terse command to knock it off. Then Joe was opening the door and looking at her as if he'd just found his favorite centerfold on his threshold. Seventeen and full of himself, he propped a shoulder against the doorjamb and looked her up and down with wicked, dancing eyes. "If you've come to borrow a cup of sugar, I'm the only sweet thing in the house." Grinning, he held his arms wide. "Take me. I'm yours."

Sabrina laughed and shook her head at him. It was an old joke between them, his flirting with her, and she never took him seriously. She liked his sense of humor and enjoyed jawing with him, but even if he hadn't been ten years her junior, she wouldn't have been interested in Joe. The teenage girls that followed him around like puppies might be impressed with his flagrant macho antics, but Sabrina didn't find them the least attractive and would have never stood for them from any man, young or old.

"Sorry, Joe, but I'm on a diet. No sweets allowed."

"Well, hell, honey, don't let that stop you. Cheat."

"I don't think so," she said, grinning. "Anyway, that's not why I'm here."

Just that quickly, his smile vanished. "Oh, boy, here it comes," he groaned. "The third degree about that mugging over on McCullough." Glancing over his shoulder to make sure his grandmother had heard nothing of the conversation, he quickly stepped outside and shut the door behind him. "You think I had something to do with it, don't you? Just because I knew old lady Walters stopped there every Monday to get money for her bratty grandson doesn't mean I told anyone about it."

Amused, Sabrina lifted a brow at him. "You sound just the teensiest bit defensive, Joe. Did I accuse you of anything?"

"No, but—"

"*Should* I be accusing you of anything?"

"No!"

"Then what's the problem? The mugger was caught. I just wanted to talk to you about some tires."

"Tires?" he echoed, frowning. "Now what would I know about tires?"

Another reporter might have been fooled by the scowl and innocent tone he adopted in the blink of an eye, but Sabrina had known him too long to be taken in by such a display. Grinning in appreciation of the act, though, she said lightly, "Oh, nothing. I just thought you might put the word out for me that two Michelins taken off a certain black, 4X4 Chevy pickup belonged to a friend of mine."

"No kidding? You talking about that tall dude that was down here earlier in the day? Somebody stole his tires?"

"Apparently so. And I'd really appreciate it if they were returned."

Slipping his hands into the back pockets of his tattered jeans, he rocked back and forth on his heels, considering the matter with a twinkle in his eye. "I don't know anyone who's into that kind of thing, you understand," he finally confided, "but I can see how tempting two new tires would be to someone running around on retreads. Life's tough, you know."

Sabrina just barely managed to hold back a smile. "And two new tires don't come rolling by every day. You think if I offered a reward it might convince whoever took them to give them up?"

At first, she thought he was going to jump at that, but after careful thought, he shook his head. "Nope, that'd only encourage whoever did this to try it again. Just sit tight. I'll drop a hint in a few ears."

That was all Sabrina could ask for. Beaming, she said, "Thanks, Joe. I knew I could count on you."

"Yeah, yeah," he snorted. "I'm a regular prince."

"That's what all the young girls around here say," she said with a laugh as she took the porch steps. "'Bye, Joe. Behave yourself."

He wouldn't—the kid just didn't seem to have it in him—but he would do as he promised. And that was all Sabrina could ask for.

* * *

When she came home from work late the following afternoon, the tires were sitting on her front porch with a big red bow on them. And suddenly a day that hadn't been all that good got better. Pulling into her driveway, Sabrina laughed. Glancing down to the corner, she thought she saw a movement in an upstairs window at Joe's grandmother's house. It was Joe, of course, but she knew he wouldn't come out for her thanks, or even admit that he was the one responsible for getting the tires back—that would clash with his bad-boy image. But without his help, those tires would be on the back of somebody's low-rider, and they both knew it. Waving gaily, she saw the curtain swish again and grinned.

Five minutes later, she was headed for Blake's place with the tires loaded in the trunk of her Honda. She'd leave them by his front door, she decided, and let him wonder how they had gotten there. It would drive him nuts. Her eyes starting to sparkle at the thought, she turned into his apartment complex and found a parking spot within a few feet of the stairs to his second-floor apartment. Seconds later, she was rolling the first tire up the steps.

As quiet as a mouse, she propped it against the doorjamb, then went back to her car for the second. She would have sworn she didn't make a sound, but just as she leaned the second tire against the first one, the door was suddenly jerked open and both tires fell across the threshold with a soft thud. Caught red-handed, she glanced up, a quick explanation already forming on her tongue, only to find herself face-to-face with Blake's grandfather.

"Oh! Mr. Finnigan! You startled me. I didn't think anyone was here."

"Pop," he automatically corrected her. "I thought you were Blake." His green eyes, so like his grandson's, lit with mischief as his gaze slid from her to the tires and back again. "You know, in my day, I had a few women surprise me with a cake or two, but I don't believe one ever showed up on my doorstep with a load of tires. Have you got a car hidden somewhere to go with those?''

Sabrina laughed. ''No, but Blake does. These are his— the ones stolen off his truck yesterday. They sort of showed up on my doorstep.''

''Just like that?'' he asked, arching a brow at her. ''Why do I have a feeling you're leaving something out?''

''Well, I did sort of feel responsible since it happened in my neighborhood,'' she admitted. ''So I put the word out that Blake was a friend and I'd like them back. But I'd prefer that he didn't know that,'' she added quickly.

''Didn't know what? That you consider him a friend or that you're the one who got his tires back for him?''

He was, Sabrina thought, fighting a blush, altogether too sharp for her peace of mind. ''Let's just say this is our little secret,'' she suggested with a smile. ''I wouldn't want Blake to feel beholden or anything. Especially since we're both usually fighting for the same stories. He might feel like he has to step back and let me have an exclusive, and that's not what I want.''

''You want to beat him fair and square at his own game.'' It wasn't a question, but a statement from a man who obviously read her like a book. Grinning, he pulled the door wider. ''I like your style, missy. Since Blake's not going to be able to thank you for the tires, the least I can do is offer you a drink after you carted those dirty things up the stairs in this heat. Come on in.''

''Oh, that's not necessary,'' she began.

''Then humor an old man,'' he said with a shrug, blatantly playing on her sympathies. ''I don't get a chance to talk to a pretty girl very often. Blake doesn't bring too many home, and when he does, they're not interested in jawing with an old geezer like me.''

The pitiful look might have worked on somebody else, but Sabrina wasn't buying it. ''Nice try, Finnigan, but somehow you don't strike me as a lonely old man who roams around an empty house talking to himself all day. You've lived here all your life, haven't you? You probably know more people than God.''

Laughter deepening the wrinkles lining his weathered face, he nodded. "Probably. But most of them are on the downhill side of seventy, and all they want to talk about is aches and pains and where they've got their money invested. I bet you can tell some stories that are a sight more interesting than that. So, you coming in or not?''

She should have said "Thanks, but no thanks," then come up with a quick excuse to get out of there. She already knew all she wanted to know about Blake Nickels—he kissed like something out of one of her dreams—and the less she saw of him and his family, the better. But she really did like his grandfather, and what harm could a few minutes do?

"Well, it is hot, and I would like to wash my hands," she said, finding more excuses than she needed to ignore her common sense. "But I can't stay long."

Thirty minutes later, she was still there. Sitting at Blake's kitchen table and on her second glass of iced tea, she couldn't remember the last time she'd enjoyed herself more. Pop Finnigan had a real gift for storytelling, and more than once, she laughed so hard, she cried. He told her outlandish tales about his stint in the navy as a cook and his travels around the world, stories, she was sure, that he'd carefully edited for her delicate ears. She could have told him that there wasn't much she hadn't heard covering crime in some of the city's worst neighborhoods, but she appreciated his old-fashioned courtliness. He was a wonderful old man and Blake was lucky to have him for a grandfather.

He was also sneaky as a fox. Without Sabrina quite realizing how it happened, he cunningly shifted the focus of the conversation to Blake. One minute he was telling her about shore leave in Italy, and the next, he was confiding that as a child, Blake had traveled all over the world with his parents, who were career diplomats.

"That kid had a ball," he said with a grin. "He could speak French and German fluently by the time he was eight and knew Rome like the back of his hand when he was fourteen. Karen—that's my daughter—really thought he would go into politics." Laughing softly at the thought, he shook his head. "She'd better thank her lucky stars he didn't. Blake always did have a nose for secrets. With all the intrigue in international politics, he would have asked questions he had no business asking and ended up starting a war or something by now. The kid's a born reporter."

"I'll give him his due," Sabrina said, eyeing him knowingly. "He does seem to know what he's doing."

"You're darn right he does," the old man agreed promptly. "He always knew what he wanted and went after it. Of course, his mother still thinks this writing stuff is an act of rebellion on his part, but you won't find a better man anywhere. When Karen and Richard got assigned to France for a year, she had this crazy notion that I was too old to live alone. I told her I was just fine, thank you very much, but you know how daughters are. She worried, so Blake quit his job in New Mexico and moved here to watch over me. I told him I didn't need a babysitter, but he still checks in with me every day. I know what he's doing, of course, but I don't say anything because I don't want Karen to worry."

Fighting a smile, Sabrina nodded solemnly. "Of course. I'm sure your daughter sleeps a lot easier at night knowing Blake is here to watch over you."

"Sure she does. She'd sleep a lot better, though, if he'd settle down with a wife and a couple of kids. A man his age needs a good woman in his life, don't you think?"

A blatant matchmaker, he winked at her, just daring her

to disagree with him, and it was all Sabrina could do not to laugh.

Lord, he was outrageous—and as bold as his grandson! She didn't have the heart to tell him that he was talking to the wrong woman. "Mr. Finnigan—"

"Pop," he corrected her, flashing his dimples at her.

"Pop," she repeated with a smile. "Blake's marital status is really none of my business—"

"It could be."

"Stop that!" Sabrina laughed. "If Blake wanted a wife and children, I'm sure he'd have them. You said yourself that he always knew what he wanted and went after it. Anyway, that has nothing to do with me. I just came over to deliver his tires. And now that I've done that, I really do need to get out of here."

He tried to talk her into staying a little longer, but she was adamant. Thanking him for the tea and the entertaining conversation, she headed for the door. But she'd waited too long. The sound of a key in the lock stopped her in her tracks. A split second later, Blake pushed open the door with his shoulder and stepped into the apartment carrying the two tires she'd left on his doorstep.

Surprised, he lifted a brow at the sight of her as a slow smile stretched across his face. "Well, look who's here. And you came bearing gifts. At least I assume I have you to thank for these," he said, dropping the Michelins on the floor next to the door. "And I didn't think you cared, Jones. That just goes to show you how wrong a man can be about a woman."

"Don't let it go to your head, cowboy," Sabrina returned sweetly. "I just didn't want you to have an excuse when I won our bet."

Pop, watching them with a broad grin, stepped into the conversation at that. "Bet? What bet?"

"We have a little wager over who can bring in the most new subscribers by the end of the month," Blake informed him without ever taking his eyes off Sabrina. "Right now, I'd say it's a dead heat."

"In your dreams," Sabrina snorted. "I just checked the numbers this morning, and I've got nothing to worry about where you're concerned, Nickels. I'm so far ahead of you, you'll never catch up."

Not the last bit concerned, he only grinned. "I'm a patient man, sweetheart. And the month's not over with yet. With a little luck, you just might have to eat those words, not to mention buy me the thickest steak in town."

"Speaking of which," his grandfather cut in smoothly, "I think I smell my roast cooking. How about staying for dinner, Sabrina? There's plenty."

"Oh, no," she began. "I couldn't."

"What's the matter?" Blake teased. "Scared of breaking bread with the competition?"

"No, of course not!"

"Maybe she has another date," his grandfather supplied.

"No—"

"Then there's no reason why you can't stay," Blake said easily. "After all, feeding you is the least I can do after you got my tires back for me."

Put that way, there was no way she could gracefully refuse, and he knew it. "All right, all right," she said, laughing. "I'll stay. I just feel guilty about showing up here at suppertime without an invitation. I should have waited until later."

"That's okay," Blake assured her, his smile crooked. "If it'll make you feel any better, we'll make you work for it. You can do the dishes."

The meal that followed was one that Sabrina knew she would remember until her dying day. The food was delicious, but it was the company that was superb. Unlike most men she knew, who were reluctant to show their emotions,

Blake made no attempt to hide his affection for his grand-father. And the old man was just as affectionate with Blake. They teased and cut up and traded stories about each other until Sabrina could hardly eat for laughing. Long after the meal was finished and the roast was just a memory, they sat at the table talking and reminiscing about old times, fascinating Sabrina. Enthralled, she could have sat there for hours and just listened to them talk.

Which was, in fact, what she did. No one was more surprised than she when she glanced at her watch and saw how late it was. "Oh, my God, it's going on ten o'clock! And I still haven't done the dishes yet."

"You don't have to do that," Pop said when she jumped up and started collecting the dirty plates. "Blake was just teasing."

"Oh, but it's the least I can do," she argued. "I can't remember the last time I had such a wonderful meal. It was delicious, Pop."

Pleased, he grinned. "I'm glad you liked it. You'll have to come again. Won't she, Blake?"

Blake, recognizing the mischievous glint in his grand-father's eyes, shot him a quelling look behind Sabrina's back, and said easily, "Sure. Maybe next time, you can make that stuffed-pig dish you learned to make in Fiji."

"I don't know," the old man said. "That sort of smokes up the house. And I wouldn't want to go to all that trouble when you never know when you're going to be called out on a story. Maybe you should just take her out instead."

"Oh, no, that's not necessary—"

"Pop—"

Ignoring Sabrina's automatic refusal and his grandson's warning tone, the old man said innocently, "Weren't you looking for someone to go with you to the awards cere-mony at the National Newspaper Convention next week-end? Sabrina's probably going, too, so why don't you go together? It seems kind of dumb to go in two cars."

Under ordinary circumstances, Blake would have agreed. If he and Sabrina had just been rivals, he wouldn't have hesitated to suggest the same thing. Just because they worked for competitive papers didn't mean they couldn't be friends. But there was nothing friendly about that kiss they'd shared or the way the memory of it made him ache in the middle of the night. He was having a damn difficult time getting her out of his head, and taking her out, even to an awards ceremony, would only make the situation worse.

But before he could think of an acceptable reason to sidestep his grandfather's suggestion, Sabrina came up with one for him. "Thanks for the offer, Pop, but I wasn't even planning on going. I don't get much out of those kind of things, and even if I did go, I'd sit with the *Daily Record* staff. Arriving with Blake could be...awkward."

As far as excuses went, it was a good one, and Blake knew he should have been thanking his lucky stars for it. But she'd come up with it damn quick. And what the hell did she mean...arriving with him could be *awkward?* He was no Cary Grant, but he wasn't some homeless guy off the street, either. He knew a lot of women who would jump at the chance to go out with him!

Perversely irritated, his ego bruised, he should have let it go. But a man had his pride, dammit, and she'd just stepped all over his. "Why don't you tell him the real reason you don't want to go with me?" he challenged her. "This has nothing to do with work or your boss and co-workers seeing you with me. You're chicken."

It was the wrong thing to say to a woman who prided herself on being gutsy. Gasping as if he'd slapped her, she carefully set the dirty plates she'd collected back on the table, drew herself up to her full five foot four inches, and planted her hands on her hips. "Let me get this straight, Nickels. You think I'm afraid? Of *you?*"

His grandfather's presence forgotten, he nodded. "You got it, sweetheart. You can't take the heat."

"I can take anything you can dish out."

"Then prove it. Go to the awards banquet with me."

"I told you—I can't sit with you!"

"That's okay. I'll pick you up and take you home. Is seven o'clock okay?"

He knew the exact moment she realized she'd walked into a trap. Her brown eyes widened slightly with panic, then in the next instant, snapped with fire. If she could have gotten her hands around his throat, she, probably would have squeezed the life out of him, but she apparently had more self-control than that. Her nostrils flaring as she drew in a calming breath, she nodded curtly. "Seven will be fine."

For the span of ten seconds, Blake savored the victory and started to grin. Then it hit him. Sabrina wasn't the only one who'd walked into a trap. He'd sworn the last thing he was going to do was ask her out, then he'd turned around and done just that. And it was all his grandfather's fault! Turning to glare at the old man, he found him watching the two of them with glee dancing in his eyes. If Blake hadn't been so disgusted with himself, he might have laughed. Lord, he was going to have to watch Pop. If he wasn't careful, he'd have him married with children before he even knew what hit him!

She had to be out of her mind.

Standing in front of the mirror on the back of her bedroom door, Sabrina stared at her image and, for the fifth time in as many minutes, gave serious thought to calling Blake and claiming that she was too sick to go anywhere. It wouldn't be a lie. Her stomach was in a turmoil, her nerves jumpy, and she was definitely sick in the head. She had to be. Why else would she be standing here decked out in a new dress wondering if Blake would find her pretty?

Dear God, what was she doing?

Turning away from the sight of herself in a red silk dress that showed more skin than she'd ever showed in her life, she nervously paced the length of her bedroom. This was crazy. *She* was crazy! She didn't even know how she had gotten talked into this madness. She didn't like these kinds of shindigs, even if she was up for one of the most prestigious awards in the business. And she didn't go out with men who made her heart skip in her chest. It just wasn't smart when she had no intention of getting emotionally involved.

Turning back toward the mirror, she caught sight of herself again and winced. What had ever possessed her to wear red? It made her look...hot. Lord, she had to change!

But before she could even think about going through her closet for something more subdued, the doorbell rang and time ran out. Her heart jumping into her throat, she froze, every instinct she possessed urging her to run.

Why don't you tell him the real reason you don't want to go with me? You're chicken.

She stiffened, heat spilling into her cheeks. What was she doing? she wondered, disgusted with herself. She wasn't afraid of Blake Nickels or the feelings he stirred in her. After all, it wasn't as if they were even going out on a real date. For most of the evening, they would be seated at separate tables and she wouldn't even have to look at him if she didn't want to. So what was she getting into such a stew for? He was basically giving her a ride, nothing more. She could handle that—and him—with one hand tied behind her back.

Or so she thought until she opened the front door and caught sight of Blake Nickels in a tux.

No man had a right to look so mouth-wateringly good in formal wear. Or so comfortable. He should have been pulling at his collar or at the very least grimacing at the fit of the rented tux, but instead, he looked like he'd just stepped off the cover of *GQ*. Relaxed, one hand casually buried in the pocket of his black slacks, he grinned down at her with that familiar devilish sparkle in his green eyes and had no idea what he did to her heart rate. Stunned, Sabrina knew she was staring, but she couldn't take her eyes off him. How could she have ever thought this man was just an average Joe?

His grin suddenly tilting boyishly, he glanced down at himself and patted his bow tie. "What? Have I got this thing on crooked, or what?"

"No, I..." Unable to stop herself, she reached up and straightened his tie. When her eyes lifted to his, something passed between them, something hot and intimate and private. A wise woman would have stepped back then and run for cover, but she couldn't seem to make herself move. Her pulse was skipping, her legs less than steady. And he hadn't even touched her.

Her breath lodging in her throat, she struggled for a light tone, but her voice was revealingly husky when she said, "You know, Nickels, you clean up real good when you put your mind to it."

He should have come back at her with a smart remark that would have eased the tension sizzling in the air between them, but his brain was in a fog and had been ever since she opened the door to him. He'd expected her to be dressed up—formal wear was required for the banquet—but nothing could have prepared him for the sight of her in that dress. There was nothing the least bit risqué about it, but it made him think of satin sheets and candlelight and touching her everywhere.

She'd put her hair up, confining her usually wild curls in a sophisticated, provocative style so that only a few wisps tumbled down to sweep the nape of her bare neck. Lord, how he envied those curls! His fingers curling into fists to keep from reaching for them, he dragged his eyes away from her hair and immediately regretted it. Her skin was like the silk of her dress, soft and smooth. The rich fabric hugged her breasts and waist, revealing every curve before flaring out to a full, flirty skirt that fell to just below her knees. A man could spend hours just wondering what she had on underneath it.

His mouth suddenly as dry as west Texas, he said hoarsely, "Thanks. You don't look half bad yourself. Ready to go?"

She nodded. "Just let me get my purse and lock up."

He waited for her on the porch, then escorted her to where he'd parked his pickup at the curb. When he opened the passenger door for her, Sabrina stopped in surprise, her eyes impish as they lifted to his. "Why, Blake, I didn't know you had it in you."

"There's a lot about me you don't know," he retorted, flashing a wicked smile at her. "You ain't seen nothing yet, sweetheart."

They were both grinning when he closed the door and walked around to the front of the truck to climb behind the wheel. But the second he slid in beside her and started the motor, their smiles faded. In the close confines of the pickup cab, they weren't touching, but they might as well have been. Scents, tantalizing and sexy, mingled and teased, and every time one of them moved, the other felt it deep inside. It was only five miles to the convention center, but it seemed like a hundred.

Breathless, her palms damp and every nerve ending attuned to Blake's nearness, Sabrina should have been relieved when they finally reached the banquet hall. The place was already packed, crowded with reporters and newspaper publishers from all over the country. And somewhere in the mass of humanity, her boss and the rest of the *Daily Record* staff were waiting for her to join them.

But instead of hurrying off when it was time for them to part, she found herself reluctant to leave Blake.

"Well," he said as she hesitated at the entrance, "I guess this is it. I'll meet you here after this shindig's over." Suddenly noticing her silence, he frowned down at her. "Hey, you okay?"

Forcing a smile, she moved closer to him as the crush of people coming through the doorway jostled them. "I just don't care for this sort of thing. In fact, I wouldn't be here now if you hadn't dared me."

"Don't blame me." He chuckled. "It's not my fault you rose to the bait like a trout after a fly. Anyway, what are you worried about? I know the guys you're up against for the best crime story, and they can't hold a candle to you."

Surprised, she smiled. "My, my, Nickels, that sounds an awful lot like a compliment. Are you sure *you're* feeling all right? You must be coming down with something."

He grinned in appreciation and caught her hand before she could feel his forehead for a temperature. "Don't let it go to your head. You'll win. *This* year. Next year's a different matter. Then you'll be competing against me, and I'll warn you right now, I like to win." Giving her hand a squeeze, he dropped it and urged gruffly, "Go on and find your table before your boss sees you standing here holding my hand. I'll see you back here in a couple of hours."

Sabrina could have pointed out that *he* was the one who'd been holding *her* hand, but honesty forced her to admit that she'd started it by trying to touch him first. And she wanted to do it again. Color stealing into her cheeks, she stepped away from him while she still could. "Okay, okay. But we're going to talk about this later, Nickels. You're not the only one who likes to win."

She found the *Daily Record* staff at a large table near the stage at the far end of the room and wasn't surprised when her attire drew a few friendly wolf whistles. Most of the crew had never seen her in anything more sensuous than a business suit, and she took their ribbing in her stride. Then the master of ceremonies, a well-known television news journalist, stepped up onto the stage, and the awards ceremony began.

He was an entertaining speaker, but the awards were what everyone was waiting for, so he quickly got to them. Reporters from all over the country were nominated for everything from the best entertainment column to best obit, with each category divided into subcategories based on the size of the newspaper. With nominations restricted to work done over the course of the past year, Blake was up for sports coverage he'd done for the *Hidalgo County Gazette* in Lordsburg, New Mexico, while Sabrina competed with other police-beat reporters from larger papers.

She hadn't lied when she'd told him she didn't care for awards. It was the tracking down of stories and the writing itself she enjoyed, not the accolades of her peers, but when Blake's category came up and he was announced as the winner, she was thrilled for him. Sitting back in her seat, she found herself smiling as he strolled up to the microphone with an easy grace she couldn't help but admire. Relaxed and at ease, he joked with the crowd, then eloquently thanked the association for the honor.

Then it was her turn. Just as Blake had predicted, she was the winner. Unlike her *date,* she didn't shine at public speaking, so she kept her thanks short and sweet and got off the stage as quickly as she could. Back at her table, Fitz and the other reporters from the *Record* gave her high-fives and hugs, then it was time to party.

She should have stayed right where she was and celebrated with her friends until it was time to leave—but the only person she wanted to celebrate with was Blake. Later, she knew that was going to worry her, but for now, all she could think of was finding him in the crowd.

With the ceremony itself over, people were milling

about, renewing old friendships, congratulating winners and commiserating with losers, and it seemed like everywhere she turned, someone wanted to talk to her. Struggling to hang on to her patience, she finally reached the *Times* table, but he was nowhere in sight.

Seeing her frustration, Vivian Berger, a crusty old gossip columnist who made a healthy living out of knowing who was seeing whom around town, grinned at her knowingly. "Well, hello, Ms. Jones. You looking for Blake?"

Sabrina didn't ask her how she knew—the woman had eyes in the back of her head and had probably seen them come in together. Cursing the color that spilled into her cheeks, she said casually, "As a matter of fact, I was. I thought I'd congratulate him on his win."

"Then you're going to have to get in line," the old lady said with a cackle, gesturing behind her. "He's right over there."

Turning, Sabrina expected to see him accepting the backslaps and handshakes of the other sports writers he'd beat out for the award. Instead, she found him in the arms of another woman.

Chapter 6

She wasn't the possessive type. She never had been. When it came to men, she didn't get jealous or catty; it just wasn't in her. She'd caught Jeff talking to attractive women dozen of times during their short-lived marriage, and she'd never even lifted a brow—not because she hadn't cared, she'd assured herself at the time, but because she'd trusted him. But the man hugging the pretty redhead across the room wasn't Jeff. It was Blake, and for some reason she didn't want to examine too closely, that made all the difference. Something that felt an awful lot like jealousy slammed into her, knotting her gut and heating her blood, stunning her. This wasn't even a date; she was hardly entitled to an explanation, she reminded herself. But that didn't stop her from taking a step toward them anyway.

Before she reached them, however, someone in the crowd stepped around her, jostling her and bringing her back to earth with a thud. Mortified, she stopped in her tracks. What in the world was she doing? She had no claim to Blake and didn't want one. He was a free agent and could hug a dozen women for all she cared—it was nothing to her.

Then why are your eyes green right now, Sabrina? a mocking voice whispered in her head. *You'd like to scratch that woman's eyes out and you know it.*

God, she had to get out of there!

But before she could turn away, Blake looked over the woman's shoulder and saw her. He grinned broadly, murmured something to his companion, then he was hurrying toward Sabrina. "There you are! I was just going to come look for you." Surprising her, he swept her into a bear hug. "Congratulations, Jones. I knew you could do it."

He was so exuberant, she couldn't help but smile. With his arms tight around her, squeezing her close, all she could think of was how good it felt to be held by him again. Then she caught the faint scent of perfume that clung to his tux jacket—perfume that belonged to the redhead he'd hugged just seconds ago. Unable to stop herself, she stiffened.

"Congratulations to you, too." Suddenly needing to get out of there, to think, she quickly drew back. "The party looks like it's going to drag on awhile and you probably have a lot of friends you want to talk to—"

"Yeah, I do," he cut in, grinning down at her. "The whole gang's here from New Mexico, and I didn't even know they were coming. C'mon, I want you to meet them." Not giving her a chance to object, he grabbed her hand and dragged her through the crowd after him.

And before Sabrina was quite ready for it, she found herself face-to-face with the redhead. Up close and personal, she was just as beautiful as Sabrina had feared. Dressed in a pale mint-green sheath of a dress that showed off her petite figure to perfection, she was positively glowing. And she didn't seem to mind in the least that Blake had left her to return with another woman. Her smile friendly, her big blue eyes alight with expectation, she waited patiently for him to make the introductions.

"Sabrina, this is Sydney O'Keefe Cassidy. We used to work together at the *Gazette* in Lordsburg," Blake confided with a grin.

"Actually, he used to pester the *H* out of me," Sydney corrected, her blue eyes dancing as she shook hands with Sabrina.

"I was just keeping you in line until Dillon came along," Blake retorted, and nodded to the tall, lean man who stood behind Sydney, towering protectively over her. "The big guy there is Dillon Cassidy, Sydney's husband," he told Sabrina. "God only knows why, but he's crazy about her."

A slow smile stretched across Dillon's square-cut, good-looking face. "I think it's the red hair—"

Huffing, Sydney said, "It's not red—"

"It's strawberry blond," her husband and Blake said together, laughing. "Anyway, it's nice to meet you, Sabrina," Dillon said, smiling down at her. "I don't know what plans you two have for the rest of the evening, but we were talking about getting out of here and partying on the River Walk. I hope you'll come with us."

"Hey, that's a great idea," Blake said, grinning. "Let's go."

Sabrina hesitated, wanting to go, but knowing she didn't dare. Not after the jealousy that had sunk its claws into her. And over a married woman, too—a friend who was obviously very much in love with her husband. How, dear God, had this happened? When had she begun to think of Blake as hers? She had to be out of her mind!

Hanging back, she immediately drew a frown from Blake. "You go ahead," she told him huskily. "I'm sure the three of you have a lot to catch up on, and I've got to be at work early in the morning. I'll just call a cab—"

"Don't be ridiculous!" Blake said. "I'll get you home

before midnight. I promise.'' The matter settled, he linked his fingers with hers and pulled her outside after him.

It was a beautiful night. The heat of the day had passed, and a lover's moon lit up a clear sky filled with stars. Not surprisingly, the River Walk was packed with summer tourists and locals who were drawn to the music and lights and the cooling breeze that rippled over the slow-moving water of the San Antonio River as it wound its way through downtown.

Walking hand in hand with Blake, Sabrina felt as if she'd stepped into a dream and any second now, she was going to wake up. She hadn't even planned to go out with him, yet here she was on what was virtually a double date with him and the Cassidys. And in spite of the voice murmuring in her ear that she was going to regret this, she was having too much fun to even think about calling it a night.

Any reservations she had about Sydney had died the second her husband stepped forward to claim her, and it hadn't taken Sabrina long to realize that she and the other woman had a great deal in common. Sydney, too, was an investigative reporter who, according to her husband and Blake, didn't know the meaning of the word fear. She had once worked in Chicago, covering the crime beat, as Sabrina did in San Antonio, and had some fascinating tales to tell. Chatting like old friends, they could have talked for hours if the men hadn't interfered.

''No shoptalk,'' Dillon said as they finally got a table at the Hard Rock Cafe, which was packed to the rafters. ''This isn't a night for blood and guts.''

''Dillon's right,'' Blake agreed. ''We came here to party. C'mon, Jones, I want to dance.''

And with no more warning than that, he pulled her out onto the dance floor. Chagrined, Sabrina stood flat-footed in front of him and felt like a duck out of water as the crowd gyrated around them to the heavy beat of the ten-year-old hit blaring on the speakers. There were a lot of things she could do well, but dancing wasn't one of them. She loved music, but she just couldn't loosen up enough to move in time with it.

But Lord, she hated to admit it. Especially to someone who appeared to dance as well as Blake. His body already starting to languidly move in time to the beat, he looked as if he didn't have a bone in his body. Just watching him made her mouth go dry. Embarrassed color stinging her cheeks, she reached up to slip a hand behind his neck and pull his head down so he could hear her over the throb of the music. "There's something you should know about me, Nickels."

Casually draping his arms around her, he smiled down into her eyes. "What's that, Jones?"

"I've got two left feet."

His gaze, sparkling with amusement, dropped to her feet. "No, you don't. You've got a lefty and a righty just like everybody else."

She grinned, she couldn't help it, and struggled to give him a stern look. It wasn't easy when his mouth was only scant inches away from hers and he was so close that she could almost feel his body swaying against hers. "Blake, I'm trying to be serious."

"Don't," he growled low in his throat as his arms tightened around her to pull her more fully against him. "You can be serious tomorrow. Tonight, let's just…dance."

"But I can't!"

"Sweetheart, nobody who moves like you do has two left feet. Trust me. You're doing fine."

She wasn't—they both knew it—but when his voice turned all rough and deep and seemed to reach out and physically stroke her, warming the dark, secret recesses of her being, she found it impossible to care that she was a step behind everyone else on the dance floor. She was in his arms, her cheek pressed against his chest, with his heart knocking out its own erotic rhythm in her ear, and nothing else mattered. Like Cinderella, she was at the ball with a make-believe prince and it would all come crashing to a close at the stroke of twelve. For now, at least, she intended to enjoy herself.

Midnight, however, came and went and she never noticed the passage of time. They left the Hard Rock and checked out Planet Hollywood, then stopped in at a little jazz place where the music was as low as the lights. When they weren't dancing, the four of them were talking and laughing and trading stories about everything from high school to first dates to their most embarrassing moments. By the time they called it a night, it was going on three in the morning.

She'd talked all evening without once having to search her brain for a topic of conversation, but the second she and Blake were alone in his pickup and headed for her house, silence slipped into the truck with them. For the life of her, she couldn't think of a single thing to say to break it. Downtown was left behind, the odometer clicked off the miles, and the quiet, accompanied by a growing tension, thickened.

Desperate, she broke it just as Blake turned down her street. "I liked your friends. They were fun."

His smile flashed in the darkness. "They liked you, too. Dillon doesn't open up like that for everyone, you know. When he and Sydney first met, he was pretty much a loner, and wanted to stay that way. She's brought him out of it, but I've never heard him tell stories about his days in the DEA like he did tonight."

Breaking to a stop in front of her house, he cut the engine and turned to her. She'd left the porch light on, but it hardly touched the shadows filling the truck. "He must have really been taken with you," he said huskily. "I can't say I blame him. Did I tell you what a knockout you are in that dress?''

He didn't move so much as an eyelash, but Sabrina could feel his touch as surely as if he'd reached out and trailed his fingers across her bare neck. Between one breath and the next, her heart was hammering and the temperature in the cab seemed to have risen ten degrees.

Blindly, she fumbled for the release to her seat belt. ''Not in so many words, but I sort of got the general idea, thanks,'' she said in a voice she hardly recognized as her own. ''I'd better go. It's late.''

''Wait! I'll walk you to the door.''

She opened her mouth to tell him that wasn't necessary, but she was too late. He was out of the pickup like a shot and walking around to open her door for her before she could tell him that was the last thing she wanted. Left with no choice, she stepped out and joined him on the sidewalk.

The walk to her front porch had never taken so long. With the neighborhood quiet, asleep, they could have been the only two people in the world. Her pulse skipping every other beat, Sabrina half expected him to take her hand, but he seemed content to shorten his strides to match hers and walk along beside her without touching her. Then they reached the porch.

''Thank you for a wonderful—''

''I had a great—''

They both spoke at the same time as they turned to face each other. Normally, Sabrina would have laughed, but in the glare of the porch light, there was nothing comical about the heat in his eyes. It stole her breath and weakened her knees and set off alarm bells in her head. He was going to kiss her. She knew it as surely as she knew her own name, and if she had a single ounce of self-preservation, she'd get inside while she still wanted to.

But she just stood there, her heart knocking against her ribs so loudly that he had to hear it, and waited. In the quiet of the night, it seemed like an eternity, but something of her need must have shown in her eyes because in the next instant, he was reaching for her and she, God help her, was stepping into his arms. "Blake..."

All she said was his name. Just that. She didn't use his first name often, and had no idea what it did to him when she called to him in quite that way. He considered himself a civilized man who could easily control his passions, but she'd been driving him crazy for hours. They'd laughed and talked and casually touched and all he'd been able to think of was this moment, when he'd take her home and finally have her all to himself. He'd been so sure that he would sweep her up into his arms and ravage that beautiful mouth of hers the first chance that he got, but the hunger he heard in the simple calling of his name—and the trepidation she couldn't quite conceal—echoed the confusing mix of emotions churning in his own gut. God, he wanted her, even when she scared the hell out of him. He should back off and give his head time to clear, but he couldn't, not when she was this close.

Silently cursing himself, aching for her in a way he had for no other woman, he found himself murmuring reassurances as he gathered her closer. "It's okay, honey. It's just a kiss."

But the second his mouth settled on hers, nothing was quite that simple. Not with Sabrina. Not since that first kiss that had tied him in knots and left him wanting for days now. Did she know how soft her mouth was? How hot? How giving? He could have spent days just learning the taste and texture of her, and still it wouldn't have been enough. Not when she was flush against him like a heat rash, her arms climbing around his neck, her tongue sweetly welcoming his in the liquid heat of her mouth. If he never kissed her again, a month from now, a year, he would still be able to taste her.

That thought alone should have brought him to his

senses, but at that moment, every sense he had was occupied with the woman in his arms. His blood rushing through his veins, need like a fist in his gut, he wanted her. In his bed. Under him. Her arms and legs and body surrounding him, taking him in, holding him like she would never let him go. Uncaring that they were standing under her porch light in full view of anyone who cared to look, he slanted his mouth across hers to take the kiss deeper.

Her head spinning, Sabrina clung to him as if he was the only solid thing in a world that had suddenly turned topsy-turvy. All her life, she'd promised herself she would never lead with her heart the way her mother and grandmother had. She just wouldn't let herself be that weak. But Blake was a man who could shatter convictions she would have sworn were carved in stone. If she hadn't known that before, she knew it now, when he kissed her as if she was something infinitely precious that he needed more than he needed his next breath. That alone should have had her fighting her way out of his arms, but his hands seduced, even while his mouth wooed her, and her mind blurred. As if from a distance, she heard the whisper of silk as he blindly caressed her, then his fingers were closing over her breast, his thumb searching out her nipple. Lightning, sweet and warm, streaked through her, and with a soft moan, she melted against him.

For long, breathless moments, she held on tight as their kisses turned hot and wild and desperate. She couldn't think and didn't want to. Then his hands slid to her hips and pulled her against him, trapping his arousal between them. Urgency firing her blood, she whimpered.

At that moment, she would have given just about anything to be the type of woman who could enjoy the moment for the pure sake of pleasure and not ruin it by thinking too much. But she couldn't. She just couldn't.

She never remembered moving, but suddenly she was pushing out of his arms. "No! I can't do this!"

Stunned, Blake instinctively tried to pull her back into his arms. "Sweetheart, wait—"

"It's late," she said huskily, gliding out of reach as she fumbled for her keys. "You should be going."

The only place he wanted to go was inside with her, but when he ducked his head to get a look at her face, he knew that wasn't going to happen. She was pale except for the wild color that fluctuated in her cheeks, and her eyes were dark with what looked an awful lot like panic as she tried to avoid his gaze. His desire-fogged brain abruptly clearing, he frowned. "In a minute. First I think we should talk about what just happened here."

"There's nothing to talk about," she said curtly, turning away. "You kissed me. I kissed you back. End of story."

End of story?! She'd just knocked him loop-legged in front of God and any of her neighbors who cared to look at that hour of the night, and she thought that was the end of the story? The hell it was!

Wanting to strangle her, he followed her across the porch to her front door. "If you really think that, then maybe I should kiss you again because that sure didn't feel like it was the end of the story to me, honey. In fact, it damn well felt like the beginning. Dammit, Sabrina, will you at least look at me?" he fumed.

She didn't even bother to answer him. Her back to him and ramrod straight, she just stood there, staring at something in front of her. Frowning, he stepped around her and swore when he saw that she was as white as a sheet. "What is it? What's wrong? What are you looking at?"

"The door," she whispered, her gaze focused on the latch. "It's unlocked."

His eyes following hers, Blake saw that not only was it unlocked, but it was slightly ajar, pulled to, but not quite closed. "Are you sure you locked it when we left? We were both distracted. Maybe you just thought you pulled it shut.''

Shaking her head, she hugged herself, suddenly chilled. "No, I know I locked it. This isn't the kind of neighborhood where you can leave your doors unlocked. I always check it twice just to be sure.''

"Then someone's been here." His face grim, Blake moved between her and the door. "And for all we know, they could still be in there. Stay out here while I check it out.''

It was the wrong thing to say to a woman who made her living covering crime. "Not on your life, Nickels," she said quietly. "In case you've forgotten, this is my house. If someone's still in there, they're damn well going to have to answer to me!''

Ignoring his muttered curses, she was right behind him as he stepped into the entrance hall and soundlessly switched on the light. Tension scraping against his nerve endings like a jagged piece of glass, Blake cocked his head and listened for sounds of an intruder, but nothing moved. The old house, in fact, seemed to be holding its breath and didn't even creak. Whoever had been there was, in all probability, long gone.

Still, he had no intention of bumbling through the house like an idiot in search of trouble. His pace slow and measured, his eyes watchful as he moved from room to room with Sabrina just a half step behind him, he flipped on lights and patiently waited for her to inspect the contents of each room and take a quick inventory. Nothing had been moved, let alone stolen.

By the time they reached the kitchen, Sabrina was beginning to wonder if maybe she *had* forgotten to lock the door. Considering how nervous she'd been about going out with Blake, it was a logical explanation. She'd taken one look at Blake in his tux, and evidently everything else had gone right out of her head, including locking the door.

Granted, she'd never done such a thing before, but that made more sense than a thief breaking into the house and leaving without taking anything.

An invisible weight lifting from her shoulders, she almost laughed at her own foolishness. Then her gaze drifted to the kitchen table and a piece of paper that hadn't been there when she'd left. A piece of paper that was folded in half with her name scrawled on the outside.

She froze, her blood chilling in her veins at the sight of that familiar jagged handwriting. She'd only seen it twice before, but she would have recognized it in the depths of hell. "Blake...there's a note...."

He followed her gaze to the table and swore, reaching it in two strides. Touching only one corner, he flicked the unlined piece of paper open and quickly, silently, scanned the typed message inside. When he finally looked up, his face was set in harsh lines. "I think you'd better call the police."

Her heart in her throat, she stepped closer. "What does it say?"

"It doesn't matter," he retorted grimly, moving to block her path. "Call Kelly."

Ignoring him, Sabrina tried to move around him, but he anticipated her and once again stepped in front of her. Scared and hating it, she knew what he was doing and couldn't even be angry with him. "You can't protect me from this, Blake," she said gravely. "Whoever wrote that damn thing was in my house! He knows where I work, where I live, where I go and when. Do you have any idea how that makes me feel, knowing he's out there somewhere, watching my every move? He's a sicko, a murderer, and I've got a right to know what kind of threats he's making, especially when they're made in my house."

Hesitating, he stood his ground. "It's just trash. Not worth worrying about."

"I deal with garbage every day on the streets," she

retorted. "I can handle it. Just because I'm wearing silk tonight doesn't mean I'm soft."

He didn't like it, but she saw something flare in his eyes and knew she had won. "All right," he said with a sigh. "Read the damn thing if you insist. I'm calling Kelly." Striding across the room, he picked up the phone.

For all of ten seconds, Sabrina almost reconsidered. But if she could be intimidated by a simple note, how could she ever look herself in the mirror again? She was a reporter, and if the innocent-looking paper on the table really was from the murderer, which it certainly appeared to be, then it was news. And she didn't cower behind anyone when it came to covering a story.

Squaring her shoulders, she approached the table as if it was a nesting ground for rattlers and cautiously lifted the same corner of the note Blake had, careful not to put any more of her prints on the paper than she had to. The pounding of her heart loud in her ears, she braced herself and began to read.

You slut! I thought you were different, that you cared, but you're just like all the rest. You got your story and your headlines—headlines I gave you!—but it was him you went out with. And it should have been me, damn you! It should have been me you dressed up for in that pretty red dress, but you couldn't see anyone but him. Did you sleep with him when you got home? Just thinking about the two of you together made me sick to my stomach. I won't allow it! Do you understand? You're mine! That's why I killed her, the girl in the red dress like yours. Now you have another story to write, and you don't have to think of anyone but me. Just me. I'll kill them all if I have to to make you happy.

Horrified, Sabrina dropped the note, snatching her hand back as if she'd been burned. "No!" she said hoarsely. "It isn't true! He couldn't have killed someone else just because I went out. That's crazy!"

Finished with his call, Blake hung up and said, "Of course he's crazy! Why do you think I didn't want you to read the damn thing? He's a sicko who doesn't know reality from a hole in the ground. For all we know, he could be making the whole thing up."

"But what if it's true?" she whispered, stricken. "What if he really did go out and kill a girl in a red dress because he was angry with me? You read the note. Some poor girl could have died tonight because I went out with you."

"Bull!" he growled. Placing his hands on her shoulders, he swore at the guilt he saw already darkening her eyes and gave her a shake. "Don't you dare blame yourself for this, Jones! You didn't do anything wrong. If the bastard really did kill again tonight, he did it because he wanted to, not because of anything you did. Dammit, Sabrina, he's a loony tune! This isn't your fault."

Deep down inside, she knew that, but that didn't make her feel any better. The killer had been there tonight, not only in her home, but watching her from the shadows somewhere like a panther waiting to spring. He could have been anywhere…hiding in the bushes in some neighbor's yard, mingling with the crowd on the River Walk, following her all night and growing angrier by the second as he'd watched her laugh and dance with Blake and his friends. And she hadn't even known it.

Damn him, who was he? And what did he want from her?

"It might not technically be my fault, but I can't help but feel that I should know who this jerk is."

"What about the list you came up with for Kelly?" he asked as she kicked off her high heels and began to pace in her stocking feet.

She laughed, but there was little humor to the sound. "Believe it or not, the list wasn't that big. And somehow I can't see the guy I turned down for the senior prom in high school doing something like this ten years later. It's got to be somebody else, but who? He's leaving clues all over the place, just daring me to figure out who he is. Why can't I put it all together and come up with a name?"

"Because he's just playing with you the way a cat does with a mouse, Jones," he said flatly. "He hasn't given you that much information, just enough to tease you and drive you crazy. If you let yourself, you'll spend hours just thinking about him, and that's what he wants...your total attention. Don't let him win that kind of head game with you."

Sam Kelly arrived then with two uniformed officers. While the officers searched the house for signs of a break-in that would explain how the killer got into the house, Sam read the note, his expression stony, then silently slid it into an evidence bag. "Since you're both dressed fit to kill, you obviously went out tonight," he said as he dropped the bag on the table with a grimace of distaste and pulled out a chair. "Tell me about it. When you left, where you went, when you got back. Everything."

Unable to sit, Sabrina roamed around the kitchen, her words jerky as she began to recount the events of the evening. "It didn't start out as a date. Since Blake and I were both going to the awards banquet for the National Newspaper Association, we decided to go together. Blake picked me up—"

"What time?" Sam asked sharply.

"Seven," Blake said, answering for her. "It was still light out. A man down the street was mowing his lawn, and a couple of ladies two houses up were gossiping over the fence between their yards. There was a jogger passing the house just as I drove up, but I didn't get a look at his face. He was about six foot, a hundred and seventy pounds, with blond hair.''

Jotting down notes, Sam nodded. "I'll check it out. Go on.''

Amazed that Blake had noticed such things when all she'd been able to see was him, Sabrina told the detective about their arrival at the convention center, where they'd parted company until after the awards ceremony. "The banquet hall was full,'' she added. "But everyone seemed to belong there. If someone was watching either one of us, I didn't see them.''

"From there we went to the River Walk,'' Blake told him, picking up the story. He gave him a list of every night spot they hit, including the Hard Rock Cafe and Planet Hollywood. "We were with friends until about three,'' he concluded. "Then I brought Sabrina home. She didn't notice the front door was unlatched until she started to unlock it.''

His expression shuttered, Sam scribbled notes, then made them both go over the details again, questioning them sharply about who might have seen them leave together, then followed them. Unfortunately, Blake wasn't familiar enough with Sabrina's neighbors to know if there'd been any strange cars parked within view of the house, and Sabrina hadn't paid attention. If anyone had followed them—and someone obviously had—they'd been damn discreet about it.

They appeared to be back at square one again, with no clues but the note itself, when one of the uniformed officers stepped into the kitchen and informed Sam quietly, "There seems to be no sign of a break-in. All the screens and windows are securely latched, and neither the front or back doors were jimmied.''

"What are you saying?'' Sabrina asked sharply. "That whoever left the note had a key? That's impossible!''

Sam shrugged. "Maybe. Maybe not. Have you had your

car worked on recently or loaned it to anyone who might have had the opportunity to have a copy of your house keys made?''

"No. Nothing. I haven't even had the oil changed, though God knows it needs it.''

"What about a spare key to the front door?'' Blake asked. "Do you keep one hidden somewhere in case you lose your keys?''

"Well, yes, but nobody would be able to find it without knowing where it was.''

That was all Sam needed to hear. "Show me,'' he said, and pushed to his feet.

Obediently, Sabrina lead the way to the front porch. "It's here,'' she said. "Behind the mailbox. The box is loose, but you can't tell from just looking at it. So I put a small magnet on the back of the box and just stuck the key to it.''

She started to show him, but the detective quickly stopped her, grabbing her hand before she could touch the small metal box that was attached to the wall right next to the front door. "Don't touch it,'' he said curtly. "I want to dust it for prints first.''

Stepping around her, he examined the black mailbox in the light of the front porch light, then dusted the entire area for prints. "Most of these are probably yours and the mailman's,'' he said when the task was complete, "but we can't take any chances. Now, where's the key?''

It was just where Sabrina had said it would be, held in place by a small magnet that was about the size and thickness of a dime. Relieved, she let out the breath she hadn't even known she was holding and smiled shakily. "See, I told you no one could find it.''

Sam wasn't so sure. "Not necessarily. Whoever left the note for you could have put the key back to make you think he didn't know where it was or he could have already had himself one made at another time. Either way, we can't assume that your locks are secure. You need to get a locksmith over here in the morning to change them for you."

"Then see about having a security system installed," Blake added, his face carved with harsh lines in the glare of the porch light. "In fact, you should have already done that. Dammit, Sabrina, this neighborhood isn't safe! Especially for a woman living alone."

Put on the defensive, she frowned. "Crime happens everywhere. You know that. And at least here, I know my neighbors, which probably wouldn't be the case if I moved into some newer, fancier subdivision where people don't even talk to each other." Wound up, she would have said more, but she suddenly spied the circle of neighbors that had collected in her front yard, drawn there by the flashing lights of the patrol cars. "See?" she told Blake triumphantly. "Everybody cares about each other here. I'm perfectly safe."

"Sabrina? Is there a problem?" Martha Anderson called worriedly. Her iron-gray hair in rollers and a hot-pink cotton robe wrapped around her rounded figure, she hugged herself and stepped closer to the porch. "When I saw the police lights, I came running as soon as I could. What's wrong?"

"It's nothing," Sabrina assured her. "Just a break-in. Nothing was taken."

"A break-in! Oh, my!"

"Did any of you see anyone lurking around Ms. Jones's house this evening between seven and three-thirty?" Sam asked the group as he moved to join them.

"No, but I did hear a dog barking around eleven-thirty," Martha said. "I thought it was Louis's, but I didn't get up to check. When he quieted down after only a few minutes, I just thought he was after a cat or something."

"It was a jogger," Louis said quietly, pushing up his wire-rimmed glasses from where they'd slid down his thin nose. "I had just turned out the lights to go to bed when Lady starting throwing a fit. I thought it was a cat, too— she really hates them—but when I looked out the front window, all I saw was a jogger trotting down the street."

Blake lifted a dark brow at that. "At eleven-thirty at night? Do you usually have people running through the neighborhood at that hour of the night?"

Suddenly chilled, Sabrina felt goose bumps ripple down her bare arms. "No, of course not. Can you describe the man, Louis? And which way was he running? Toward my house or away from it?"

"Away," he said reluctantly. "And I'm sorry to say I didn't have my glasses on, so I didn't get a very good look at him in the dark. He was tall, with sort of a lanky build and dark hair. Sort of like Jeff."

"Jeff?" Blake repeated sharply. "Jeff Harper, her ex-husband?"

"I'm sure it wasn't him, dear," Martha told Sabrina when Louis nodded reluctantly. "I know you two had your differences, but I can't see him breaking into your house. Not after all this time."

Sabrina didn't think so either, but when she saw Blake and the detective exchange speculative looks, she had no choice but to come to Jeff's defense. "Louis didn't say it *was* Jeff, just that the jogger was built like him. There must be hundreds of men in San Antonio who fit the same description. And it was dark, and Louis didn't have his glasses on. It could have been anyone."

"She's right about that," the older man agreed. "I'm the first to admit that I'm blind as a bat without my glasses. Anything more than three feet away tends to be rather blurry. I guess that doesn't do you much good, does it?"

"I wouldn't go so far as to say that," Sam Kelly said with a smile as he closed his notebook. "You've given us a general description of the man and the approximate time of the break-in. If you or any of the rest of you think of anything else, I'd appreciate it if you'd call me at the station.''

They all promised to do just that, then reluctantly returned to their homes. Sam conferred with the two uniformed officers, then sent them on their way. When he turned back to Sabrina, his face was set in somber lines. "Considering the circumstances, I think you'd better find some place else to stay for a while. At this point, we have to conclude that that note is from the same person who killed Charlene McClintock and the others, and if he's to be believed, he killed again tonight. We can't be sure until a body's found, but one thing is for sure—he's furious with you. For your own safety, you need to get away from here for a while.''

Blake couldn't have agreed more. "She can stay at my place until the bastard's caught. No one will bother her there.''

"Oh, no! I couldn't!''

Sabrina's response was automatic and held more than a trace of panic. Watching the color come and go in her pale cheeks, Blake could understand her reservations. He didn't have to read her mind to know that her thoughts, like his, were on the kisses they'd shared on that very porch less than an hour ago. He wanted her. More than he should, considering the painful lessons Trina had taught him. And Sabrina, in spite of her claims to the contrary, wasn't exactly indifferent to him. Together, the two of them could set a forest ablaze, they were that hot. Living with her, even for a day or two, and keeping his hands to himself, would be impossible.

"Yes, you can,'' he said, throwing caution to the wind. "I'll stay with my grandfather, and you'll have the whole place to yourself. No one will know you're there but me and Sam and Pop. You'll be perfectly safe as long as you make sure no one follows you there after work every evening.''

Safe. Just thinking about it made her want to jump at the chance to get away, but she'd never been one to run from a threat before, and she couldn't start now. "I appreciate the offer, Blake, but you haven't talked to your grandfather. He told me himself how independent he was. He may not want you to move in with him."

He laughed at that, his grin rueful. "Are you kidding? He'd do just about anything for you, even put up with me for a couple of weeks."

"But it could take longer than that," she argued. "And I don't like the idea of letting this monster, whoever he is, drive me out of my own house."

"What's more important?" he tossed back. "Your life or your pride?"

Put that way, she had no argument. Left with little choice, she gave in. "All right, you win. Give me a minute to pack some clothes, then we can leave."

Chapter 7

It was nearly four-thirty when Blake unlocked the door to
his apartment and waited for Sabrina to precede him inside. Tired, her nerves frayed from an evening that had
had more emotional highs and lows than a roller coaster,
she stepped over the threshold and could have sworn she
heard her heart pounding in the dark, intimate silence that
engulfed the place. Moving past her, his shoulder just
barely brushing hers, Blake switched on a light, but it
didn't help ease the sudden tension. Standing just inside
the door, she stopped, her mouth dust-dry. This was a mistake. A terrible mistake.

What was she doing here? she wondered, hugging herself. It wasn't as if she were destitute or friendless. She
could have gone to a hotel. And any one of her co-workers
would have been happy to put her up for as long as
necessary.

She stopped short at the thought. She couldn't drag her
friends into this mess, any more than she could afford to
go to a hotel for an extended stay. And with the police not

even close to making an arrest in the case, it could be weeks, months, before it might be safe for her to go home again. She couldn't impose on even the best of friends for that long.

So she was stuck, left with no choice but to be beholden to Blake. And there didn't seem to be a darn thing she could do about it, either. She'd tried to explain to him before they'd left her place that she couldn't, in good conscience, put him out of his apartment indefinitely, but the stubborn man had flatly refused to listen. He'd hustled her into her car, warned her that he was going to take a circuitous route to make sure they weren't being followed, and like a lamb to the slaughter, she'd followed him.

She shouldn't do this. She couldn't! She was already having trouble handling the emotions he stirred in her. How was she going to put the man out of her head when she would be living among his things—sleeping in his bed, for heaven's sake!—for God only knew how long? She had to be out of her mind.

But if Blake noticed her sudden trepidation or was the least bit shaken at the thought of her living among his things, he gave no sign of it. Striding toward the short hall that opened off the far end of the living room, he opened one of the two doors there and set her suitcase inside. "The bedroom's through here, and the bathroom's right across the hall," he told her. "There's a laundry room off the kitchen, and clean sheets and towels in the linen closet in the bathroom. Feel free to use whatever you need."

She shouldn't, she was already taking advantage of him—but she hadn't thought to bring her own sheets and towels. Nodding, she whispered, in no mood to argue with him tonight, "Thank you."

"Well, then, I guess I'd better pack some things, then get out of here if either one of us is going to get any sleep tonight. Another couple of hours, and it'll be time to get up."

Sabrina could have told him she didn't expect to sleep much anyway, but he'd already disappeared into the bedroom. When he returned to the living room a few minutes later, all he carried was a single duffel bag. "This'll do me for now," he told her as he headed for the front door. "I'll drop by in a couple of days for the rest."

Her throat tight, she forced a smile that wasn't nearly as breezy as she would have liked as she followed him across the living room. "It's your apartment. Drop by whenever you like."

Stopping just short of the front door, Blake barely stifled a groan at the suggestion. No, he thought as he stared down at her, he wouldn't be dropping by, not without a damn good reason. Not if he had a brain in his head, which at this point was doubtful. She looked damn good there. The only place she would look better was in his bed.

Images hit him then, hot and intimate and seductive. His teeth grinding on a curse, he told himself to get the hell out of there while he still could. His blood pressure was already through the roof, his fingers itching to reach for her and haul her close. But even as his head ordered his feet to move, he came up with reasons to linger.

"Are you sure you're not going to be scared here?" he asked in a voice that was as rough as sandpaper. "I know we weren't followed, but it is a strange place and you don't know any of the neighbors."

Her face lifted to his, her eyes meeting his in the shadows near the door, she murmured, "I'll be fine, Nickels. Really. You don't have to worry about me."

She might as well have asked him not to breathe. Like it or not, he was worried, and he didn't like leaving her. He hadn't realized how much until just now. "If you have any problems, you can reach me at Pop's. The number's in the directory by the phone in the bedroom."

She nodded, her voice as hushed as his. "I don't think that's going to be necessary, but thanks."

Seconds passed, long moments of silence that seemed to hum and throb with expectation. Fumbling for his keys, he held them out to her. "The silver one is for the dead bolt, the other one for the main lock. Make sure you use them both."

Her gaze never leaving his, she reached for them and, in the process, brushed her fingers against his. It was an innocent touch, over in the blink of an eye, but he felt the warmth of it all the way to the soles of his feet. And she was just as stirred by it as he. He watched her eyes darken, heard her nearly silent gasp as her breath caught in her lungs, and keeping his hands to himself was almost more than he could stand. With no conscious decision on his part, he started to reach for her, only to let his arm fall back to his side. He couldn't. She was a guest in his home, there because he'd promised her she'd be safe and have the place all to herself. If he kissed her now as he longed to, as his body cried out for him to, he'd never be able to walk away from her.

Cursing himself for being a man of scruples, he had to content himself with cupping her cheek in his hand and rubbing his thumb with painstaking slowness across her bottom lip. "Lock the door behind me," he said thickly. When she nodded, dazed, he gave in to temptation and brushed his thumb across her sweet mouth one more time. A split second later, he was gone, quietly shutting the door after him.

For what seemed like an eternity, Sabrina just stood there, the thunder of her racing heart roaring in her ears. She never remembered reaching for the dead bolt, but suddenly her hand was on the latch, shooting it home. From the other side of the door, she heard Blake whisper a husky good-night, then the fading sound of his footsteps as he walked away.

She *almost* called him back. Her hand was on the dead bolt, the words already trembling on her tongue, when she realized what she was doing. Muttering a curse, she snatched her hand back as if she'd been burned. Dear God, dear God, dear God! What was she doing?

"Sabrina Jones, stop this!" she said out loud to the empty apartment as she whirled away from the door. "You're not here to drool over the man, so just get him out of your head right here and now."

It was sound advice, but she soon found that it was almost impossible to follow. Too wired to even think about going to bed, she wandered around the apartment and saw Blake everywhere she turned. The refrigerator was filled with hot dogs and Twinkies and enough cholesterol to choke a horse. With no effort whatsoever, she could picture him drinking directly from a half-gallon carton of whole milk, then flashing a grin at her as he wiped his mouth with the back of his hand. And then there was the bathroom. His shampoo was there...and his cologne. She didn't open it, but she didn't have to. She only had to close her eyes and he was holding her again, kissing her again, the clean, spicy, sexy scent of him surrounding her as surely as his arms.

"Don't start, Sabrina," she muttered, heading for the bedroom. "Don't you dare start."

She should have gone to bed, but she unpacked her suitcase instead, which meant she had to go through Blake's dresser and closet to find space for her things. Touching his clothes was like touching him. Shaken, she felt like she was peering into his soul. There were some things, she decided, that a woman had no business knowing about a man she'd claimed she wanted nothing to do with. Like the way he arranged his sock and underwear drawer.

Lord, she needed to get out of there. But there was no place to go except to bed. She told herself she was tired— she would be more in control of her thoughts tomorrow. But when she pulled on a sleeveless cotton gown a few minutes later, turned out the lights, and crawled into

Blake's queen-size bed, she knew she wasn't going to get any sleep in the remaining few hours that were left of the night. Not when his scent clung to the sheets, making it impossible to think of anything but him.

Her heart thumping crazily, she couldn't stop herself from clutching at his pillow, muttering curses all the while. Tomorrow, she promised herself, she was going to wash every sheet and towel in the place with her own laundry detergent. Maybe then she'd be able to at least bathe and sleep without her senses clamoring for a man who wasn't there.

How long she lay there like that, she couldn't have said. The deep, dark silence of predawn enveloped her, surrounding her like a blanket, weighing her down. Exhaustion pulling at her, she should have slept, but her mind was too busy, her pulse too erratic. Restless, she couldn't even seem to lie still. She was all over the bed, searching for a comfortable spot that just wasn't there. Finally giving up in defeat, she rolled over with a disgusted sigh and stared up at the darkened ceiling. Maybe she should just forget the whole thing and get up.

When the phone on the bedside table suddenly rang, shattering the silence, she nearly jumped out of her skin. Instinctively, she reached for it without turning on a light, her heart slamming against her ribs. It was nearly five o'clock. Who could possibly be calling Blake at that hour of the morning? "Hullo?"

"Did I wake you?"

Blake's deep, rough voice rumbled softly in her ear, as clear as if he was there in the bed beside her. With a will of its own, her heart slowly turned over and picked up speed. Just that quickly, she was smiling and couldn't for the life of her say why. "Do you make a habit of calling women at five o'clock in the morning, Nickels?" she teased softly.

"Only ones who arc sleeping in my bed when I'm not

there," he countered smoothly, chuckling. "You are in my bed, aren't you?"

She should have said no, that she'd decided to just stay up the rest of what was left of the night, but the truth popped out in the most provocative way. "Yes, cowboy, I'm in your bed," she murmured huskily. "I've been hugging your pillow for the last fifteen minutes trying to get to sleep."

He groaned and admitted thickly, "I don't think I needed to know that part, Jones. Now *I* won't be able to sleep."

She laughed, not the least bit repentant. "Don't expect any sympathy from me. You're the one who insisted on giving up your bed for me."

"Only because I was worried about you. Are you okay?"

"I'm fine. Really," she assured him. "Anyway, if you want to worry about someone, you'd better worry about yourself. Once word gets out on the street that you've got a knight-in-shining armor complex, you're going to have damsels in distress from all over the city beating a path to your door. If I were you, I'd get out of town while I still could."

His chuckle vibrated in her ear, warming her inside and out. "I'll have you know I don't pull out the armor for just anyone. Only a particularly feisty female reporter I have a bet with."

"A bet you're going to lose," she reminded him sweetly.

"Time will tell. Speaking of time," he said gruffly, "I guess I should get off of here and let you try to get some sleep. You know where I am if you need me, Jones."

She should have made some lighthearted, breezy comment, but his raspy words seemed to reach right through the phone line to squeeze her heart. Her smile faltered, and emotions, thick and warm, clogged her throat. "I know," she whispered. "Good night, Blake."

His soft good-night echoing in her ear, she hung up and hugged their conversation to her breast as fiercely as she did his pillow. It was a long, long time before she finally fell asleep.

The morning sun was bright and cheerful, and if he'd had a shotgun, Blake would have shot it out of the sky. Slamming his eyes shut against the glare, he cursed long and low, damning his throbbing head, the too-small twin bed in his grandfather's guest room, the hot, sensuous dreams of Sabrina that had haunted the few hours of sleep he'd finally been able to snatch from what was left of the night.

In spite of his best efforts, a reluctant smile propped up one corner of his mouth as he thought of their whispered phone conversation while most of the rest of the world slept. It was, he realized, a good thing that they'd been almost two miles apart, or he would have had a damn difficult time keeping his hands off of her. God, what was he going to do about her?

She was tying him in knots, taking over his thoughts, his dreams, haunting him. And that didn't even begin to touch the emotions that gripped him every time he thought of the note that had been left for her on her kitchen table. Just the thought of some sleazeball following her, watching her every move, wanting her, enraged him. She was in danger, more than she seemed to realize, and every instinct he had urged him to lock her up somewhere safe, out of harm's way, until the bastard was in custody.

Slinging an arm over his eyes to blot out the sun, he rolled to his back and tried to laugh at the thought of anyone trying to protect Sabrina Jones when she didn't want to be protected. She'd take his head off if he even suggested such a thing. The lady was a fighter, with more guts than any woman he knew. He didn't doubt for a minute that in most circumstances, she could take care of herself, but that gave him little comfort. There was nothing ordinary about her current situation. She had a serial killer on her tail, and that wasn't something she or any other woman should have to deal with alone.

And *that* was something he could do something about. Rolling over onto his side, he reached for the phone. A few seconds later, he grinned as a familiar voice drawled, "Alamo City Investigations. This is Adam Martin. May I help you?"

"Well, that depends. How much is it going to cost me?"

"Blake?" his friend said, shocked. "Is that you? Son of a gun! I tried calling you last week in Lordsburg, but your number had been disconnected. Where the hell are you?"

"Some P.I. you are," Blake teased, his green eyes twinkling. "I'm right here in town. I've been working at the *Times* ever since the beginning of August."

"Hey, man, I've been working my tail off. Who's got time to read the paper?" An old college friend, Adam gave him a hard time about not calling sooner, then proceeded to catch up on the latest news. "So what's going on?" he asked finally. "And don't tell me you need a P.I. I told you before if you ever wanted to give up reporting, I'd hire you in a second. I've got employees with ten years' experience who can't hold a candle to you when it comes to investigating. Say the word, and you've got a job."

Blake's smile faded. "Actually, I do need your services," he said seriously. "I want you to watch Sabrina Jones for me."

"Sabrina Jones, the reporter for the *Daily Record*?" he asked in surprise. "Why? Is she stealing your stories or what?"

"I can hold my own with the lady when it comes to reporting. This is something else. I guess you've heard

about the serial killer going around town killing professional women?''

"Of course. Every woman I know is as jumpy as a
scalded cat, and I can't say I blame them. What's that got
to do with Sabrina Jones?''

"The killer's become fixated on her. The bastard's sending her notes, threatening her. Last night, she came home
to find one on her kitchen table. The police think he has
a key.''

"Damn! And she doesn't have a clue who he is?''

"No. Detective Kelly and I finally convinced her that
she needed to stay someplace else until the son of a bitch
is caught, so she's taking over my place until it's safe for
her to go home. I'm staying at Pop's.''

"So she's still alone at night and roaming all over the
city during the day,'' Adam concluded. "If the jerk really
wants to get her, she's an easy target, Blake.''

"I know. That's where you come in. I want you to
watch her night and day and not let her out of your sight.''

"And the lady's agreeable to this?''

"Are you kidding?'' Blake laughed. "She'd be all over
my case in a heartbeat if she suspected that I was even
talking to you about her, let alone hiring you. So you're
going to have to be damn discreet. She's no dummy.''

"Hey, discreet's my middle name,'' Adam joked.
"Give me all the particulars, and I'll put someone on her
right away. And don't worry. She'll never suspect a
thing.''

Relieved, Blake gave him a detailed description of Sabrina, his address, and the license-plate number of her red
Honda. When he hung up a few minutes later, a worry that
he hadn't allowed himself to acknowledge lifted from his
shoulders. She'd be furious if she ever found out he'd put
a tail on her, but for the first time in what felt like days,
he knew she was safe. Maybe now he could get her out
of his head and sleep at night.

* * *

Her head sluggish from what amounted to a little over an hour of sleep, her eyes bloodshot, and her stomach rolling at the mere thought of food, Sabrina reported to work on time, but God only knew how. She didn't remember dressing, or for that matter, actually driving to work. And things only went downhill from there. On a day when she would have liked nothing better than to trade places with someone on the obit desk, Fitz sent her all over town, chasing one breaking story after another. By three in the afternoon, all she wanted to do was drag herself back to Blake's apartment, crawl into bed, and not move for another twenty-four hours.

"Jones, get over to Comanche Courts," Fitz yelled across the city room at her. "There's been a drive-by shooting. Go see what you can get on it."

She groaned, but she went, hanging on to the thought that in another couple of hours, she could call it a day. Just two more hours. Surely she could get through that.

Comanche Courts was a housing project on the near east side of downtown, mere blocks from the River Walk and Alamo and the hundreds of thousands of tourists who visited the city every year. Since it was so well-known to her, Sabrina could have driven there with her eyes closed. A hotbed of poverty and crime, the courts had, over the years, been the site of more drug busts, murders and shootings than Sabrina could hope to remember. And she'd covered almost all of them.

It was not a place where you dropped your guard, but Sabrina had never been scared there. As usual, the police were present in intimidating force, the lights on top of their patrol cars silently whirling as they questioned possible witnesses. No one had been hurt—this time—but too many times before, she'd arrived to find an innocent victim lying in his own blood while his family screamed and wailed, helpless to save him.

Making her way through the crowd, Sabrina started questioning people, but if anyone had seen anything, they weren't willing to talk about it. Then she found herself next to a young girl who couldn't have been older than twelve. An innocent with dimples, she looked like a baby—until you got a look at her eyes. Dark and knowing and *old*, they had obviously seen things that no twelve-year-old should have even dreamed about, let alone witnessed firsthand.

"It was the Demons," she said in a voice so low that Sabrina had to bend her head to hear her. "They were after Joshua Cruz because they think he joined a rival gang."

At the mention of one of the most dangerous gangs in the city, Sabrina arched a brow. "I thought the Demons stuck to the west side."

"Not anymore. They declared war on the Devils."

"So this is the start of a gang war?" Sabrina asked in surprise, jotting down notes. "Is the Cruz boy a member of the Devils?"

Hugging herself, goose bumps rippling across her skin in spite of the heat of the afternoon, the younger girl shook her head, tears of frustration gathering in her dark eyes. "No, but they don't care. Franco Hernandez is a bully and a killer. He doesn't care who he hurts as long as it makes him look tough."

Studying her, Sabrina asked quietly, "Are you saying you saw the shooting? Was Franco the shooter?"

For a minute, she could almost see the word *yes* hovering on the girl's tongue. Then fear crept into her eyes and she clammed up. "I'm sorry. I can't say any more." And before Sabrina could even ask her her name, she disappeared into the crowd.

"Damn!" Muttering curses under her breath, Sabrina knew her one shot at getting anyone to talk to her had probably just slipped through her fingers. The people in the courts had their own brand of justice that had nothing to do with the legal system, and that, unfortunately, led to more shootings, more deaths, a catch-22 without end.

Still, she couldn't give up. Not when there was a chance that someone among the fifty or so people milling around might give her a little more information. And she still needed to question the officers investigating the shooting.

All her concentration focused on pulling information from witnesses who wanted nothing to do with her, it was a long time before Sabrina felt the touch of someone's eyes on her. Frowning, she turned, half-expecting to find Blake watching her with a mocking grin, but he was nowhere in sight. And no one else seemed to be paying the least attention to her. In fact, no one even made eye contact with her.

"You're losing it, Jones," she muttered to herself. "That's what happens when you only get an hour of sleep. Chill out."

She tried, but when she turned back to the rookie officer she'd just started to question, the fine hairs at the back of her neck rose in warning. Suddenly chilled, her heart lurching in her breast, she fought the need to glance over her shoulder.

"Something wrong, ma'am? If you don't mind me saying so, you look a little green around the gills."

Sabrina winced at that *ma'am*. She must look more haggard than she realized, she thought with a groan. She couldn't be five years older than the fresh-faced officer, and he was treating her like his grandmother.

Forcing a smile, she said, "Actually, I'm fine, just a little paranoid at the moment. You're going to think I'm crazy, but could you do me a favor?"

"Sure, if I can. What is it?"

"Just casually look behind me at the crowd. Do you see anyone watching us?"

Rubbing the back of his neck, he glanced around with a nonchalance that would have done an Academy Award winner proud, then shrugged, his smile crooked, as he turned his attention back to Sabrina. "People always stare when the police show up, but I don't see any suspicious characters if that's what you mean. Why? Has someone been bothering you?"

"Not bothering me exactly. Just…watching me." Unable to explain the disquiet that had her pulse jumping in her veins, she laughed shakily. "Just forget I said anything. I didn't get much sleep last night—I guess it's catching up with me. If you hear anything else about the shooter, I'd appreciate it if you'd give me a call."

She gave him her card, then drove back to the paper, double-checking her rearview mirror every couple of blocks. The traffic shifted and flowed normally enough around her, giving her no reason to think that she was being followed, but her gut was churning, the back of her head itching in awareness, and nothing she could say would reason her growing uneasiness away. Her fingers curling tightly around the steering wheel, she hit the gas, zipped around the car in front of her, and made a sharp right turn at the next corner without bothering to use a signal. Horns honked and someone threw an obscene gesture at her, but she didn't care. The *Daily Record*'s fenced-in parking lot was a half a block away, the security guard clearly within sight. Sending up a silent prayer of thanks, she raced into the lot like the devil himself was after her.

It wasn't until she braked to a stop and cut the engine, however, that she realized she was shaking like a leaf. Laying her head back weakly against the headrest, she let her breath out in a rush. "This isn't like you, Jones," she lectured herself in a voice that wasn't nearly as firm as she would have liked. "You don't jump at every shadow like a 'fraidy-cat. Those notes must really be getting to you. Maybe you really should think about taking a long vacation and letting someone else deal with this for a while."

It sounded good, but she knew she wasn't going anywhere. Whoever had left those notes for her could threaten her as much as he wanted, stand in the dark and stare at her, try to follow her if he thought he could keep up with her, but it wasn't going to do him any good. She was scared—only a fool wouldn't be—but there was no way she was letting a sniveling coward of a murderer scare her off the story of a lifetime.

The matter settled, she strode into the city room of the *Daily Record* with her chin at a confident angle. If her knees still had a tendency to knock and her heartbeat wasn't as slow and steady as she would have liked, no one knew that but her.

"Hey, Jones," Fitz called out the minute she stepped into the city room. "Did ya get the skinny on that drive-by?"

She nodded, holding up her notebook. "Got it right here, boss. Give me a few minutes to transcribe my notes, and I'll have it to you by five."

"Atta girl! Now if I can just light a fire under the rest of the bums around here, we just might be able to put out a paper tomorrow."

Sinking down into the chair at her desk, Sabrina grinned at the old man's familiar litany. He'd been with the paper for nearly forty years, and as far as she knew, he'd never yet missed a morning edition. But he still worried like an old woman, pacing and grumbling and fretting until the paper was put to bed every night. That kind of stress might have eaten away the lining of someone else's stomach years ago, but Fitz seemed to thrive on it. It was, she knew, what made him so good at his job.

The city room was, as usual, mayhem, with her co-workers coming and going and putting the last finishing touches on stories for tomorrow's edition. Flipping open her notebook to her notes, Sabrina hardly noticed. With the ease of years of practice, she blocked out everything but her thoughts and started to pound out the story on her computer keyboard.

Concentrating, she couldn't have said when she first became aware of the fact that someone had stalked into the city room and crossed directly to her desk, where he stopped and glared down at her, waiting for her to notice him. Her gaze trained on her computer monitor, she caught sight of movement from the corner of her eye and figured it was one of the copyboys. "Just a minute," she said absently. "I'll be right with you."

Frowning, she closed her eyes, searching for the ending to her article, and suddenly there it was. Her fingers flew over the keys. Saving it, she smiled in satisfaction. "There! Now, what can I do—"

Her eyes widened, the words dying on her tongue as she looked up into her ex-husband's furious face. "Jeff!" Straightening in shock, she blurted out, "What are you doing here?"

"Looking for you," he said through his teeth. "I want to talk to you."

Taken aback by his hostile tone, Sabrina blinked in surprise. Jeff was a man who prided himself on his self-control. He didn't get angry—he just got very very quiet, and his gray eyes took on a coldness that chilled you to the bone. But something had his shorts in a twist. From the looks of the hot, red flush staining his cheeks and throat, he was more interested in yelling at her than talking, but she wisely kept that thought to herself. One wrong word just might push him over the edge and she had no intention of doing that while they were the object of at least a dozen curious pairs of eyes.

Rising to her feet, she forced a smile. "Why don't we talk outside? Would you like a Coke or something from the break room?"

"No."

So much for good manners. "Okay. Let's go."

Her curiosity killing her, she led him through the maze of corridors to the rear door that opened onto the parking lot, where they wouldn't be disturbed. Before it had even closed behind them, she was demanding some answers. "Okay, Jeff, let's have it. What's going on?"

"*What's going on?*" he echoed, outraged. "Don't you dare stand there and pretend to be Miss Innocent! You know damn well what's going on. You told the police that I was threatening you!"

"What?"

"You heard me," he growled. "A Detective Kelly showed up at the office this morning asking questions about my whereabouts last night." A pained expression crossed his thin face just at the memory of it. "I don't have to tell you what Mr. Druthers thought of that. I spent two hours in his office trying to explain myself, and I don't even know what this is about. If this costs me a partnership..."

The phrase was an old familiar one that left Sabrina cold. A partnership. It was all he'd ever thought of when they were married, all he'd ever wanted. A lawyer with one of the oldest, most prestigious firms in the city, Jeff would have sold his own mother to get in the firm if he thought Mr. Druthers and the other partners wouldn't have severely disapproved.

"I'm sorry you were inconvenienced," she said coolly.

His eyes glacial, he sniffed, "'Inconvenienced' doesn't begin to describe what you did to me."

"*I* didn't do anything. Louis was the one who mentioned your name to the police, but only because someone had broken into my house and he saw someone in the neighborhood who favored you."

She tried to tell him that she had become the unwitting target of a serial killer, but as usual, he wasn't interested in anyone but himself. He didn't even hear her.

"Wasn't it convenient that you had an ex-husband to

blame?'' he said snidely. ''So what can I expect next, Sabrina? The police showing up at my house? Searching it? Just because you've gotten mixed up with a sick character who'll do anything to get his name in the paper? I don't think so. I won't have it. Do you hear me? Whatever your problems are, you keep me out of them.''

For a man who never broke a sweat if he didn't have to, he stormed off with an amazing amount of energy. Watching him disappear around the corner, Sabrina could only shake her head. She'd actually been married to that pompous ass for two years. What had she ever seen in him?

Her temples starting to throb, she headed back inside and told herself to forget him. She could not, however, forget what had brought him back into her life. The killer. For all she knew, he could be watching the parking-lot exit, waiting for her to leave. He would follow her, of course, all the way to Blake's if she wasn't careful.

Sick, her nerves jumpy at the thought of playing cat and mouse with a man she couldn't name or put a face to, she considered the idea of working late. But what good would it do? She would have to leave eventually. It would be better to do that now than after dark when she couldn't see who might be watching her, tailing her, from a distance.

Still, that didn't make driving out of the secured parking lot any easier. Her heart in her throat, she turned left instead of right, away from Blake's apartment, then spent the next half hour trying to make her way unobtrusively back to it. It was nerve-racking business. By the time she finally pulled into the apartment complex and pulled the door down on Blake's private garage, hiding her car from prying eyes, she was shaking.

Deep down inside, she found herself hoping that Blake would be waiting for her in the apartment. She hadn't seen him all day, not even when she'd gone to Comanche

Courts to cover the drive-by, and as much as she hated to admit it, she'd missed him. She wanted to see that crooked grin of his, that spark of devilment in his eyes, and, just for a minute, walk into his arms and feel them close around her. Later, she would deny it, but for now she just needed to be held.

But when she unlocked both locks and pushed open the door, she knew before she ever stepped over the threshold that he wasn't there. The apartment was too quiet, the air too stale. She'd turned off the air-conditioning when she'd left that morning, and the place was like an oven. Disappointed, she shut the door and shot the dead bolt home and tried to find comfort in the sound of it clicking into place.

Instead, all she felt was lonely, and that horrified her. Flipping on the air conditioner, she told herself to knock it off. Just that afternoon, she'd had an excellent reminder of why she didn't need a man in her life. She was just like her mother and grandmother when it came to the male of the species—she was a lousy judge of character. If she didn't want to be married a zillion times like they had been, then she was going to have to resign herself to living alone. That didn't mean she couldn't be attracted to Blake or enjoy his kisses. She had the same needs as any other woman. She just had to be on guard and make sure her romantic heart didn't trick her into thinking there was anything more between them than physical attraction.

Satisfied that she'd finally resolved that issue, she headed for the bathroom and a cool shower in the hopes that it would wash her nagging headache down the drain. It didn't. She knew it was just a combination of exhaustion and tension, but she found it impossible to relax. For her own safety, she was virtually a prisoner here until the following morning, and the walls were already beginning to close in on her.

Outside, the sudden yapping of what sounded like a terrier broke the quiet. Figuring it belonged to one of Blake's neighbors, who was no doubt walking the dog after it had been locked up in the apartment all day, she strolled over to the window and looked out. The dog was nowhere in sight, and at first glance, the street outside the apartment seemed to be deserted except for tenants on their way home from work. Then she saw the man blending into the shadows beneath an Arizona ash tree across the street.

He was just standing there, during the hottest part of the day, watching her.

Chapter 8

"**Y**ou ought to go check on that girl and make sure she's okay."

Hardly tasting the meat loaf his grandfather had made for supper, Blake only grunted. Pop had been hounding him about Sabrina from the moment he stepped in the front door from work, blatantly playing matchmaker, and had no idea how close to success he was. Over the course of the day, he'd had to force himself to stay away from her, to let someone else cover stories where he knew he might run into her. Knowing Adam or one of his men was watching over her had eased his mind considerably, but not enough. He wanted to see her with his own two eyes, touch her, pull her into his arms and assure himself that she really was okay.

Which was why he was staying the hell away from her.

His jaw set, he pushed the food around on his plate, his appetite nonexistent. It was that late-night phone call that had done him in, he decided, and knew he had no one to blame but himself. He'd lain on that torture device that was disguised as a bed in Pop's guest room and listened to her murmur in his ear, his body hard and aching and hurting. Given the chance, he'd have done it again in a heartbeat.

And that was what had him worried. She'd gotten under his skin, into his head, and was in danger of worming her way into his heart, and he couldn't just stand by and let it happen. He'd learned the hard way that you never really knew a woman, no matter how good a friend or lover you thought she was, and that wasn't a lesson he had to learn twice.

So he was staying well away from Sabrina Jones. He'd done what he could to make her safe; that was all he could do. From here on out, she was on her own. If he couldn't sleep for thinking about her, well, that was just too damn bad.

"I just don't understand you," his grandfather complained. "In my day, when a lady was in trouble, a man didn't leave her to fend for herself. Have you even talked to her today? How do you know she's not lying dead in a ditch somewhere?"

"She's fine, Pop."

"You don't know that. What if that bastard who's leaving her all those notes found out she was staying at your place? He could have surprised her like he surprised those other women."

Knowing how his grandfather would jump to all the wrong conclusions, he hadn't meant to tell him about his arrangement with Adam, but if he didn't, he'd hound him until he finally gave in and gave Sabrina a call. "That's not going to happen, Pop—"

Scowling at him, he growled, "And just how the heck do you know that? She's a gutsy girl—"

"Too gutsy for her own good sometimes," Blake agreed. "Which is why I called Adam Martin today."

His mouth already open to argue, his grandfather

snapped it shut as his green eyes started to twinkle. "You put a P.I. on her? Oh, boy, are you going to be in hot water when she finds out!"

"Hopefully, she'll never know," Blake said just as the phone rang. Glancing at his grandfather, he lifted a brow. "You want me to get that?"

"Yeah, it's probably your mother. She calls just about every day at this time to remind me to take my blood-pressure medicine. You'd think I was a senile old man or something," he grumbled.

"You?" Blake laughed as he rose from the table. "You'll be as sharp as a tack when you're a hundred, and you know it." Snatching up the phone, he said, "Finnigan residence."

"Blake, is that you?"

Recognizing Sam Kelly's voice, he stiffened. "Yeah, Sam, it's me. What's up?"

"I thought you'd want to know that Sabrina just placed a 911 call from your place. Evidently she spied someone watching her from across the street. I'm heading over there right now."

Blake's heart stopped in midbeat. "I'll meet you there." Hanging up, he hurriedly told his grandfather what was going on, then headed for the door. "I don't know when I'll be back."

He drove like a madman, breaking every posted speed limit without a thought, just daring a cop to try and stop him. But if there were any black-and-whites in the vicinity, he didn't see them. Within three minutes of rushing out of his grandfather's house, he braked to a rough stop in front of his apartment.

In spite of the fact that he'd made the short drive in record time, Sam Kelly was already there. His unmarked car was parked at the curb across the street, the portable red light he'd slapped on the roof whirling. He was standing in the shade of an Arizona ash talking to a man who was dressed like a jogger in T-shirt, shorts and running shoes. One look at him and Blake knew the fat was in the fire. It was Adam Martin.

"Well, damn!" Muttering curses, he got out of his pickup and crossed the street, a sheepish grin curling the corners of his mouth as he approached the two men. "I guess I don't have to introduce you two. Dammit, Adam, you weren't supposed to let Sabrina see you!"

"I know," he said with a grimace. "I blew it. But I wasn't expecting her to be staring out the window. I was just going to sit under the tree and pretend I was catching my breath, but she caught me looking. The next thing I knew, the police were driving up. I'm sorry, Blake. I guess you're going to have to tell her now, huh?"

"If he doesn't, I will," Sam said, shooting Blake a reproving look. "You should have told her the minute you put somebody on her tail."

"I didn't think it would be necessary. Anyway, she never would have agreed to it." Glancing up to the apartment's living-room window, he wasn't surprised to see Sabrina standing there, a worried frown furrowing her brow. "Who's on the next shift, Adam?"

"Mitch Hawkins, then Don Sanchez," he said, then gave him a description of both men. "I take it you're not going to pull them?"

"Hell, no. She's not going to like it—in fact, I can pretty much guarantee she's going to read me the riot act—but that's just too damn bad. She'll be safe, and that's all that matters. Well, I'd better get this over with."

Amused, Sam drawled, "If she tosses you out the window, at least there'll be a witness to call for an ambulance. Keep up the good work, Adam."

Blake's mouth twitched, but he wasn't smiling when he crossed the street and took the stairs to his second-floor apartment. If all she did was toss him out the window, he'd be damn lucky.

* * *

Standing at the window, watching the three men laugh, Sabrina frowned as Blake crossed the street toward the apartment complex. When she'd seen Sam drive up, she'd expected him to immediately arrest the man across the street posing as a jogger, not chat with him like this was old home week. Couldn't he see the man was definitely stalking her? What in the world was going on?

Troubled, she was seriously considering going down there to find out for herself when there was a knock at the door. She didn't have to check through the peephole to know that it was Blake. Crossing to the door, she snatched it open. "Thank God you're here! I was just going down there," she said as she pulled him inside. "Who is that man? I couldn't believe it when I looked out the window and saw him watching me. Why isn't Sam arresting him?"

"It's all right. It's not what you think—"

Turning back toward the window, she hardly heard him. "I've had this feeling all day that someone was following me. It was like an itch at the back of my neck. I thought I was going crazy, then suddenly, there he was. He never tried to get into the apartment, but he scared me to death."

"I'm sorry about that. I should have told you—"

Frustrated, she cried, "What does he want? He just stands there...." His words suddenly registering, she whirled back to face him. "What do you mean, you should have told me? Told me what?"

He hesitated, and when he did, a flush started at his throat and slowly worked its way up to his face. Sabrina didn't like the suspicions suddenly stirring in her head. Her eyes narrowing dangerously, she stepped toward him. "What have you done, Nickels? What do you know about that man down there?"

There was no help for it—he had to tell her. "He's a friend," he began reluctantly.

"A friend!"

"His name's Adam Martin. We went to college together."

"College," she repeated, sounding like a broken record. "You went to college with a stalker?"

Here it came. Bracing himself, he said bluntly, "He's not a stalker. He's a P.I. I hired him to watch you."

"You *what?!*"

"I hired him—"

She waved him off, not needing to hear the words again.

Stunned, outrage and confusion warring in her eyes, she just stared at him. "Why? Why would you do such a thing? Who gave you the right?"

"No one, but—"

"You're damn right no one did!" Working herself up into a fine temper, she started to pace, muttering half to herself. "God, I can't believe you did this! Jeff, yes—he didn't think I had the sense to get off the tracks when a train was coming. But I do the same work you do, go to the same sleazy places in this town that you do. I've never been hurt, never been shot at, never even been scared. But you think I need a bodyguard."

Blake told himself to keep a tight rein on his own temper. She was entitled to her anger. He just had to let it blow itself out. But damn, he didn't like being compared to her jerk of an ex-husband in any way, shape or form. "You never had a serial killer after you before, either," he pointed out tersely.

"Whether I have or haven't isn't the point. *You had no right!*"

"I don't see it that way," he said flatly. "Three women are dead. Three women who were probably just as independent as you are. Right or wrong, I wasn't going to stand around flat-footed while you became the fourth, so I did something about it."

Her hands on her hips, she glared at him. "Without so much as a by your leave."

It wasn't a question, but an accusation, and he didn't flinch from it. "You're damn right. It was easier that way. You would have just given me a hard time about it when there was nothing left to discuss. I hired the tail and I'm the only one who can fire him."

Too late, Blake realized he probably should have found a more diplomatic way to put that. It was nothing less than the truth, but he didn't have to rub her nose in it. She started to sputter, her brown eyes sparking fire. He should have been backpedaling, trying to soothe her ruffled feathers, but instead, he found himself perversely struck by the humor of the situation. Grinning, he said, "Go ahead and blow a gasket, but if you're going to get mad, get mad at the right person. This is all your fault."

That stopped her in her tracks. "*My* fault? How the heck do you figure that? You were the one who took it upon yourself to hire that man," she snapped, motioning in the general direction of the street. "I didn't do anything."

"Except bring out the caveman in me."

The admission came out of nowhere to steal her breath. Caught off-guard, her heart lurching in her breast, Sabrina blinked, sure she must have heard him wrong. "I beg your pardon?"

Wry humor glinted in his eyes. "You heard me. I've never considered myself a chauvinist, but there's something about you that just seems to bring out the caveman in me. Logically, I know you can take care of yourself, but this doesn't have a whole hell of a lot to do with logic."

"Blake—"

"I know, it's crazy, but there it is. So if it'll make you feel any better, I didn't hire Adam for you—I hired him for me. So I don't have to worry about you when I'm not around."

Not sure what he was admitting to, Sabrina couldn't seem to drag her gaze away from his. He was still smiling, but there was something in his eyes, an emotion that drizzled through her like honey, warming her to her soul and alarming her at one and the same time. With no effort whatsoever, he was slowly, bit by bit, carving a place for himself in her life, in her heart. She'd only known him for a matter of weeks, yet she was already living in his apartment, sleeping in his bed. Granted, he wasn't in there with her, but for how long? How long before she lost her head, then her heart?

Dismayed, she shook her head. "No," she whispered hoarsely. "I appreciate your concern, but you aren't responsible for my welfare. If you're getting ideas about me just because I'm staying here, you can forget it right now. I can find somewhere else to stay."

She started to brush past him, but he grabbed her, hauling her in front of him. "Oh, no you don't," he grated. "You're not going anywhere until we get this settled."

"There's nothing to settle!" she insisted, tugging at her arm. "Let me go, Blake. I've got to get out of here."

That should have gained her her release. Instead, he drew her inexorably closer. "I don't think so," he murmured. "You can't walk away from this any more than I can. Not this time."

Her spine ramrod straight, she didn't bother to tug at her arm again. "Did I ever tell you that I've never cared much for Neanderthals?" she purred. "You might remember that."

He *almost* laughed. Lord, she was something! He watched her try to stare him down and couldn't for the life of him look away. Or let her go. Not when he had her this close and he was aching to kiss her again. She was probably going to be furious with him, but he'd just have to risk it. Murmuring her name, he leaned down and took her mouth with his.

Half braced for a struggle, he felt her stiffen, felt every muscle go perfectly still as her breath seemed to catch in her lungs. Her palms were flat against his chest, wedged there to push him away—with the slightest pressure, she could have won her release. Because as much as he wanted her, he would have never forced her. But instead of shoving him away, her fingers curled into the material of his shirt. It was just a faint movement, a caress that she probably wasn't even aware of. But it told him far more about what was going on in her body than she knew.

She couldn't fight the attraction between them any more than he could.

A wise man would have stopped there, content with the small victory. But the emotions raging within him had nothing to do with contentment, and there was no way in hell he could stop now. His mouth gentling, softening, cajoling, he planted tiny, nibbling kisses at the corners of her mouth, the curve of her cheek, the sweet, sensitive hollow at the base of her throat. "God, I want you, Jones," he breathed huskily into her ear. "Can't you feel how much? Tell me I'm not the only one going crazy here."

"No," she whispered, but even as she denied it, her mouth lifted to his.

"Yes," he insisted in a rough growl. Swooping down, he pressed her lips open with his, seducing her with his tongue in a series of long, slow, drugging kisses that were guaranteed to drive her quietly out of her mind. He was the one, however, who felt his control slipping. His breathing ragged, he tore his mouth from hers, but he didn't let her go. He simply couldn't. His arms tightening around her, he held her close, his eyes locked with hers. "Tell me, honey."

Dizzy, the thunder of her heart loud in her ears, she couldn't for the life of her look into those forest-green eyes of his and deny what he did to her. Not when her pulse was all over the chart and her knees had long since lost the ability to support her.

Her arms tightening around his neck, she muttered,

"Damn you, Nickels, I don't know how you keep doing this to me. I can't think when you kiss me like that."

She didn't know another man she would have trusted enough to make that admission to. One more kiss, and he could have turned her to putty in his arms, but he didn't take advantage. A half smile curling one corner of his mouth, he lifted a hand to her cheek and admitted thickly, "I seem to be having that problem myself. What do you think we should do about it?"

Her senses beginning to cloud, she leaned into his hand. "Talk about it later," she murmured, pulling his mouth down to hers. "I can't think right now."

Later would be too late. She didn't give her heart lightly, and instinctively she knew that Blake could hurt her in ways Jeff never had. But they had, by fits and starts, been racing toward and fighting this moment from that first day when he'd stepped in her path and tried to protect her from something she didn't need protection from. She couldn't deny it any longer. Couldn't fight it any more. She wanted him. Here. Now. In every way a woman could want a man. Just once, she promised herself dreamily as she gave herself up to his kisses. She would have him just this once and get him out of her system. Maybe then she could sleep at night without reaching for him in her dreams.

But if she thought they were just going to have sex, she soon discovered how wrong she was. Nothing that they stirred in each other was that simple, that uncomplicated. His hands moved slowly over her, charting every dip and curve with a touch she somehow knew as well as the beat of her own heart, and intimacy was there between them, strong and sweet and sure. The world was just outside the apartment, waiting to intrude, but all she heard was the sigh of his breath, the thunder of his heart, the whisper of their clothes as they strained against each other, wanting more as need coiled tight between them.

"Blake—"

His name was all she could manage, the only thought in her head. How long had she been waiting for this, for him? He scared and thrilled her and shook her with the way he seemed to know her better than she knew herself. He nuzzled her ear and smiled softly when her breathing changed. And there were her breasts. She never said a word, never indicated by so much as a gasp how sensitive her breasts were to the play of his fingers even through the cotton of her shirt and bra, but he knew. Gently, tenderly, he trailed a finger around the crest of her nipple, circling, circling with infinite slowness, until all her attention was focused just there.

Shuddering, throbbing deep inside, she held her breath, waiting. Then, just when she thought she couldn't stand the torture any longer, he brushed against the tight bead he had created with a touch that was as soft as the brush of an angel's wing and heat streaked like an arrow straight to the core of her. Moaning, she turned into his hand, her breast filling his palm. Nothing had ever felt so good.

Holding her, caressing her, Blake told himself he'd been waiting too long for this moment to rush it. But, God, she made it difficult! She was so sweet, so responsive, that it was all he could do not to strip her clothes from her, drag her down to the living-room floor and take her like the caveman she so easily turned him into.

Tearing his mouth from hers, struggling for the control that was suddenly as elusive as a snowflake on a hot summer day, he forced himself to release her breast, but only so he could lock his arms around her and mold every soft, beautiful inch of her to him. But that, too, was agonizing. Snuggling close, her arms trapped between them, she plucked at the buttons of his shirt, undoing them one by one. Then she was touching him, running her hands under his shirt, stroking him like a cat and kissing him wherever she could reach, and in ten seconds flat, he was hotter than a two-dollar pistol.

Even then, he might have found the strength to stop. But when he burrowed his fingers in her dark, wild hair and turned her face up to his to ask her if she had any idea what she was doing to him, her brown eyes were nearly black with passion and lit from within by a fire that burned just for him. Staring down at her, he felt something shift in the region of his heart, something he couldn't control, something that swamped him with emotion and stole the breath from his lungs. His control going up in flames, he swept her up in his arms and carried her to his bed.

The last rays of the setting sun were streaming through the blinds at the window, striping the sheets with bars of golden light, but all he saw when he laid her on the bed and came down next to her was Sabrina. Her lips slightly swollen from his kisses, her cheeks flushed, her hair spread out across his pillow, she looked like something out of a fantasy, the answer to a lonely man's dreams.

He hadn't realized just how lonely he had been for her until then.

Urgency filling him, tearing at him, he fought out of his shirt and jeans. Before they even hit the floor, he was reaching for the buttons to her blouse. He couldn't remember the last time he'd fumbled with any kind of fastenings on a woman's clothing, but suddenly his fingers were shaking. That should have stopped him cold, set him back on his heels, made him think, but he wanted her too badly. Swearing, he tugged at her blouse, then her hands were there to help him, as impatient as his, and in seconds, she was bare and reaching for him.

She was beautiful. Another time, he could have spent hours just looking at her, touching her, delighting in her small, perfect breasts and slim hips and the impossible softness of her skin, but not now. Not when she pulled him into her arms, nipped at his ear and rasped softly, "Hurry."

As the day aged, the light shifted and mellowed and the

shadows grew long. Outside, the sound of laughter from the apartment pool floated on the early evening air, but in the bedroom, the only sound was of Sabrina's soft, fractured moan as he slipped into her. Then her legs were closing around him, her wet, hot heat welcoming him, and his mind blurred. He moved, and she was there with him, catching his rhythm, taking him deeper. And as he took her like a man possessed, and she started to come apart in his arms, his name a keening cry on her lips, his only thought was that he had finally come home.

In the silence afterwards, their breathing was rough, the racing of their pounding hearts slowly easing. His face buried against her neck, feeling more satisfied than he'd ever felt in his life, Blake held her close and couldn't seem to make himself let her go. Not yet. Not when he could still feel the little aftershocks that rippled through her. He was crushing her, but even when he managed to roll to his side, he took her with him, his arms twin bands of steel around her. He couldn't stop touching her, caressing her, assuring himself she was real.

It had been a while for him, he told himself. It was just chemistry. And loneliness. Trina had been a part of his life for a long time, and he hadn't even looked at another woman until Sabrina had crossed his path and the sparks had flown between them. After such a long dry spell, it hadn't taken much to light a fire. But now that they'd made love, he could get her out of his head.

But even as he tried desperately to believe that, she stirred in his arms and dropped a kiss to his chest, and just that quickly, he wanted her again. More than before, in a hundred different ways. Shaken, he drew in the scent of her and knew he could have spent hours just exploring her, learning her secrets, loving her again and again and again, until they were both too tired to move.

Dear God, what had she done to him? he wondered as

the light outside gradually darkened with twilight. When Trina ran off with that trucker the night before he'd planned to ask her to marry him, she'd ripped his heart out by the roots. Like a damn fool, he hadn't known that she was even seeing anyone else. And it had hurt, dammit!

Never again, he'd promised himself. He was never going to open himself up to that kind of pain again. Especially with a woman who had made it clear that she wasn't interested in anything that even hinted at long-term commitment. If he was going to get involved—and he still wasn't sure that he was—he wouldn't settle for anything less than the long haul.

Even as his hands trailed over her, loving the feel of her, he knew he had to get out of there. Now, while he still could. He had to think, figure out where he was going, where the hell *they* were going, if anywhere.

But leaving her wasn't nearly as easy as he would have liked. His arms didn't want to release her. His jaw clenched on an oath, he rubbed his cheek against the top of her head and said quietly, "I've got to go. I rushed over here like a madman when Kelly called, and Pop is probably worried sick by now thinking you've been murdered. You going to be okay by yourself?"

His hard, sinewy body pressed close from shoulder to thigh, Sabrina nodded, dazed. "Mm-hmm."

What in the world had just happened here? She'd been married, divorced; she'd made love more than enough times to know what to expect. But nothing and no one had ever swept the ground right out from under her the way Blake just had. For the first time in her life, she'd actually felt the earth move and she didn't know if she wanted to call AP with the news or run for cover.

Something of her inner agitation must have shown because Blake was suddenly pulling back to get a better look at her face, a frown worrying his brow as his eyes searched hers. "You're awfully quiet."

Heat burning her cheeks, she ducked away from that all-too-discerning gaze of his, afraid he could read her like a book. "Actually, I was just about to doze off," she said with forced lightness. "You make a nice pillow, Nickels."

His mouth quirked, but he didn't smile. "My pleasure," he said gruffly. "About what just happened—"

"We're both consenting adults," she said hurriedly, cutting him off. "There's nothing more to discuss."

She moved then before he could stop her, dragging the covers up to her breast as she turned to face him with half the width of the bed between them. Her smile breezy, she prayed that he couldn't see how fake it was in the gathering twilight. "Go on now, get out of here. It's getting late. Your grandfather will be worried."

He should have been pleased, she thought. After all, didn't most men worry about a woman getting the wrong idea after sex? He wanted out and she was making it easy for him, but instead of acting grateful, he was looking at her as if she'd just insulted him.

"All right, all right," he said stiffly. "I'm going."

Throwing off the covers, he rose naked from the bed and had no idea what the sight of him did to her. Her mouth dry, her heart skipping every other beat, she watched as he tugged on his clothes, the frown that wrinkled his brow growing darker with every article of clothing he pulled on. By the time he was completely dressed, he was positively scowling at her. "We're going to talk about this tomorrow," he warned, then stalked out.

The second the front door slammed behind his stiff back, Sabrina wilted like a week-old rose, the need to call him back almost more than she could bear. She wanted him to hold her, to reassure her that she wasn't the only one who'd been shattered by their loving. And that alone terrified her. What if he, too, had experienced the same free fall through space and he was just as thrown by it as she? What then? Where did they go from here?

The possible answers shook her to the core.

Her heart slamming against her ribs, she climbed out of bed and grabbed a robe, chiding herself not to lose her head. It was just lust. It had to be. Simple, basic desire. The kind that made fools of the women in her family and caused them to make all the wrong decisions about men and love and life. She wouldn't, couldn't get caught up in the wonder of it. Her mother and grandmother might love walking down the aisle so much that they were willing to risk the divorce that inevitably followed, but she couldn't handle it. Once was enough. Some people just weren't cut out for marriage, and she was one of them.

Not that Blake had asked her to marry him, or was even thinking about doing such an outrageous thing, she quickly assured herself. He wasn't the type of man to get caught up in the emotion of the moment and lose his head. But he also wasn't, she decided, the kind of philandering low-life who jumped from woman to woman, bed to bed. According to his grandfather, his family had high expectations for him in politics and that meant nothing short of marriage to the right woman would ever be acceptable. She was not, and never would be, that woman.

Still, there was a part of her, deep in the heart of her, that remembered his loving and cried out for more. He'd touched something in her that no one else had, stirred something in her that she'd dreamed of without even realizing it until now. She didn't want to lose that. Didn't want to lose *him*. God, what was she going to do?

Torn, she spent the rest of the evening prowling around the apartment in search of a distraction from her own thoughts. But everywhere she turned, she was reminded of Blake. She tried reading, even television, but nothing seemed to help. She couldn't even look out the window without being reminded that there was a man out there, watching the apartment for Blake, keeping her safe. Her head told her that her safety wasn't his responsibility—her heart whispered that he cared.

Frustrated, exhausted, she finally went to bed, and though she slept, she didn't really rest. She couldn't. Not when her heart and mind spent the hours between midnight and dawn arguing like a couple of eight-year-olds. By the time the alarm went off at seven, she knew she had to go back home. Blake wouldn't be happy about it and neither, for that matter, would Sam Kelly, but she needed her own things around her—if only for a little while—to remind her of who and what she was.

She called in to work and asked for a couple of hours off, then headed to her place an hour later. Not surprisingly, Blake's hired gun followed her the whole way, never letting more than one car get between them during the drive, not even on the freeway. Scowling at him in her rearview mirror, Sabrina recognized him from Blake's description as Mitch Hawkins—a blond surfer-type who looked like he had more brawn than brain. He'd smiled and nodded at her when she'd first emerged from the apartment, but she hadn't made the mistake of thinking that he took his job lightly. Before coming to work for Adam, he'd been a border-patrol agent and could, according to Blake, track a scorpion across solid rock.

Not surprisingly, he didn't follow her into her driveway, but parked at the curb two houses down and across the street. By the time she stepped out of her car, he had already shut off his motor and slumped down in his seat. If she hadn't known he was there, she would have never seen him.

"Hey, gorgeous! Where you been hiding out? I ain't seen you in a while."

At Joe Gomez's sexily growled greeting, Sabrina turned to find him pushing a battered Harley toward her down the street, his brown eyes, as usual, sparkling with devilment.

As far as Sabrina knew, he didn't own a motorcycle, and there was a good possibility he'd burrowed this one from a friend without asking, but he looked so refreshingly normal that she wanted to hug him. Restraining herself, she grinned fondly at him. "Hey, yourself," she said, striding down the driveway toward him. "What do you mean, hiding out? I've been around."

"Yeah, right. And I'm the Easter bunny." Hurt, he gave her a chiding look, his eyes, for once, dead serious. "Do I look like I'm stupid or what? In all the years I've known you, you've always come home at night. The word on the street is that dude killing all those women has got it in for you."

Alarmed, Sabrina stiffened. "Where'd you hear that?"

"I've got my sources, don't you worry about it. And they're right, aren't they? You're in deep—"

"Joe!"

At her sharp warning tone, he widened his eyes innocently. "What? All I was going to say was you were in deep trouble."

"Sure you were."

He grinned. "I don't know why everyone jumps to the conclusion that my mind is in the gutter...."

He would have said more, but before he could, a black Chevy pickup came roaring around the corner at the end of the street and slammed to a stop in front Sabrina's house. A split second later, Blake was striding toward where they stood talking, so angry steam was practically pouring from his ears. Sabrina took one look at him and felt her heart start to knock in her breast. She didn't have to ask how he'd found her—her watchdog had obviously called Adam Martin, who had reported to Blake.

"If you've come to chew me out, you can save your breath," she began quickly.

That was as far as she got. "There's been another murder,'' he said tersely. ''Apparently the killer made good on his promise to you in his note. The body was found less than three blocks from here.''

Chapter 9

The murder scene was a particularly gruesome one. The victim, Denise Green, a florist who had just opened her own shop and was still struggling to get the business off the ground, had been shot in the head and the heart in her own kitchen and had died immediately. Then the killer, going on a rampage, had ransacked her house with a viciousness that he'd made no attempt to hide. In his rage, he had paid particular attention to the bedroom, ripping the sheets and mattress with a kitchen knife, then shredding every piece of clothing in the room.

There was no note, but none was necessary. Denise Green's general description was the same as Sabrina's...she was slender and petite, with curly black hair and brown eyes. And the similarities didn't stop there. Not only did she live in the same neighborhood in a house that was almost identical in style to Sabrina's, she also, as a florist, loved flowers. Her yard and front porch, like Sabrina's, were overflowing with them. And though her body had only just been found, she had, apparently, been dead for several days. Her neighbors thought she had gone to a floral convention in Phoenix and only started to wonder if something was wrong when they noticed that her dog was still in the backyard instead of at the kennel.

The police wouldn't know for sure until they got the report from the medical examiner, but she appeared to have died the night Sabrina went with Blake to the awards ceremony at the convention center. The same night the killer had slipped into Sabrina's house and left that note on her kitchen table. He had, to put it mildly, had a busy evening.

Stricken, Sabrina stood in Denise Green's bedroom with Blake and Sam and stared at the bed, at the ruined clothes, and felt the rage that had been directed squarely at her. Chilled to the bone, she hugged herself, nausea backing up in her throat. It should have been her, she thought numbly. As much as she wanted to deny it, she couldn't miss what was right there in front of her eyes. She should have been the one lying stone-cold dead in her own kitchen with two bullets lodged in her head and her heart. She was the one the killer had been furious with, the one he'd struck out at, the one he would have killed if he could have gotten his hands on her. But she hadn't been available, so he'd gone out and murdered an innocent woman instead just because she'd had the misfortune to remind him of Sabrina.

Dear God, when would this end?

"We're still going through the house for prints," Sam said, breaking the shocked silence that had fallen over them at the sight of the bedroom. "The perp's been damn careful up to this point, but it looks like he lost it when he did this. If we're lucky, he slipped up and made a mistake."

And if they weren't, there would be more deaths, more of the same, before the killer was caught. "What about the neighbors?" Sabrina asked stiffly. "Did any of them see or hear anything? Whoever did this didn't do it quietly.''

"Not that we've been able to discover so far, but the body wasn't found until after most people had already gone to work. We should know more later in the day.''

Noting the condition of the bedroom in his notebook, Blake glanced up with a frown. "What about signs of forced entry? Whoever this bastard is, he can't have keys to all these women's houses.''

"No, there was no key this time," the detective said flatly, leading them back to the kitchen. The body had already been removed and taken to the morgue, but there was still dried blood everywhere. Motioning toward a bouquet of wildflowers on the counter, he said, "We think that was how he got in.''

"You mean the flowers?" Sabrina asked in surprise. "Like a delivery boy?''

He nodded. "The card was still on the flowers, unopened, and the body was found right by the counter. She was still clutching her open purse....''

"Digging for a tip while he shot her right between the eyes," Blake concluded, creating an image of the murder that they could all see with sickening clarity. "God, that's cold.''

Sabrina shuddered. "If he had to use a delivery to get in the door, then he didn't know her.''

"Probably not," Sam agreed. "Which means he's changed his M.O. slightly, and I don't like the sound of that. Up until now, he's taken out his rage with you on women he appears to have known who remind him of you—that makes it personal. Now he's killed a stranger, someone he knows nothing about and really can't pretend is you, and that can't give him nearly as much satisfaction. That's only going to increase his rage, which might be what he needs to finally work up the nerve to come after you. For your own safety, you really do need to get out of town for a while."

As the last of the blood drained from her cheeks, Sabrina had to give him credit. When he issued a warning, he shot straight from the hip and didn't pull any punches. "Believe me, Sam, nobody would like to do that any more than I would, but I just can't afford to walk away from my job and hide out somewhere until this weirdo is caught. Anyway, you said yourself it's me he wants. I'm the one he really wants to kill. If I just disappear, he might go underground until I show up again."

"If you're thinking of offering yourself up as a decoy, you can just forget it," Blake said harshly before the detective could so much as open his mouth. "It's not going to happen."

Just days ago, she would have bristled at his tone, but the loving they'd shared last night had changed her, and to her horror, she couldn't stop her heart from lurching at the possessive, protective glint in his eyes. What had he done to her? She should have been setting him straight on the fact that only one person was in control of her life and it wasn't him, but all she wanted to do at that moment was walk into his arms.

Instead, she said huskily, "Nobody said anything about being a decoy."

"Good. Just so we understand each other."

His eyes, as green as a high-mountain forest, snared hers and held them captive, setting the pulse at her throat jumping crazily. The rest of the world faded from her consciousness, and for a split second in time, it was just the two of them, alone and needy.

Clearing his throat, Sam said dryly, "Now that we've got that cleared up, we still have the problem of keeping Sabrina safe. Considering how reckless this bastard's getting, I think he's ready to snap. I wouldn't put it past him to go after her in broad daylight."

"That's not going to be a problem," Blake said, never taking his gaze from Sabrina. "From now on, I don't intend to let her out of my sight."

"What?" she exclaimed. "What are you talking about?"

"You heard me. You're not going anywhere from now on without me."

"But you've already hired a P.I.—"

"And he's doing a good job," he replied. "But he can't watch over you the way I can."

His lips twitching, Sam glanced from the grim resolve in Blake's eyes to the sudden flush stinging Sabrina's cheeks and had the good sense to cut and run. "Well, I can see you two need to discuss this. I'll just get out of your hair and let you at it."

Blake never spared him a glance. "There's nothing to discuss," he told Sabrina flatly once they were alone, "so don't even think about arguing with me."

"The hell I won't," she hissed, keeping her voice deliberately low so it wouldn't carry to the policemen in the other rooms of the house. "Dammit, Blake, have you lost your mind? You can't go with me everywhere I go!"

"I don't know why I can't. Who's going to stop me?"

"Well, my boss, for one," she snapped. "What are you going to do when I report to work in the morning? Go with me?"

Not the least daunted by the idea, he nodded. "Every morning until the creep who's after you is behind bars."

"But that could be weeks! Months! Do you honestly think Fitz is going to sit back meekly and let me bring someone from the *Times* into the city room when we're in the middle of the biggest subscription war ever? He'll have a fit!"

Grinning, he pushed away from the counter to sling a friendly arm around her shoulder. "Better watch it, Jones," he teased. "Anybody hearing you just might think you're worried about me.'' When she only sniffed at that, he chuckled and steered her out the door. "I can take care of myself and you, too, sweetheart. Are you through around here? Good. So am I. Let's get back to work.''

He followed her back to his apartment, left her car there, then drove her downtown to the ninety-year-old building that housed the *Daily Record*. In spite of that and his claims at the murder scene, Sabrina still didn't expect him to go inside with her...until he got out of the truck and started to follow her toward the employee entrance, his hand riding protectively at the bow of her back.

Fighting the sudden need to melt back into his touch, she stopped in her tracks. "Blake, this is crazy! Even if you can somehow get Fitz to agree to this, what about when you need to report in at the *Times*? Your editor's not going to be exactly pleased to see me, you know.''

"Don't worry about Tom. He's an old friend. I'll square it with him.''

"But what if you can't?''

His green eyes twinkling with devilment, he teased, "In the words of a talented writer I happen to have the good fortune to know, 'We're in the middle of the biggest subscription war ever.' Do you really think your boss or mine is going to fire either one of us when we're the two best reporters they've got?''

"Well, no, but—''

"I rest my case.'' Reaching past her shoulder, he pulled open the heavy steel door for her and waited for her to precede him. "Let's go.''

Stepping inside, she was sure that they'd be stopped any second for an explanation. But Blake's presence didn't raise so much as an eyebrow. The few reporters that they did encounter who recognized Blake only nodded and went on about their business, and those in the city room didn't even glance up from their computers. Relieved, Sabrina dropped into her desk chair and sighed like a woman who had just made it through an obstacle course.

Chuckling, Blake took the chair opposite her desk, out of sight of her monitor, and pulled his notebook out of his pocket. "Go ahead and work, honey," he said, shooting her a smile that would have made her grandmother's heart jump in her breast. "I'm going to organize my notes. Then when you're finished here, we'll go over to the *Times* so I can write my piece."

Sure she wouldn't be able to write a word with him sitting right there, Sabrina cast him a suspicious look, but he was frowning at his notes and never noticed. Turning her attention back to her computer screen, she didn't even have to close her eyes to find herself back in Denise Green's bedroom, the carnage there sickening her. Suddenly, her fingers were flying over her keyboard as the words just flowed.

Lost in her own thoughts, Sabrina never saw her boss walk into the city room, but suddenly he was standing three feet away from her desk and scowling from her to Blake and back again. "You want to tell me what the hell is going on here, Jones?" he growled.

She jumped, her heart in her throat, and sent a line of *S*s running across her computer screen. "Fitz! You scared the life out of me! This is Blake—"

"I know who it is," he said curtly. "What I want to know is what's he doing here?"

"He's with me—"

"I can see that. Any particular reason why? And this better be damn good."

He had that look on his weathered face, the one that warned Sabrina that he had already made up his mind not to like what he was about to hear, and it was all she could do not to shake him. "Now don't go getting your back up before you've even heard what's going on, Fitzy. I know this looks odd, but I can explain everything if you'll just give me a chance—''

"I didn't give her a choice in the matter," Blake cut in, pushing to his feet to tower over the elderly editor. Quickly and concisely, he filled the other man in on the latest developments. "The psycho's obviously after her and I'm not letting her out of my sight until he's caught. So you'd better get used to seeing me around, Fitz," he warned with a cocky grin. "You're going to be seeing a lot of me. From now on, Sabrina and I will be going everywhere together."

Known more for his bluster than his bite, the editor scowled. "Let me get this straight, Nickels. You're telling me you're going to waltz into my paper whenever you feel like it and I'm supposed to get used to it?"

Even to his own ears, it sounded damn arrogant, but Blake had no intention of backing down to Fitz or anyone else when it came to Sabrina and her safety. His jaw set like stone, he nodded. "You are if you expect Sabrina to come in personally to file her stories. Otherwise, she can call them in from my place. The choice is yours."

His cheeks flushing with temper, Fitz opened his mouth to tell him exactly what he could do with those choices, but something in the depths of Blake's eyes must have warned him he was making no idle threat. Closing his mouth with an audible snap, he expelled his breath in a huff. "You really think she's in that kind of danger?" he asked gruffly.

"Yes, sir, I do," Blake replied quietly. "Detective Kelly asked her to leave town but she refused because she knows how you need her right now."

Sabrina sniffed at that, frowning. "You don't have to make me sound like a martyr, Nickels. I had other reasons for staying besides that—like the fact that I happen to need this job. And no coward of a murderer is going to run me out of my town."

She might as well have saved her breath. Neither man

spared her a glance. "I don't like the idea of anyone from the *Times* walking in and out of here like they own the place, but if I've got to put up with one of Edwards' crew, I guess I'd just as soon it be you. I can trust you not to use any insider information you pick up while you're here against us."

It wasn't a question, but Blake treated it as one anyway. Lifting his hand to his heart, he said solemnly, "On my word as a Boy Scout."

The old man nodded. "Good enough. Jones, don't take any more chances than you have to. That's an order."

Giving her one last stern look to make sure she got the message, he strode off, leaving Sabrina staring after him in amazement. He'd practically given Blake carte blanche to come and go as he pleased. She never would have believed it if she hadn't heard it with her own ears.

Shaking her head, she frowned up at Blake. "Were you really a Boy Scout?"

Shrugging, he grinned. "What do you think?"

Over the course of the day, they covered a robbery involving a tourist near the River Walk, a bank hold-up, investigated the rise of gang activity in one of the city's more affluent high schools and looked into a money laundering scheme among some businesses near Fort Sam Houston. Half expecting Blake to hover over her like an overprotective parent, Sabrina was pleasantly surprised at the first crime scene when he gave her plenty of space to do her job. Interviewing the investigating officers while she spoke to the victim, he kept an eye on her, but never got close enough to overhear her questions.

Walking back to his truck with him when they were both finished, she couldn't help but tease him as he opened the passenger door for her. "You know, Nickels, I think there really must be some truth to this Boy Scout stuff. I gotta tell you—I'm impressed. I didn't think you had it in you."

Playfully tugging on her hair, he grinned. "Don't let it go to your head, Jones. I still plan on winning our bet—this is just a temporary lull in competition. Once things are back to normal, you'd better watch out. I'm going to eat your lunch."

"Oh, yeah?" she tossed back, her own eyes starting to sparkle. "You and whose army? You're good, cowboy, I'll give you that. But I'm better and you know it. I guess it's a man thing."

Confused by the sudden shift in her reasoning, he frowned. "What?"

"Not being able to accept when you're beaten," she said sweetly. Flashing her dimples at him, she dared to reach out and pat him on the cheek. "Poor baby. Men have such fragile egos."

Lightning-quick, his fingers trapped hers against his face, and suddenly, neither one of them was smiling. His blood starting to warm in his veins, Blake deliberately reminded himself that he'd sworn not to touch her again. Not after he'd gone up in flames with her and come damn close to losing his soul to her. After he'd forced himself to leave her last night, he'd lain in his narrow bed at his grandfather's and spent what was left of the night convincing himself that he'd blown their lovemaking all out of proportion. It was just good sex, nothing more. His emotions weren't involved. They couldn't be. Then he'd heard about the fourth murder and called Adam to find out where Sabrina was. When he'd learned that she'd gone back home, his heart had stopped in his chest.

He'd broken all speed limits to get to her, and ever since then, he'd been fighting the need to snatch her close. Damn, she tied him in knots! He wanted her—she didn't want commitment. So where the hell did that leave them? Until he had the answer to that, he had no business touching her. But he couldn't seem to stop himself.

Holding her hand to his jaw, he said in a voice that was

sandpaper rough, "My ego's just fine, thank you very much. And I wouldn't count my chickens before they hatch, honey. You just might end up with egg on your face."

Her eyes darkened, and becoming color stole into her cheeks. "I can handle whatever you dish out, Nickels," she promised huskily. "And don't you forget it."

Staring down at her, his heart beginning to knock against his ribs, Blake told himself they were talking about the bet, nothing more. But as he slammed her door and walked around the hood of his truck to slide in beside her, all he could think about was that she could handle him, all right. Anytime she damn well pleased, better than any woman ever had before. All she had to do was say where and when and he'd be there.

Awareness humming on the air between them, they both gave a start as Blake's police radio crackled to life and a disembodied voice called all available patrol cars within the vicinity of Loop 410 and Broadway to Texas State Bank for a hostage situation. With a muttered curse, Blake started the motor and pulled away from the curb with a squeal of tires. Seconds later, they were racing across town, each of them sending up silent prayers of thanks for the distraction of work.

When they ended up at the *Times* right before quitting time, Sabrina couldn't believe how well things had gone. After Sam Kelly's grim warning earlier that morning, she'd expected to spend the day looking over her shoulder, wondering when the killer was going to make his presence known. But it was usually Blake her eyes found whenever she looked around, and he didn't give her time to wonder about anything. When he wasn't discussing the stories they'd just investigated, he was distracting her with some tall tale that invariably made her laugh.

For a woman who valued her independence, she should

have been more than a little exasperated with him—after all, he hadn't given her any choice when he'd designated himself her personal bodyguard, and she wasn't used to a man just taking over her life that way without so much as a by-your-leave. But he hadn't crowded or pushed or in any way interfered with the way she worked. He'd just been there, a protective shadow who worked alongside her as if he did it every day of the week. And as much as her head hated to admit it to her heart, she'd liked having him there. He was a man a woman could get used to having underfoot.

When they'd first walked into the *Times*, she'd expected his boss to demand an explanation once he discovered her identity, but Tom Edwards only lifted a brow in surprise, told her that something big had to be in the works if Blake was conspiring with the competition, then offered her a job if she ever decided to jump ship and come work for a real paper. She'd liked him on the spot.

Seated at the chair Blake had drawn up for her at his desk, she watched him pound out three stories in record time and couldn't help but be fascinated. He used two fingers—just two—and never looked at his computer screen until he was finished. And even then, he only made a few changes before he flipped to his notes for the next story.

Unabashedly reading over his shoulder, Sabrina had to admit the man was darn good at what he did. She could knock out a story in record time when she had to, but it always took her a few stops and starts before her writing really got going and she got out of the way of her own muse. Blake seemed to have no such problem. What came off the top of his head was pretty much what he turned in as his finished work, and there was a grittiness to it that reached out and grabbed her with the first word. She couldn't help but be impressed, and knew that long after he was out of her life, she would carry in her heart a picture of him sitting at his desk, his forehead wrinkled with concentration and his eyes intently focused on something she couldn't see, hammering out a story.

Then, as quickly as he had begun, he was finished. Turning to her with that wicked grin of his that never failed to jump-start her heart, he said, "Now that you've seen a master at work, what d'ya say we blow this joint and get out of here, Jones? I don't know about you, but I'm starving."

Feeling a little hungry herself, she started to agree with him, only to frown with mock indignation. "Hold it right there, Nickels. What was that crack about a master at work?"

His eyes crinkling with amusement, he rose to his feet and reached down to pull her from her chair. "The truth hurts sometimes, Jones. But hey, look at it this way—now that you've seen me in action, maybe some of my genius will rub off on you. Of course, some things you just have to be born with—"

Laughing, she playfully punched him in the gut. "Yeah. Like modesty and talent and true greatness. When I get my Pulitzer, you can say you knew me when."

Enjoying himself, he only snorted and hauled her after him toward the nearest exit. "I've been meaning to have a serious talk with you, honey, about these delusions of grandeur you've been having," he teased. "I know this good doctor—"

Glancing over his shoulder to laugh down into her eyes, he pushed open the outside door and never noticed that while they'd been inside, the sky had turned dark and threatening and the wind had picked up. The minute they stepped outside, the rain that had been forecast all day started to fall with just a scattering of drops.

Surprised, Blake glanced up as thunder rumbled threateningly overhead. "Uh-ho. Better hurry. We're in for it."

Well used to summer storms that could blow up out of

nowhere, Sabrina knew better than to linger. Practically running to keep up with Blake's long stride, she dodged raindrops like bullets and rushed across the parking lot. They were halfway to Blake's truck when the heavens opened up like a floodgate. By the time they threw themselves into the pickup's cab, they were both soaked to the skin.

Laughing, Sabrina shook her wet hair out of her face and turned to Blake, intending to make a crack about not having to wash her clothes when she got home, but the words died unspoken on her tongue. His shoulder almost rubbing hers, Blake sat as if turned to stone behind the steering wheel, totally oblivious of his wet clothes as he stared down at her, his green eyes hot and intense and devouring as they moved over her.

The thud of her heartbeat, along with the dancing of the rain on the roof of the truck, was suddenly loud in her ears. Sabrina automatically glanced down...and gasped. Drenched by the rain, her thin, white cotton blouse, normally sedate enough for church, was nearly transparent and molded her breasts like a wet T-shirt. Embarrassed color firing her cheeks, she hastily moved to cover herself.

Blake, however, was faster. Reaching behind the seat, he pulled out a lightweight cotton jacket. "Here. This'll help." His voice as rough as a gravel road, he draped it around her shoulders, then couldn't seem to stop touching her as he adjusted the collar and pulled it snugger around her. "Are you cold? I can turn on the heater."

Cold? Sabrina thought shakily, swallowing a moan of laughter. Even if it hadn't been a sticky ninety or more degrees, the brush of his hands would have warmed her if it'd been thirty below. Everywhere he innocently touched—and a few places he didn't—she burned.

"No," she choked. "I'm fine. Really. Just embarrassed to death."

"Don't be," he growled, lifting her chin so that she was

forced to meet his gaze. "You're beautiful. And no one saw you but me."

And he had already seen all of her there was to see. The knowledge was there in his eyes, in the tension that curled between them like a lick of fire, in the breathlessness that suddenly seized them both. His hand slid from her chin to her throat in a slow glide, and just that quickly, they were back in his apartment, in his bed, and she was aching for another kiss.

His own need was just as fierce—she could see it in his eyes, feel it in his hands, which weren't quite steady as he moved to draw her closer, his head already lowering to hers. Then, on the street that ran in front of the *Times*'s parking lot, they heard the blare of a horn and the sudden screech of tires as a BMW, going too fast on the wet streets, narrowly missed a van that pulled out right in front of it.

Stiffening, Blake drew back abruptly and swore, remembering nearly too late that they were sitting in a public parking lot in full view of anyone who cared to look. "Let's get out of here," he muttered. A muscle ticking along his clenched jaw, he started the motor with a sharp twist of his wrist.

They didn't speak all the way home.

There was no question that he was staying the night. Or that he was sleeping in his own bed...with her. Neither one of them said anything, but the knowledge was there in his eyes, in the accelerated thump of her heart, in the expectation that filled the air like a gathering storm.

Restless, all her senses attuned to his every move as he followed her into the apartment, Sabrina knew that making love with him again could be nothing but a mistake. He was coming to mean too much to her. He made her want things she knew she couldn't have. When he touched her, kissed her, took her into his arms, she felt that anything was possible, that together they could single-handedly defeat the curse that made it impossible for the women of her family to find lifelong happiness with one man. He made her ache to believe in fairy tales and happily-ever-after and the love of a good man.

Wrapped close to his heart, it was so easy to believe that anything could happen, that he would be with her forever and grow old with her. She hadn't realized until now how desperately she wanted that, ached for that. She knew, though, that was just her emotions crying out to her. With nothing more than a heart-stopping grin, he stirred the romance in her soul. In her family, romance didn't last. Deep down inside, she knew that. But still, she couldn't send him away.

"You need to get out of those wet things," he said gruffly from behind her, shattering the silence that engulfed them. "Why don't you climb into the shower, and I'll start supper?"

His jacket still around her shoulders, she nodded, hugging herself as a blast of air from the air conditioner hit her, raising goose bumps on her damp skin. "I think I will. With the rain and everything, I am kind of cold."

"Then I'll put on some soup. Take your time. It'll be ready when you are."

If he'd touched her—just once—she wouldn't have needed soup or a shower to warm her, but he turned toward the kitchen and didn't see her need. So she headed for the bedroom to collect clean clothes, then stepped across the hall to the bathroom. She'd just started the shower and was adjusting the water temperature when there was a soft tap at the door. Her heart starting to knock like an out-of-balance washing machine, she called huskily, "Come in."

Without a sound, the door glided open to reveal Blake standing on the threshold, his expression solemn as his eyes met hers. "Sorry to interrupt, but I just remembered the city has a serious water shortage, what with the drought and everything.''

Caught off guard, Sabrina almost smiled. The mayor had asked all citizens to practice voluntary conservation methods, just as he did every summer, but the water supply wasn't close to critical and they were hardly in a drought, especially considering the fact that it was currently pouring outside and showed no signs of letting up.

"A water shortage," she repeated in bemusement. "I hadn't realized the problem was that bad." Struggling to keep her expression as serious as his, she felt her heart shift into a heavy, primitive rhythm and could do nothing to quiet it. "What do you suggest we do about it?"

Without a word, he crossed the threshold and shut the door. A half step was all it took to leave only a few inches between them. Slowly, giving her time to object, he lifted his hands to the jacket she still wore and began to ease it from her shoulders. "We both need to take a shower," he said hoarsely. "If we took one together, think of the water we'd save."

Her eyes locked with his, she felt the jacket slide to the floor and found herself holding her breath, waiting for his eyes to drop to her wet blouse, but his gaze never left hers. He didn't touch her again, but simply stood there, waiting as the bathroom filled with steam. The next move, if there was going to be another one, was clearly hers.

A wise woman would have taken a moment to step back and give herself time to think. A smart one would have insisted on it. But right from the beginning, she hadn't been wise or smart when it came to this man. He tempted her past all bearing, confused her, haunted her, made her long for the impossible. And in the end, he was going to hurt her. Oh, he wouldn't do it intentionally, but she knew him well enough now to know that there would come a time that he would want to talk of the future. And they didn't have one.

Still, she couldn't deny herself—deny them—these precious moments stolen out of a lifetime of being alone. Swallowing the lump that had risen to her throat, she lifted fingers that were far from steady to the top button of his shirt. "I suppose, then," she murmured, "that you could say it's our civic duty."

He nodded, a whisper of that wicked, wicked smile of his flirting with his mouth as his hands copied hers and reached for the top button of her blouse. Between one heartbeat and the next, he slid it free. "No question about it," he agreed huskily, turning his attention to the next button. "It's the only right thing to do. We save time…" His hands still busy with her buttons, he leaned down and nuzzled her ear. "And water. And—"

"Soap," she finished for him softly as her head fell weakly back and her eyes grew heavy with desire. "I could rub it on you. Then you could rub against me…."

She didn't finish the suggestion, but she didn't have to. He growled in approval, his hands fisting in her partially opened blouse as he pulled back to stare hungrily down into her eyes. "Is this one of your favorite blouses?"

Thrown by the sudden shift in conversation, she frowned. "Not particularly. Why?"

"I'll never forget it, but right now it's in the way." His fingers tightening in the material, he gave a quick jerk of his hands and sent the remaining buttons flying.

"Blake!"

He grinned. "There. That's much better. Do you mind?"

How could she mind when he was looking at her as if he'd just gotten three wishes for his birthday and all of them were her? His eyes scorched her, his hands worshiped her, and his mouth…she couldn't even think when he stripped her bra from her and kissed his way down to a nipple that pouted for his possession. Her cry of pleasure echoing above the drumming of the shower, she clutched his head to her breast and felt her bones melt one by one.

When he finally kissed his way back up to her mouth, she couldn't even remember her own name. Giving her a quick, hard kiss, he tore at his own clothes and what remained of hers until they were both naked. His green eyes dark and intense in the mist that shrouded them, he pulled her into the shower with him, laughing as the warm spray immediately soaked them both. Then he was pulling her in front of him, his back to the shower head, blocking the water from hitting her in the face. "Now what was that you were saying about soap?"

His eyes sparkled with a dare; his grin said she flat-out didn't have the nerve. He should have known better. With him, her heart was quickly discovering, she would dare just about anything. Happiness bubbling up in her like the clear, laughing water of a spring, she picked up the bar of soap from its holder on the side of the shower stall and slowly lathered it between her hands, her smile hot and sultry and wicked. "It seems to me," she murmured huskily, "that I mentioned something about rubbing...."

His grin broadening, he spread his hands wide, the outrageous man not the least bit self-conscious when it came to his body. "Start anywhere you like, honey. I'm all yours."

She could have started with his very obvious arousal and brought him to his knees, and she knew he wouldn't have offered a word of complaint. Instead, she reached for his hand—his left—and folded it between her palms.

"I like your hands," she said simply. Hugging his wrist to her bare breast, she gently transferred the soap on her hands to his, and all the while she talked. "Sometimes at night when I'm sleeping, I picture them touching me, undressing me, then slowly driving me out of my mind." Rubbing her fingers over the back of his hand in slow-moving circles, she looked up and asked in a sexy rasp,

"Have you ever done that? Pushed a woman right over the edge with nothing but your hands? Stroking? Caressing? Everywhere?"

Staring down at her, her fingers lighting a slow burn deep in his gut, Blake could only nod. Did the little minx know what she was doing to him? She had to—he certainly had no way of hiding it from her—and all she was doing was soaping his hand! And seducing him with the kind of love talk that no man with any blood in his veins could resist. With infinite care she took his other hand, giving it the same attention to detail as she confided how she liked his hands on her breasts and sliding down her belly.

There was no doubt that she knew exactly what she was doing—her eyes were alight with naughtiness as she lathered her hands again, then carefully soaped each arm all the way to his shoulders, all the while telling him how safe she felt with his arms around her, how she knew nothing and no one could hurt her as long as he was holding her.

He'd thought he was a strong man, but with nothing more than that, she broke him. Groaning, he reached for her. "Come here, witch."

"Wait." She laughed as he hauled her against his chest where she belonged. "Don't you want me to wash your back?"

"Later," he rasped, kissing her senseless. "Much later."

On fire for her, he gave her no time to tease or argue or even catch her breath. Pushing her up against the shower wall, he tried to hang on to patience, tenderness, but he was beyond that. His hands were shaking—*shaking!*—his lungs straining. He could feel the fire in her, the need, and by God, he ached. Then her hands were on him, right where he'd wanted them, and something in him just seemed to snap. Sweeping her up, her urged her legs around his hips.

"Blake! What—"

"I've got you, sweetheart," he said thickly, surging into her before she could do anything but gasp. "I won't let anything happen to you."

He wanted to say more—that he hoped to God she hadn't been teasing when she'd said how safe she felt in his arms—but she moved, clutching him tighter, taking him deeper, and his entire universe shrank to the wet, hot heat of her surrounding him, her breasts slippery with soap as she slid against him, her name a chant, a promise, that called to him in his head. The world could have stopped and started turning the other way, but, lost in the wonder of her, he never would have noticed. There was nothing except Sabrina, pulling him toward paradise, taking him as he'd never been taken in his life.

Chapter 10

Too spent afterwards to do much more than clumsily drag a towel over both of them, Blake carried her to bed and crawled in beside her in the dark, dragging the sheet and bedspread up around them as the cool air from the air conditioner brushed over their still-damp bodies. Shivering slightly, Sabrina scooted back against him, her soft sigh a whisper in the night as he draped an arm around her waist and anchored her close. Outside, the rain drummed against the roof and dripped from the eaves, and occasionally, thunder rumbled far off to the east. Sated, content, they slept.

They turned to each other again in the night as naturally as if they'd been doing it for years, lazily exploring each other with slow hands and drugging kisses. The white-hot flash of heat that had driven them before was now a glowing ember that warmed instead of burned. This time, they had the patience to linger, to stroke, to pleasure each other until they were weak with the wonder of it. And when he swept her under him and she welcomed him with a soft moan, they looked into each other's eyes in the dark and couldn't seem to stop smiling. Whatever happened in the future, they had now, tonight, and nothing could ever take that away from them.

Still buried deep inside her, unable to let her go, Blake drifted back to sleep with her in his arms. Exhausted, replete, more relaxed than he'd ever been in his life, he never heard the rain stop or the nurse who lived next door come home after working the three-to-eleven shift. Not wanting anything to disturb this night with Sabrina, he'd remembered to shut off the phone on the nightstand after they'd made love in the shower, so he never heard the one in the kitchen ring around two in the morning. Ten rings later, it finally stopped, but his face was buried in Sabrina's hair, his dreams filled with her, and the rest of the world had long since ceased to exist.

When someone pounded on the front door at three, he frowned in his sleep, fighting wakefulness. It was thunder, he told himself groggily. Another storm had rolled in—it would blow itself out in a little while and be gone by morning. But the pounding continued, and he came awake with a start to realize that someone was hammering at his front door loud enough to wake the dead. Muttering a curse, he eased away from Sabrina, careful not to wake her, and reached for his jeans.

"Hold your horses," he grumbled as he quietly shut the bedroom door and hurried barefoot across the living room. "I'm coming, dammit! And this damn well better be good."

His jeans zipped but not buttoned, he glanced through the peephole and lifted a brow in surprise at the sight of the uniformed policeman standing there pounding on his door as if he intended to do so for the rest of the night if he had to, to wake him up. "What the hell!"

Turning the dead bolt, he jerked open the door and scowled at the fresh-faced cop who looked like he was hardly old enough to shave. "You want to tell me what the hell you're doing, Officer?" he growled. "Besides waking up everybody in the complex. Dammit, it's three o'clock in the morning!"

Flushing, the younger man said stiffly, "I know that, sir. I'm sorry to disturb you, but I'm just following orders. Are you Blake Nickels?"

"Yes, I am," he retorted, scowling. "Whose orders?"

"Detective Kelly's, sir. When he couldn't reach you on the telephone, he told me to hammer the door down if I had to to wake you up. There's been an arrest in the serial-killer murders, and he was sure you would want to know about it as soon as possible."

"An arrest!" Surprised, Blake cast a quick look over his shoulder to make sure the bedroom door was still shut, then stepped outside onto the open cement balcony that connected all of the second-floor apartments to the garden patio below. The gutters still dripped, splashing raindrops on his bare toes, but he never noticed. "I had no idea Kelly was that close to making an arrest. Who is the bastard?"

"His name's Jeff Harper. He was picked up a little over an hour ago at his home on the north side—"

"Jeff Harper!" Blake exclaimed, stiffening. "Are you sure about that?"

"Yes, sir," he said grimly. "He's downtown right now being booked, and he didn't come easily. From what I heard, he fought like the devil. It took four officers to bring him in."

Stunned, Blake couldn't believe it. Jeff Harper. Granted, he didn't like the son of a bitch or the thought of him coming anywhere near Sabrina, but she had trusted him once, loved him enough to risk marrying him in spite of her family history. She might not love him any longer—she couldn't, dammit!—but she didn't hate him, either. Harper had disillusioned her and hurt her, but finding out that he was the one who had stalked and terrorized her

while she had defended him to the police was going to
tear her apart.

God, how was he going to tell her?

She would have to know, of course. And then there was
the story to write. They had to get downtown, find out
what the hell had happened to break the case wide open
tonight, and get some answers from Sam. "Thanks for the
information, Officer Johnson," he said, noting his name
tag. "Sabrina and I'll get downtown as soon as we can. Is
Kelly at the station?"

"The last I saw him, he was at the suspect's house su-
pervising the collection of evidence," the other man said.
"But he expected to be back at the station within the hour.
I can check if you like."

"That's okay," Blake said. "I'll find him. Thanks for
your help."

His mind already jumping ahead to what he was going
to tell Sabrina, he stepped back into the apartment and shut
the door behind him and never saw her standing in the
darkened living room until he started toward the bedroom
and she switched on a light. She'd pulled on a robe and
stood hugging herself as if it was the middle of winter, her
brown eyes huge and haunted in her pale face, and he
knew she knew.

"I woke up and you weren't there," she said huskily.
"When I couldn't find you, I noticed the front door was
ajar...."

So she'd heard it all, every damning word. Watching
the hurt darken her eyes, he would have given just about
anything short of his first-born child to have five minutes
alone with Jeff Harper in a dark alley. Stepping toward
her, he reached for her and hauled her into his arms.
"Honey, I'm sorry."

"I can't believe it," she said against his chest, clutching
at him. "Not Jeff. There has to be a mistake."

He shouldn't have been surprised by her defense of the

bastard—even when his car had been spotted near her house and her neighbor had given a description of a jogger that had sounded like the twin of her ex, she'd still refused to believe that Jeff could be involved—but it still twisted in his gut like a rusty knife. Stiffening, he said, "Why? Because you still care about him and you can't believe that someone you have feelings for would want you dead?"

"No, of course not," she began, only to suddenly become aware of his coolness. Drawing back, she looked up and gaped in amazement at the rigid set of his jaw. "You're jealous!"

"I am not! Don't be ridiculous."

He scowled, glaring at her, just daring her to repeat such nonsense, but she only laughed, not the least bit intimidated, and stood on tiptoe to loop her arms around his stiff neck. "If I weren't so surprised by the idea of you being jealous of anyone, I just might be insulted, Nickels. Do you really think I could have done what I did in that shower with you if I cared two cents about another man?"

His lips twitched, but he stood unbending before her, softening only when she melted against him, giving him an excuse to hold her again. "You were awful damn quick to defend him," he grumbled, stroking her hair as if he couldn't help himself.

"Only because I thought I knew him," she said quietly, sobering. Her heart suddenly aching, she laid her cheek against the hollow of his bare shoulder and fought the crazy need to cry. "Try to understand," she said softly. "It wasn't all that long ago that I was married to him, Blake. For two years, I slept with him, cooked for him, even washed his damn underwear. How could I have been so close to him and never sensed the violence in him? Was I that blind? Or just insensitive? What did I do to make him hate me so?"

"You didn't do anything," he said roughly, tightening

his arms around her. "You aren't the one with the problem, honey. He is. The man's sick. He has to be. And you aren't the only one he fooled. He has friends, family, people that have known and worked with him a heck of a lot longer than you have. If none of them saw this coming, how could you?"

"But the Jeff Harper I knew couldn't even take a sick dog to the vet. How could someone like that kill four women and terrorize me?"

He shrugged. "People change."

"But not that much. There's been a lot of pressure on the police to make an arrest. Maybe someone made a mistake—"

He drew back, his hand cupping her chin to lift her gaze to his. "You know better than that. Kelly was the one who made the collar, and he never would have done that without a hell of a lot of evidence. You know how careful he is. Especially where this case is concerned. The whole state's watching, not to mention his superiors. He wants a conviction too badly to risk making a mistake."

He was right, but that didn't make it any easier to accept. Jeff. Dear God, how could it be Jeff? She hadn't lied when she'd told Blake that she didn't care two cents about him, but he was still the first man she'd ever loved, the first man she'd ever given her heart and body to. They hadn't parted friends, but she hadn't thought they were enemies, either. Obviously, she'd been wrong.

"I know," she said thickly, forcing a halfhearted smile that did nothing to conceal the pain squeezing her heart. "It just makes no sense. Why would he do such a thing now? If he was going to try to kill me, why didn't he do it when I divorced him?"

As short on answers as she, Blake shrugged. "I don't know, sweetheart. I wish I did. Who knows what pushes somebody over the edge? It might not have had anything to do with you at all—he could have just been looking for somebody to strike out at about something and your name came to mind. You know yourself that these types of crimes don't always make a lot of sense.''

''Do you think Kelly will let me talk to him?''

Blake stiffened at that. No! Now that they knew Harper was responsible for terrorizing her, he didn't want her anywhere near the man. But she was the intended victim here, and he knew her well enough by now to know that this would eat at her like a cancer until she got some answers.

Still, his first inclination was to lock her up in the bedroom until Harper was tried and convicted and behind bars for a good, long stretch. She'd fight him on that, however, and he couldn't say he'd blame her. She had a right to know what was going on in Harper's head. But if she was hurting now, that could damn well rip her apart, and there wasn't anything he could do to protect her from that kind of pain. Except be there for her.

Slinging an arm around her shoulder, he turned her toward the bedroom. ''Let's get dressed and go downtown and find out.''

By the time they rushed into the central station downtown, it was going on four. Normally at that hour of the morning, the only ones about were cops and the lowlifes of society—drunks and brawlers and an occasional scumbag who got his kicks punching the woman in his life. But not tonight. Somehow, the word had already gotten out that there'd been an arrest in the serial killings, and the place was crawling with press. There were at least three field reporters from the local television stations, complete with camera crews, hassling the officer at the front desk for the story, not to mention radio and print reporters from every town within a fifty-mile radius. By dawn, there'd probably be some from Dallas and Houston as well.

Swearing at the sight of them, Blake shouldered his way through the crowd, pulling Sabrina after him. Finally reaching the front desk, he flashed his press badge at the scowling sergeant and said, "We need to see Detective Kelly."

"So does half the world," he drawled. "You're going to have to wait just like everybody else. He's called a press conference for seven. You can ask him anything you like then." Suddenly spying Sabrina where she was half-hidden behind Blake, his weathered face cracked into a smile. "Hey, Jones! What are you doing down here? The last time you covered the graveyard shift, you were still writing obits."

Sabrina grinned, affection lifting the heavy boulder that seemed to be sitting on her heart. Stoney Griffen had been sitting at that desk the first time she walked into the police station as a nervous cub reporter. He could have made things hard for her, but he'd gruffly taught her the ropes and had been a friend ever since.

"There's not a whole lot of things I'd crawl out of bed for at this hour of the night, Stoney, but this is one of them."

Suddenly remembering who the suspect was they had in the lockup, his teasing smile faded. "Aw, jeez, Sabrina, I'm sorry." Snapping at the other reporters to back off, he waited until they'd stepped back a couple of paces before he confided quietly, "I don't know what I was thinking of. Of course you'd be here. Are you okay?"

"Well, I can't pretend it hasn't been a shock, but I'm dealing with it." Introducing Blake to him, she said, "We really need to talk to Sam, Stoney. Isn't there some way we could see him before the press conference?"

Sighing heavily, the older man shook his head. "Sorry, darlin'. He's not even here right now. He's still over at Harper's house with the evidence guys. And I wouldn't go over there if I was you, either—he won't have time to talk to you. The last I heard, they were taking the place apart brick by brick."

"Then when he gets back—"

"He's got a meeting lined up with the chief. There ain't no way in hell I'm interfering with that."

"He's meeting with Travelino at this hour of the morning?"

The older man nodded. "The chief's been keeping a close eye on this one. In fact, Kelly hasn't made a move without letting him know about it. The old man wants to go over the evidence the minute Kelly walks through the door."

Blake swore. "It looks like we're going to have to wait just like everyone else."

If it had been any other night, any other case, Sabrina would have been more than willing to do just that. But questions hammered at her, nagged at her, pulled at her like a persistent child who refused to be silenced. Given the least encouragement from Stoney, she would have been out of there like a shot and racing for Jeff's house. But she knew police procedure as well as he did, and even though Kelly had notified her about Jeff's arrest, there was no way he was going to give her special treatment at a crime scene of this importance. Not when Travelino was waiting for him back at the station.

Reluctantly accepting defeat, she sighed. "Great. So what are we supposed to do for the next three hours?"

"Eat," Blake growled as he steered her away from the front desk and headed for the nearest exit. "In case you've forgotten, we missed supper. I'm starving. Let's go over to Mi Tierra and grab a George's Special."

She hadn't forgotten anything, least of all *why* they hadn't eaten. And in the few minutes it took for them to walk down the street to the all-night Mexican restaurant that was the heart and soul of Market Square, find a booth, and order their food, all she could think of was those moments in the shower, then later in his bed. He was coming to mean too much to her. Even as her heart swelled with joy at the thought, her head insisted that she take steps to do something about it now that she was safe again and Jeff was behind bars—

Just that quickly, her thoughts were dragged back to the murders, the notes left for her, the deliberate attempt to terrorize her, the threats to kill her. What little appetite she had vanished.

Seated across from her, Blake knew the minute he'd lost her. One second, her eyes were all dreamy, a sexy little smile playing with her mouth, and the next, her cheeks didn't have any color and she'd withdrawn into herself. And it didn't take an Einstein to figure out that her mind was back at the police station with that murdering ex-husband of hers.

And he *was* jealous. He wasn't happy about it, but he couldn't avoid the truth when it slapped him right in the face. Somehow, without quite knowing how it had happened, he had come to think of her as his.

God, he had to get this caveman stuff under control, he told himself. But even as he lectured himself to get a grip, he pushed his iced tea and place setting across the table. When Sabrina blinked in surprise, he grinned crookedly and moved around to slide in next to her on her side of the booth. "You look a little lonely over here all by yourself, Jones. Mind if I join you?"

Since he already had, she could do nothing but laugh. "Don't mind me, Nickels. Make yourself at home."

"Thanks. I think I will." Slipping an arm around her shoulders, he drew her flush against his side, unmindful of who might be watching. It wasn't until then that he realized just how badly he'd needed to have her back in his arms. "You know, Jones," he confided huskily as he trailed his fingers up and down her arm, "I could get used to holding you. You're real…touchable."

Watching her, he caught a wisp of a smile, then he felt it, that softening that always seemed to steal his breath when she leaned against him, letting him take her weight. "We're supposed to be working, Nickels."

Her tone was gently reproving—but she didn't pull away. Encouraged, Blake blatantly caressed her. "I am, sweetheart. I'm working real hard at controlling myself."

"Blake!"

"I just love it when you cry out my name that way," he growled outrageously. "Do it again."

She laughed, she couldn't help herself. "Stop that!" She giggled, casting a quick look around. "I swear, I just can't take you anywhere. We're in a public restaurant, for heaven's sake!"

Unrepentant, he leaned down to nuzzle her neck. "There's not another soul within twenty feet, and he's half-asleep. Which is what we would *not* be doing if we were back in my bed," he muttered roughly for her ears alone.

Telling her exactly what he would do to her if they were back in his apartment, he watched in growing satisfaction as the color flowed back into her pale cheeks, and her eyes lost that haunted look. And while she might have been chilled by her own thoughts only a few moments ago, the lady definitely wasn't cold now. Leaning more fully against him, she was warm and soft and responsive, and she never even flinched when the waiter brought their food, then quickly left them alone.

If he thought he was pulling a fast one on her, however, she quickly set him straight once the waiter was out of earshot. Capturing the hand that had dropped to her knee, she gave his fingers a warning squeeze. "You think you're pretty tricky, don't you, Nickels?"

"Who? Me? I don't know what you're talking about."

"You can cut the innocent act, cowboy. It's not working. The day you're innocent is the day the Alamo becomes the next Disneyland. You're not the type to seduce a woman in a public place. You're trying to take my mind off Jeff.''

Amusement glinting in his eyes, he leaned down and brushed a kiss across her mouth. "So how am I doing?"

Surprised that he even had to ask, she grinned. "I'll let you know later—when we're alone." When he groaned, she only laughed and pulled his arm from around her shoulder. "Eat, Nickels, before your food gets cold."

For the next twenty minutes, by unspoken agreement, they avoided any mention of Jeff or the murders or the evidence that Sam Kelly was even now collecting against her former husband. Concentrating instead on their food, they enjoyed each other's company as if they didn't have a care in the world. They traded stories about their childhoods and colleges and every boss they'd ever had, then argued good-naturedly over their favorite movies. By the time they stopped to catch a breath, their plates were clean and they were both more relaxed than when they had walked in.

That couldn't last, however. As they headed back to the police station, Blake shifted the conversation to the weirdest stories they'd ever covered, but Sabrina couldn't concentrate. Tension crawled along her nerves, wiring her, and her steps unconsciously slowed as the station grew closer and closer. For the first time in her life, she actually dreaded a press conference.

"You start stiffening up again and I'm going to have to kiss you right here on the street in front of God and everyone," Blake warned as he laced his fingers with hers. "You'll get through this, Jones. Just don't beat yourself up over it. None of it was your fault."

She could have told him it was too late for that—somehow, she should have seen this coming—but they'd reached the front steps of the station by then and it was time to go back to work. Resisting the sudden childish need to cling to his hand, she gave his fingers a quick squeeze, then dropped them, squared her shoulders, and marched up the steps.

When Sam Kelly presented himself to the press at seven in the morning, he didn't look as though he'd been up all night. Clean-shaven and neatly dressed in a gray suit and white shirt that didn't show a single wrinkle, he walked into the media room with a confident step and took the podium like a man who was well used to taking control. All business, he greeted the crowd with a brisk good-morning and, without bothering to glance at his notes, began to relate the details of the arrest of Jeff Harper.

"Mr. Harper was taken into custody at 2:23 this morning at his home on O'Connor Road. He initially resisted arrest, but there were four uniformed officers on the scene and he was quickly subdued. Presently, he is being charged with the murders of Charlene McClintock, Tanya Bishop, and Elizabeth Reagan."

"Why not Denise Green?" Jason McQuire, a reporter for the local ABC affiliate, called out. "Are you saying that Harper didn't kill her?"

"No," he said carefully, "I'm saying that he's not currently being charged with that murder. The M.O. in Ms. Green's murder was slightly different, and we're not booking anyone until we've had a chance to sift through the evidence more thoroughly."

Seated next to Sabrina at the rear of the room, Blake spoke up. "When did Jeff Harper become a suspect?"

His expression grim, Sam said, "Right after Sabrina Jones got the first note about Tanya Bishop's murder. We knew the murderer was somehow linked to her—it was just a matter of finding out how. As most of you may or may not know, the suspect is Ms. Jones's ex-husband."

"Did you find physical evidence linking him to the crimes?" a reporter from Austin asked. "Is that why you were at his house so long?"

Automatically taking notes, Sabrina listened as Sam described the extensive evidence found at Jeff's home. A gun—an unregistered .38 wiped clean of fingerprints—and a stash of bullets were found in the garage, wedged up in the rafters behind a box full of Christmas ornaments. They wouldn't know for sure until ballistics tests were done, but Sam and his men were pretty sure it was the same .38 used to kill the four women. The fact that it had been wrapped in various items of clothing that were believed to have belonged to the victims and were taken by the killer as trophies only added to the conviction that the gun was the murder weapon.

A radio reporter from the nearby town of Seguin said, "So the evidence you have presently is circumstantial?"

His mouth tightening, Sam nodded. "Obviously, we'd like an eyewitness or a confession, but given what we've got, we're sure we have the right man. The gun and clothes didn't just walk into Harper's garage by themselves and hide. And we have three witnesses who will testify to seeing a car matching the suspect's in the area at the time two of the murders were committed."

"What about an alibi?" Blake asked.

"Mr. Harper claims he was at home with his wife at the time of all four murders, but when we questioned the wife, she couldn't corroborate that because she was asleep each time and couldn't guarantee that he was in the house or not."

Stricken, her hand flying across her notebook as she jotted down notes, Sabrina wanted to cry out that this was all a terrible mistake. It had to be. But even as she tried to find an explanation for the facts that Kelly had so clearly laid out before them, her own professional objectivity forced her to admit that the evidence was damning. If it had pointed to the guilt of any other man but Jeff, she would have believed it in a heartbeat.

Sick at the thought, she had to force herself to concentrate on the task at hand. "What broke the case for you?" she asked Sam. "It couldn't have been the recovery of the murder weapon. You didn't find it until you went in to make the arrest, did you?"

"No, but we knew it was on the property somewhere—"

"How?"

"We got an anonymous tip around seven-thirty last night," he admitted. "And before you all start throwing questions at me, there's not a lot I can tell you about that," he said quickly when most of the inhabitants of the room perked up in interest. "The call came in over a 911 line from a pay phone across the street from the Alamo. As you know, that area is usually crowded with tourists, especially in the middle of the summer, and no one noticed anything. We do know the caller was male, but that's about it. He claimed he preferred not to give his name because he's a neighbor of Harper's and has to live on the same block with him. If he was mistaken in what he had seen, he didn't want the suspect to know that he was the one who had turned him in. That's all I can tell you."

The roomful of reporters had no intention of letting the matter drop with that, and started firing questions at him. There was, however, little else he could add. If he had any other information, it wasn't for public consumption until the trial, which wouldn't be for months. Minutes later, the press conference broke up.

They rode back to the *Daily Record* in silence. His attention divided between his driving and Sabrina's withdrawn figure, Blake ground a curse between his teeth. He'd watched her all during the press conference, watched her agitation as she jerkily scribbled notes, watched her almost visibly flinch as Kelly gave an accounting of the evidence. She hurt, and it was all he could do to stop himself from reaching for her. She hurt, and he hated that.

For the life of him, he couldn't understand how she could have any kind of feelings for the bastard who'd had her looking over her shoulder every time she stepped outside. Harper had threatened to kill her, for God's sake! For no other reason than that, Blake would have liked to hang him up by his thumbs and leave him to twist in the wind. That, however, wasn't going to make Sabrina feel any better, and that was his only concern right now.

Braking to a stop at the curb in front of the *Daily Record*, he frowned. She was safe now. It was all right for him to let her out of his sight. The rational part of his brain knew that he could let her go back to her life and not worry about some sleazeball stalking her like a hunter after his next big kill. The nightmare was over, the danger past. He no longer had to feel responsible for her.

But even as he silently acknowledged that, he was reluctant to let her go. They needed to talk. But they couldn't do it now, not when they each had to get back to their papers and write their accounts of the night's events. Over the course of the next twelve hours, there would be recaps of each murder to do and interviews with Harper's friends and neighbors. And one with Harper himself if he could get it, he silently acknowledged.

Just the thought of that should have had him making his excuses so he could get to the jail and convince the man to give him an exclusive. Instead, he said, "Do you want me to come in with you? I can wait while you write your story, then take you home so you can get your car."

Sabrina hesitated, wanting to jump at the offer, but she knew she couldn't. He had his own story to write, and she couldn't take advantage of him that way. But Lord, how she wanted to! For the first time in her career, she dreaded writing a breaking story. Just thinking about Jeff and the hatred he must feel for her made her want to jump into Blake's arms. But she was no longer in danger—she no longer needed his protection. Her heart ached at the thought of going back to an adversarial relationship with him, but she was the one who had insisted only a few weeks ago that there was no place in her future for him or any other man. She couldn't cling to him now.

Reluctantly, she shook her head. "Thanks, but that's not necessary. I don't know how long it's going to take me, and you've got your own work to do. I'll get a ride."

He wanted to argue—she could see the struggle going on his eyes—but she didn't give him the chance. Reaching for the door handle, she said huskily, "I've got to go."

He made no move to stop her, but just as she stepped out of his truck, he warned, "You haven't seen the last of me, Jones. When things calm down a little, we're going to talk."

His words carried the hint of a promise—and a threat. Her heart doing a flip-flop in her chest, Sabrina watched him drive away and bit her tongue to keep from calling him back.

Fitz told her later that her piece about Jeff's arrest was one of the best she had ever written, but Sabrina took little pleasure in the compliment. She'd tried to divorce herself both physically and emotionally from it and write it as she would any other story, but she just couldn't do it. By the time she finally finished, she was drained. Her head ached and her eyes burned, and all she wanted to do was go home and sleep around the clock.

But in spite of the fact that she had started work before four that morning, her day had hardly begun. She had a whole string of interviews she had to conduct, starting with the crime scene investigators who had uncovered the evidence at Jeff's house and continuing right down to the snow-cone seller at Alamo Plaza who might have caught a glimpse of whoever had made the anonymous phone call about Jeff to the police. But first, she had to have wheels.

When one of the sports reporters heard she was afoot,

he volunteered to give her a ride home since he was headed in that direction. She jumped at the offer, and a few minutes later, had him drop her off at the corner half a block from her house. At barely ten in the morning, it was already hot, but she didn't care. She just wanted to walk down her own street without feeling that someone was watching her.

It was heaven.

Martha Anderson was, as usual, outside in her front yard gossiping over the hedge with Gwen Richards, the widow who lived on her west side. The two were fast friends who kept an eagle eye on the neighborhood—a leaf couldn't fall without them knowing about it. Reassured that some things remained consistent, Sabrina waved gaily at them, then hurried up the porch steps to her front door. Both women waved back and continued to talk to each other as if they didn't have a care in the world, but Sabrina wasn't fooled by their nonchalance. They weren't called "the Newspapers" by the rest of the neighbors for nothing. The minute Sabrina was safely inside her house, the two old ladies would call everyone on the block to let them know she was home.

Grinning at the thought, she let herself inside. Silence closed around her immediately, clammy and thick, intimidating. Unable to stop herself, she shivered, the pleasure she expected to feel when she walked through her front door just not there. She wanted to forget Jeff and the sick murders he had committed, but all too easily, she found herself remembering the night after the awards banquet when she'd come home with Blake to find her front door unlocked and the threatening note waiting for her on her kitchen table.

She shouldn't have come here, she thought. Not yet. She wasn't ready for the memories or the nagging silence of her own thoughts. She should have just grabbed her car keys and gotten the hell out of there. But it seemed like ages since she'd been home. Her plants needed watering, and there was mail to go through. She could take a few minutes to see to those things, then grab a quick shower. Maybe then she'd be able to get through the rest of the day without going quietly out of her mind.

She had just started to water the ivy in the kitchen when there was a knock at the front door. Not really surprised, Sabrina's lips twitched. If her calculations were right, it had taken Martha all of two minutes and twenty-five seconds to get away from Gwen and make her way over there to find out where she'd been for the last two nights. That had to be a record even for her.

Her eyes starting to twinkle, she turned back to the front door. But it wasn't Martha standing on her porch, or even Gwen. It was Louis, and he looked extremely upset.

Chapter 11

"My dear, I'd just heard about Jeff's arrest on the radio when I saw you walk up. I know you're divorced and all, but you must be devastated. Is there anything I can do?"

Sabrina appreciated his concern, but she couldn't take any sympathy right now, not when her emotions felt as though they'd just been put through a food processor. He was, however, only being kind. Her smile forced, she said, "Well, it was something of a shock, but I'm coming to grips with it. And I don't have to be afraid anymore."

"That's the important thing," he agreed gruffly. "He's behind bars now and he can't hurt you. You probably have a million things to do, but I just wanted you to know that if you needed to talk, I've been told I'm a good listener."

The throbbing of her head intensifying, Sabrina reminded herself that he'd been a good neighbor to her over the years, and she couldn't be rude just because the last six hours had been rough ones. "I've got to get back to work in about an hour, but I've got a little time now. Why don't you take a seat on the porch swing and I'll fix us something cold to drink," she suggested. "I'll be right back."

Leaving him on the porch, she hurried back to the kitchen, trying to remember what she had in the house to serve him. She knew he didn't like sodas, so that left iced tea or lemonade and she wasn't sure she had the makings for either. Of course, there was always water, but—

Lost in her thoughts and wishing she could have put this off until later, she was checking to see how much sugar she had when she heard a noise behind her. Startled, she whirled and nearly dropped the sugar canister when she spotted Louis standing in the kitchen doorway. "Oh!" she laughed shakily, her heart hammering against her ribs. "You scared me."

Contrite, he immediately apologized. "I should have said something, but I thought you heard me come in. Are you all right?"

"I guess I'm still a little jumpy." Replacing the sugar canister on the counter, she decided to brew tea and moved to the sink to fill the teakettle with water. "The last week has been pretty hairy," she admitted as she crossed to the stove. "Not knowing who was threatening me was the worst. I was constantly looking over my shoulder. Then to find out it was Jeff..." She shuddered. "I still can't believe it."

His expression suddenly hard and cold, Louis nodded. "I know. I'm sure he fooled a lot of people, but there's no question that the man is a first-class bastard, dear. I hope he gets the book thrown at him. It's no more than he deserves for hurting you."

His vehemence surprised her. She knew Louis was as protective of her as an older uncle, but he'd always seemed to like Jeff, even after she divorced him. In fact, she'd never heard him say a harsh word against him. "I really think he has to be sick, Louis. Or he's on drugs or something. It's the only explanation. Four women are dead. The Jeff I was married to would have to be out of his mind to do something like that."

"I don't care if he's crazy as a loon. He hurt you, and he's going to pay for that."

Confused, she frowned. "He scared me, but he never touched me physically. It's those poor women who are the real victims—"

"They didn't suffer like you did," he said flatly, dismissing their deaths with a careless wave of his hand. "You were the one who constantly tried to please a man who couldn't be pleased. I stood by and watched you try to make that son of a bitch happy, and it made me sick to my stomach. He didn't deserve you."

Stunned, Sabrina could only stare at him. She'd never heard Louis talk like this, hadn't a clue, in fact, that he'd ever felt that way about Jeff. And how could he dismiss the death of those four women so easily, without an ounce of compassion? She'd always thought he was such a kind and gentle man, but there was a barely controlled rage in his eyes now that was more than a little scary.

Suddenly aware of the way he stood in the doorway, blocking it, she told herself to remain calm. There was no reason to get all paranoid. Obviously, something was going on here that she didn't understand. She would get him outside and they would talk about it.

The teakettle whistled then, and relief almost weakened her knees. "The tea will be ready in just a second," she said brightly. Her smile felt like it would crack her face, but it was the best she could manage under the circumstances. "Why don't you go on out to the front porch and I'll be right there?" she suggested. "I think I've got some cookies around here somewhere—"

"No."

She jumped at his sharp response, her smile slipping.

"Okay, fine," she said carefully, watching him warily. "Then we'll just have the tea."

Never budging from the doorway, he only looked at her, his pale eyes suddenly coolly amused behind the lenses of his wire-rimmed glasses. "You just don't get it, do you, Sabrina? You're not going anywhere."

Her heart jumped into her throat, but she only laughed shakily. "Of course I am. I told you, I have to get back to work—"

"I've been watching you for a long time, you know. Years, in fact," he said casually, not even hearing her as he leaned against the doorjamb. "The first day the two of you moved in here, I knew Jeff was all wrong for you. Anybody with eyes could see that he was a selfish bastard who didn't deserve you, but you tried your damndest to make it work. Do you know how hard it was for me to stand back and watch you do that?"

Transfixed, she could do nothing but mutely shake her head.

"No, of course you didn't," he said bitterly. "You never even knew I was alive. And I couldn't blame you. You were married and you should have had eyes for no one but your husband, even if he didn't deserve you. But then you divorced him, and I thought I might finally have a chance. Surely you would see then how much I loved you. But you never looked twice at me."

Shocked, Sabrina couldn't believe what she was hearing. He *loved* her? As a man loves a woman? Surely she must have misunderstood. But even as she tried to convince herself otherwise, she looked into his eyes and knew she hadn't made a mistake. He made no attempt to hide his pain—or resentment. Remorse stabbing her in the heart, Sabrina wanted to defend herself, but there was nothing she could say that wouldn't make him feel worse. He was right—she hadn't noticed, but he was over thirty years older than she was. He'd always been friendly when they spotted each other in the yard, but she'd never dreamed that he was romantically interested in her. Why would she? He was old enough to be her father!

"Louis, I'm sorry. I never realized."

"No, you didn't," he retorted, not making things easy for her. "You were young and pretty and you didn't have time for an old man. So I looked around and found myself someone else. She was a lot like you, a professional woman who knew what she wanted out of life. Unfortunately, she wasn't you."

Becoming more uncomfortable by the moment, Sabrina really didn't want to hear about his love life, but he hadn't budged from the doorway, and she knew he wasn't letting her out of there until he'd said everything he had to say. "That doesn't mean she wasn't right for you," she said earnestly, trying to reassure him. "Maybe you need to give her another chance."

"I can't. She's dead."

"Oh, I'm sorry!"

"I killed her."

He said it so easily, in the same casual tone he might use to mention that he'd mowed the grass, that, at first, the confession didn't register. Then her startled eyes met his and there was no question that he'd said exactly what she thought he'd said. Her heart starting to slam in her chest, she paled. "If this is some kind of a joke, I don't think it's very funny."

"Oh, it's no joke," he assured her seriously. "I tried to make her into you—the same perfume and hairstyle, but she kept fighting me. She said I was old-fashioned and domineering and no man was going to dictate to her what she could and couldn't wear. She didn't know her place, so I shot her."

Horrified, Sabrina realized she must have made a strangled sound of protest because he pushed away from the doorjamb, the smile that played about his mouth rueful and twisted and deranged. "Don't worry, she didn't suffer. None of them did."

A restless hand flew to Sabrina's suddenly tight throat. "None of them?"

"There were others," he said simply. "But they didn't work out, either"

"How many others?"

"Three more. I knew you would put two and two together, after the first two, and you did. Finally, you noticed me!" A pleased smile bloomed across his face. "It was wonderful. So I killed again. Then once more because I couldn't help myself. *You* made me mad." Suddenly noticing her ashen complexion, he frowned. "You should sit down. You're awfully pale all of a sudden."

Her blood roaring in her ears, Sabrina almost choked on a hysterical laugh. He'd just admitted to killing four women and he was concerned that she was a little pale?

It hit her then—*four* women. He'd claimed he'd killed four women, and the only murders she'd written about recently were those committed by the serial killer.

The logical part of her mind immediately rejected the idea. The police had arrested Jeff; they were sure they had the right man. He had motive and opportunity, not to mention a garage full of incriminating evidence and no alibi. They couldn't have made a mistake. Could they?

Dread clutching her heart, she stepped around the table before he could help her into a chair. "I don't need to sit down, but I would like to hear more about these murders," she said quickly. "When did all of this happen? And who were these women? Did you know them personally or just pick them by chance?"

Amused that she even had to ask, he chided softly, "Surely you've guessed by now, Sabrina. I can't think of anyone in San Antonio who wouldn't know their names. Charlene McClintock, Tanya Bishop—"

"But Jeff was arrested for those murders. The police found evidence—"

"That I planted," he said quite proudly. "How do you think they even knew to look for it, dear? I called in the tip."

He was serious. Even though a smile still clung to his thin lips and he spoke in a tone that was warm with affection, there was a feral gleam in his eye that a blind woman couldn't have missed. "Why?" she choked out hoarsely. "Why are you telling me this?"

In the blink of an eye, his smile vanished. "Because I love you!" he raged. "I've loved you forever, but you couldn't see it. You couldn't see *me!*" he snarled, hitting himself hard in the chest with a clenched fist. "It was your work, always your work that got in my way. Then when I finally figured out a way to get your attention there, you couldn't see anybody but *him!*"

Agitated, his mouth twisting with contempt, he turned suddenly and swept all the canisters from the counter. "Damn you, you're in love with Blake Nickels, aren't you? Don't try to deny it. Don't you dare! Do you think just because I'm an old man I can't see what's right in front of my eyes? *I saw you!*"

Startled, more frightened than she'd ever been in her life, Sabrina took a step back. "When? What are you talking about?"

"At that damn newspaper party when you couldn't keep your hands off each other. And then later on the porch when you kissed him like a slut. You left with him that night, after you found my note on the table. You left and went to his apartment, didn't you? You made love with him."

"No. Not then—"

"Don't lie to me!" he roared, jerking a very small, very ugly little revolver out of his pocket. "I won't stand for it. Do you hear me? I've killed for you, and by God, you'll love me or you'll love no one."

Trapped, caught between the locked back door and where he stood blocking the doorway to the rest of the house, Sabrina knew real fear for the first time in her life. He was going to kill her—there wasn't a doubt in her mind. If she didn't find a way to reason with him, he'd snuff her out as easily as he had Tanya Bishop and all the others. The police would know then that Jeff was innocent, but they wouldn't suspect Louis in a million years. They would look for someone with an obvious grudge, not an elderly neighbor who had never had a cross word with her.

Never taking her eyes from the gun, she slowly pulled out a chair at the table and sank down into it. Every instinct she had was screaming at her to run, but that was probably what he was hoping for, so he would have the pleasure of gunning her down. "Please," she pleaded shakily, "put the gun down and let's talk. Surely there's some way we can work this out...."

Staring at his computer screen, Blake quickly read over his story about Jeff Harper's arrest. It was good, he silently acknowledged. Damn good. The kind of thing that just might win him another award. And he didn't like it at all.

Scowling, ignoring the commotion of the *Times'* city room, he dropped his hands from the keyboard and sat back, wondering what the devil was wrong. He'd checked all his facts twice, arranged and rearranged them, and started over more times than he had on any other story in the last six months. And he still couldn't shake the niggling feeling that something wasn't quite right.

The facts just didn't add up, dammit!

Tapping a pencil against the edge of his desk, he told himself he was getting as bad as Sabrina. She'd tried every way she could to find an excuse for the incriminating evidence found in her ex's garage, and now he found himself doing the same thing. And not because he cared two cents about Jeff Harper. He didn't like the man. But if he was a serial killer, then Blake was Al Capone.

Oh, all the facts pointed to Harper's guilt; there was no doubt about that. *If* you just took them collectively and didn't ask any questions. Like who called in the anonymous tip. How had the caller known there was enough evidence in Harper's garage to choke a horse? And why would a man of Harper's obvious intelligence keep damning evidence on his property just days after he'd been questioned about the murders by the police? He had to know he was a suspect and the police could return at any time. And then there was the car. If Harper really was the killer and the same man who had left those notes for Sabrina, why would he use his own car in a neighborhood where it was known and he was sure to be recognized? Only an idiot would do that.

Or someone who was trying to frame Harper.

Instinctively, he tried to dismiss the idea. Kelly was an experienced detective—he would have smelled a setup like that in a heartbeat.

But he'd also been under a lot of pressure to make an arrest in the case, a voice in his head pointed out. *Harper made it easy for him by publicly confronting Sabrina and acting like an ass. With the evidence that was found in that damn garage, what else could Kelly do but arrest him? That doesn't necessarily mean Harper actually killed anyone.*

And if he didn't, then the real killer was still out there, still after Sabrina.

His blood running cold at the thought, Blake snatched up his phone and punched out the number for the *Daily Record.* "Let me speak to Sabrina Jones," he snapped the minute someone answered in the other paper's city room.

"Hold on a minute," a disembodied, bored feminine

voice said. "I think she just stepped out for a second. Let me see if I can find her."

Blake winced as the receiver was thrown down on a desk, every instinct he possessed urging him to hurry. Too late, he realized he should have told the woman that it was an emergency, but he'd expected Sabrina to be right there. Dammit, where the hell was she?

Twenty seconds ticked by on the clock on the wall at the far end of the city room, then another thirty, before the phone was picked up again and the same feminine voice said, "Sorry, she's not here. She left about twenty minutes ago to go home and pick up her car. You want to leave a message?"

Blake felt his heart stop in his chest. Home? She'd gone *home?* Swearing, he growled, "Yeah. This is Blake Nickels. If she shows up there, tell her not to leave again without talking to me first. You got that? Don't let her leave!"

Slamming the phone down, he jerked it up immediately and called Sabrina's home number. But if she was there, she didn't answer, and with every ring, the muscles in his gut tightened. "Dammit!"

She hadn't gotten there yet, he told himself, and prayed it was true. If somebody at the *Record* gave her a ride, they could have had some errands to run before they could drop her off. If he hurried, he could beat her there. Hanging up, he ran for the door.

Her eyes locked in fascinated horror on the gun that Louis held on her with icy determination, Sabrina jumped when there was a sudden pounding on her front door. Before she could even think about screaming for help, Louis was around the table and pressing the revolver to her temple.

"One word," he snarled in a low voice, "and it'll be your last."

Her gasp quickly stifled, she nodded and felt the cold

steel of the gun's barrel slide against her skin. Nausea churned in her stomach, backing up into her throat.

"Sabrina? Are you in there?"

At the first sound of Blake's voice, she bit her lip to keep from crying out, the need to call out to him almost more than she could bear. He'd come for her. Somehow she'd known deep inside that he would, even though he couldn't possibly have known that she was in trouble. He would take care of Louis. All she had to do was scream—

"I'll kill him," Louis grated, reading her mind. "I swear to God I'll kill him if he doesn't get away from that door."

"No!" Horror choking her, she ignored the revolver at her temple and turned to him with pleading eyes. "He must have called the *Record* and found out I got a ride home. Let me talk to him. I can convince him to leave."

"Yeah, right," he drawled sarcastically. "Before or after you tell him to call the police?"

"I won't. I swear!" she promised. "You can stand right there behind the door and listen the whole time. We had a fight yesterday," she lied in growing desperation. "I'll tell him I'm still mad at him and make him leave. Please. If you shoot him, the neighbors will hear and then what will you do?"

He hesitated, clearly not trusting her, the look in his eyes wild and panicky. Whatever was going on in that twisted head of his, he obviously hadn't anticipated this kind of kink in his plans. "All right," he muttered. "But you say one wrong word, you even look at him funny, and I'll shoot you both. Get up."

Jerking her to her feet, he jammed the gun in her back and pushed her through the kitchen door into the central hall that ran all the way to the front of the house. His breath hot against the back of her neck, he stopped her three feet from the front door simply by curling his fingers into her arm until she winced. "Remember what I said. One wrong move and you won't have time to regret it. I'll make sure of it."

Her knees quaking, her heart pounding so hard she could hardly catch her breath, she nodded stiffly and took two shaky steps toward the door just as Blake knocked again. Out of sight behind the door itself, Louis thrust the revolver into her ribs. "Put the chain on and keep it on," he said between his teeth in a nearly soundless whisper.

Her fingers far from steady, Sabrina did as ordered, then waited for his nod for her to open the door. When he grudgingly gave it, she braced herself. Her heart in her throat, the cold, hard barrel of the revolver pressing threateningly into her ribs, she opened the door as far as the chain would allow, all of four inches.

"Thank God!" Blake breathed. "I was beginning to think you weren't here."

"I was in the middle of something," she said coldly, and nearly snatched the words back when she saw his eyes narrow in surprise. Please, please, let him understand, she prayed, then demanded, "What do you want?"

He took a step toward her, only to stop, his dark brows snapping together when she didn't release the chain. "I need to talk to you. Can I come in?"

"No," she said curtly. "Everything we had to say to each other was said last night. I told you then to leave me alone and I meant it. Now, if you'll excuse me, I'm going to take a bath and go to bed. Alone." Without another word, she shut the door in his face and shot the dead bolt home. Stunned, Blake stared at the closed door in disbelief. She'd slammed it in his face. As if he was some kind of door-to-door salesman who didn't know when to take a hint, he thought in growing fury. So she wanted to be left alone, did she? Well, by God, she didn't have to tell him twice. He didn't push himself on any woman.

Fury and hurt clouding his judgment, he stalked down

the porch steps to the curb and climbed into his pickup without once looking back. With a savage twist, he turned the key in the ignition and tore off down the street with an angry squeal of tires. What the hell did she mean, whatever they'd had to say to each other was said last night? He'd made love to her until they were both too weak to move and he hadn't heard a single word of complaint out of her. In fact, he would have sworn she was as caught up in their loving as he was. Dammit to hell, how could he have been so wrong about her?

Scowling, he was already turning the corner, intending to head back to the *Times,* when he realized that nothing she'd said had made sense. They hadn't exchanged cross words last night. In fact the only thing they'd come close to arguing about was Jeff, and that was only because she hadn't wanted to believe that he was capable of murder. She'd been upset, but not with him. So why was she acting now like she couldn't stand the sight of him? What the hell was going on?

Replaying the entire conversation in his head a second time, he still couldn't make any sense of it. She hadn't even taken the safety chain off! She'd stood there, pale and nervous, and stared up at him through that damn crack in the door as though he was some kind of rapist who was going to force his way in and drag her down to the floor. If he hadn't known better, he would have sworn she was scared to death. But why would she be scared of him? She had to know he wouldn't harm a hair on her head—

But the bastard who had killed four women and promised her she would be his next victim would.

His hands clenched on the wheel at the thought. No! He couldn't have gotten to her so quickly. He was just being paranoid. If she'd been in trouble, she would have said something, given him some kind of sign.

Everything we had to say to each other we said last night. I told you then to leave me alone and I meant it.

Her words echoed in his head, haunting him, chilling his blood. She'd never told him to leave her alone. Never! So why would she say that unless she was trying to relay some sort of message to him, a message she couldn't just spit out because someone else was there, listening? He hadn't seen him or heard so much as a whisper of movement from the other side of the door, but suddenly he knew in his gut that she hadn't been alone and she was terrified.

God, how could he have been so blind? Swearing, fear clutching him by the throat, he jammed down on the accelerator, uncaring that he was fairly flying down a residential street as he circled the block, his only thought to get to her before it was too late. He'd kill him, he raged. He didn't care who the son of a bitch was, if he so much as touched a hair on her head, he'd kill him with his bare hands.

Caught up in the fury burning like the fires of hell deep inside him, he turned back onto her street, just in time to see her step outside onto her front porch. With Louis Vanderbilt.

"What the hell!"

Stunned, he whipped over to the curb and jerked to a stop behind a parked car six houses from her place, unable to believe his eyes. Louis Vanderbilt was her stalker? The man who had shot four women in their own homes, then walked away and left them to bleed to death? *He* was the one who was in love with Sabrina and planned to kill her because she didn't know he existed?

Dazed, he shook his head. This case was driving him nuts and twisting his thinking. Louis Vanderbilt was an old man who wouldn't hurt a flea, let alone kill anyone. Especially Sabrina. He was clearly fond of her and watched over her with an eagle eye. He would never do anything to harm her, he assured himself.

Then he saw the gun.

He only caught a flash of it, a glint of metal in the

morning sun before Louis crowded close to her, concealing the small pistol between their two bodies as he urged her toward where her Honda was parked in the driveway. Then he was pushing her through the passenger door and making her scoot over the center console to the driver's seat. Seconds later, her face as pale as death, she backed out of the driveway and drove off in the opposite direction from where Blake was parked at the curb.

He swore and just barely stopped himself from racing after her. He couldn't do that, dammit, not without taking a chance that the old man would recognize his pickup behind them and shoot her on the spot. But, God, he couldn't just sit there! Snatching up his cellular phone, he quickly called Sam Kelly, his gaze never leaving Sabrina's red Honda as it moved slowly down the street.

The unfamiliar voice that came on the line, however, didn't belong to Sam. It was a secretary who informed him that the detective was currently out of the office but expected back at any moment. Swearing, Blake identified himself. "I can't wait for him to get back. Page him if you have to, but track him down. The wrong man was arrested for the serial killings." Rattling off his cellular number, he barked, "Have him call me the second you find him. And hurry, dammit! There's not much time."

At the end of the street, Sabrina turned right, and within seconds, her Honda disappeared from view around the corner. Muttering a curse, Blake pushed the end button, tossed the phone into the passenger seat and pulled away from the curb in one smooth, quick movement. It seemed to take forever just to reach the corner.

The cross street was a main thoroughfare that ran due north and was usually busy at that hour of the day. Several cars zoomed past before it was clear enough for him to turn right as Sabrina had, and he found himself holding his breath, afraid he'd lost her. But when he turned the corner, making sure to stay a healthy distance behind the car in front of him, Sabrina was nearly a half a mile down the road, but well within sight. Sending up a silent prayer of thanks, he started after her.

His cellular rang nearly ten minutes later, cutting like a fire alarm through the tense silence that filled the cab of his truck. Never taking his eyes from the red Honda in the distance, he snatched it up.

"What the hell's going on, Blake?" Kelly demanded in his ear. "I was in a meeting with the chief when I got your message, and it was kind of hard for me to explain to him how we could have arrested the wrong man when I don't know what the devil you're talking about. What—"

"Just listen," Blake cut in, swearing as Sabrina turned at the next light and headed west. Where the hell was she going? "Jeff Harper didn't have anything to do with killing those women—he was set up by Louis Vanderbilt."

"Louis Vanderbilt?" the other man repeated in confusion. "Sabrina's neighbor? C'mon, Blake, he's old enough to be her father!"

"I don't care if he's older than dirt," Blake snapped. "Right now, he's holding a gun on her in her car and forcing her to drive west on Hildebrand."

"*What?* Hell!" Throwing questions at him, the detective determined his location, then growled, "I've got three units on the way, Blake. As soon as they get there, I want you to back off and let them handle the situation. And don't give me a hard time about this," he added quickly, anticipating an argument. "You're unarmed and a civilian. Let my men do their job and Sabrina won't get hurt."

Silence his only answer, Blake wasn't making promises he had no intention of keeping. If the bastard hurt Sabrina, he was going to tear him limb from limb. "They're turning right on State Avenue," he retorted. "It looks like they're headed for Crocker Park. Get your men over there, Kelly. Now!"

"Dammit, Blake, don't you dare go rushing in there like John Wayne—"

For an answer, Blake pushed the button to end the call and tossed the phone back into the passenger seat. When it immediately rang again, he ignored it, his gut tightening as he, too, reached the intersection with State Avenue and turned right. Crocker Park lay less than a mile down the road. A popular recreation spot for families on the weekends, it wasn't nearly as savory a place during the middle of a workday. Occasionally, you might come across a mother with young children playing on the swings, but more often than not, the only occupants of the park were people who, for whatever reason, didn't want to be seen. They sat in isolated parts of the parking lot in cars with darkened windows, doing God knows what. Drivers using State Avenue to cut through the park seldom spared them a second glance, nobody but an occasional park ranger took an interest in what was going on, and no one seemed to care.

Wishing there were more than two cars between him and Sabrina, Blake followed cautiously, checking his rearview mirror every few seconds for the police, but there was no sign of them. Dammit to hell, where were they? Any second now, Sabrina was going to be in even deeper trouble than she was now, and the only thing he had that resembled a weapon was a tire iron. And while he'd like nothing better than to brain Vanderbilt with it, it wasn't going to do a whole hell of a lot of good against a gun.

Racking his brain for a plan, he abruptly ran out of time ten seconds later. Sabrina turned into the park entrance, and there was no way he could follow her. With so little traffic, Vanderbilt would spy him immediately. Swearing, he had no choice but to drive on past the entrance.

Daring to slow to a crawl, he cast a quick look through the park entrance as he passed and saw the red Honda disappear into some low-hanging bushes near the creek that marked the park's western boundary. When he was a teenager, it had been a popular necking spot for teenagers. Now it was deserted, with the nearest car nearly a hundred yards away. Vanderbilt could do anything he liked to Sabrina there, out of sight of prying eyes, and the few other occupants of the park wouldn't notice a thing.

God, he had to do something! The police were never going to get there in time if he didn't.

His heart slamming against his ribs, he waited until he reached the far end of the park and pulled into the parking lot of the church across the street. The need to hurry ate at him from the inside out, but this was no time to go rushing blindly in like a fool. He had to think! Grabbing the tire iron from behind his seat, he was just stepping from the truck when his cellular rang again. Muttering a curse, he almost ignored it. He had to get to Sabrina, dammit! But if it was Kelly, he needed to let him know exactly where Vanderbilt was holding her.

Answering it, he said, "Kelly? I'm at the church parking lot at the end of the park. Do you know where the old lover's lane is?"

"At the south end of the park?" the other man asked. "Opposite the main entrance?"

"Yeah, that's the one. Vanderbilt's got Sabrina back there in the bushes. I'm going in."

"Dammit, Blake, I told you to sit tight!" Kelly snapped. "My men'll be there any second. You rush in there now, you just might get Sabrina killed."

"And if I don't, that just might get her killed, too. Don't ask me to sit on my hands on this, Sam. I can't. I'm going in, and there's not a damn thing you can do to stop me."

"The hell I can't. I'll arrest your ass—"

Without another word, Blake ended the call and shut off the phone's power. Stepping out of his truck, the tire iron clutched in his hand, he soundlessly eased the door shut. Across the street, the park was deserted except for the handful of cars parked in isolated spots under the trees. The freeway was on the far side of the creek and screened out by the thick stand of oaks there, and downtown was just over the hill to the south. Still, if you hadn't known better, you could have easily sworn you were miles from the hustle and bustle of the state's third largest city.

The quiet grating on his nerves and setting his heart thumping in his chest, Blake tightened his grip on the tire iron and jogged across the street and down into the creek bed that meandered all the way to the spot where Vanderbilt had Sabrina hidden among the trees. There, out of sight of the park's occupants and anyone else who might be watching, he began to run.

Chapter 12

"This is all your fault," Louis lashed out as he forced Sabrina out of the car and dragged her through the bushes to a small clearing that was totally cut off from the rest of the park. "*I loved you!* Do you know how many women I've said that to in my lifetime? Just you." His eyes tortured behind the lenses of his glasses, he glared at her accusingly. "You're the only one. The only one I ever wanted, the only one I ever dreamed about, the only one I wanted to share my life with. But you didn't even know I was alive."

Her gaze locked on the gun he was waving wildly about, fear churning like a storm in her stomach, Sabrina struggled not to panic. If she could just get him to drop his guard—and the gun—for a second, she might be able to escape into the bushes and lose him. It was a long shot, but the only one she had. No one knew she was here or in danger. If she was going to get out of this alive, she had to do it all by herself.

Facing him in the middle of the clearing, she fought to

remain calm, but it wasn't easy, not when she could see the madness in his eyes. "That's not true," she said quietly. "I always knew you were just next door if I needed you—"

"But you never did," he cut in harshly. "The only thing you ever needed me for was to fix a leaky faucet or give your car a jump when your battery was low. You didn't need my arms about you or the security of knowing I was there beside you in the middle of the night. You didn't need anything but your job."

"I had to work, Louis. I have bills to pay just like everybody else."

"But you didn't have to love it!" Anger tightening every line of his body, he said bitterly, "You didn't have to drop everything and go running to it in the middle of the night just because some idiot beat up his girlfriend or a convenience store was held up. You shouldn't have been darting around town chasing stories at all hours of the day and night, putting yourself in danger and worrying me to death. You should have been home, with me, where you belong, talking about our future, planning children. I'm not too old to have children, you know. I used to dream about the babies I would give you...."

A loving smile playing about his thin mouth, he described the children he'd planned to have with her, the two boys and a girl that she would stay home with and take care of like a good, dutiful wife and mother, and Sabrina could do nothing but stare at him. How could she have lived next door to this man for years and not realized that he was totally and completely out of his mind? How could she have been so blind?

"Louis..."

He blinked, his expression changing from dreamy to angry resentment in a split second. "But we're never going to have those babies, are we? We're never going to have anything. Not children. Not a home together. Not a future. Because of you.''

Bitterness twisted his mouth. "God, what a fool I've been. You don't want me. You never did. You never will. All you want is Nickels."

She didn't have to justify herself to him, didn't owe him any explanation about her private life. But he was so close to snapping, she had to do something before he went completely ballistic. "Blake and I are friends—"

He snorted. "Is that why your face lights up like a Christmas tree every time he comes anywhere near you? Damn you, I'm not blind!" His thin face flushed with fury, he turned on her, brandishing the gun in her face, the haunted look in his eyes wilder than ever. "You love him," he snarled. "Oh, you might not think you do, but I know you. You don't give your heart lightly, and you've given it to Nickels. And that can't be tolerated. Not after all that I've done for you."

What had he done for her except kill four innocent women? she wondered in confusion. The coppery taste of fear thick in her throat, she said, "Please, Louis, you're twisting this all out of proportion—"

"So this is all my fault? Is that what you're saying?"

"No!" she said hastily as his silky tone slid over her, making her skin crawl. "I'm not saying anything of the kind. We're just both upset. Why don't we go somewhere and get a cup of coffee and discuss this rationally? I'm sure we could work it out if we could just—"

The sudden snapping of a branch in the bushes was as loud as a gunshot. For a second, neither of them moved, then quick as a striking snake, Louis whirled, his eyes crazed as he searched the surrounding brush for an intruder. "He's out there," he said, half to himself. "I can feel him. Go away, Nickels! Leave us alone!" And with no more warning than that, he fired into the bushes.

Sabrina screamed. "Louis, no!"

Hidden in the thick undergrowth, Blake threw himself behind a tree just as the bullet whizzed past his shoulder. Cursing himself for not watching where he was putting his feet, he leaned against the tree, waiting for his heart rate to slow. He didn't think for a second that Louis had seen him—the surrounding brush was too dense and he'd been careful to keep out of sight as he'd worked his way toward where he could hear them talking—but the old man was obviously paranoid where he was concerned. And not so crazy after all if he knew that he would eventually come after him for Sabrina.

Chancing a quick look around the oak, he spied Louis standing with his back to Sabrina, his face twisted with fury and madness as he studied the surrounding brush off to Blake's right. For the moment, at least, he was distracted and didn't even realize that Sabrina was slowly backing away from him. If Blake could keep the old man's attention away from her long enough, she just might have a chance to slip into the trees and hide.

Glancing around, he found the fallen branch he'd stepped on and picked it up. Barely two feet long and not quite as thick as his wrist, it was half-rotten but would still make a nice loud crash when it hit the ground. Silently praying that Sabrina was on her toes and ready for anything, he hefted it by one end and tossed it far to the right of him. As it came down through the trees, it sounded, at least for a few seconds, like the cavalry was breaking through the underbrush.

As jumpy as a first-time bank robber, Louis whirled, his eyes wild as he scanned the bushes for a threat he couldn't see. "Go away!" he cried, and fired wildly into the trees.

Blake didn't wait to see more. "Run, Sabrina!" he yelled, and dove into the thick stand of oaks off to his left in an effort to draw the old man's anger away from Sabrina to himself.

From the corner of his eye, Blake saw Sabrina take off

at a dead run, but she'd barely reached the edge of the clearing when Vanderbilt realized that he was losing her. "No!" His scream echoing eerily through the trees, he spun on his heel to find her racing for the concealment of the bushes. Snarling, he lifted his pistol and fired just as she threw herself into the trees.

"You bastard!" Rage roaring in Blake's ears, fury blinding him to everything but the need to kill the old man with his own hands, he threw the tire iron and hit him right on his wrist. The gun went flying, and before he could do anything but cry out in pain, Blake was on him.

"You miserable piece of trash! If you hurt her, I'll make you wish you'd never been born."

Out of his head, his only thought to get the gun, Louis was stronger—and wilier—than he looked. Kicking and scratching and ranting like a wild man, he slipped out of Blake's hold and scrambled for the pistol, which had fallen under a bush at the edge of the clearing. His breathing ragged, sweat dripping down into his eyes, Blake launched himself at him, grabbing him just as the old man's hand closed around the barrel of the gun.

"Drop it!" he growled, jamming one hand under Louis's chin while the other locked around his wrist. "Drop it or I swear I'll put my fist through your face."

Past reason, Louis only grunted, his lips drawn back in a snarl as he fought to hang on to the gun. Swearing, Blake rolled over the ground with him and finally came up on top as sirens wailed in the distance. With a vicious oath, he slammed the old man's hand down on a rock. Just that quickly, the fight was over. The pistol fell from his grasp, and in the next instant, Blake had it and was towering over him.

"Just give me an excuse to pull the trigger," he said coldly, pointing the gun right at his head. "Please...just one. That's all I need."

From behind him, there was a crashing through the underbrush, but Blake never took his eyes from Louis, who didn't even try to get up but lay in the dirt like a beaten old man. "Don't do it, Blake," Sam Kelly said as he and four uniformed officers pushed their way into the clearing. "He's not worth it. Let us take over from here."

"Only if you promise to damn well keep him away from Sabrina," he said coldly. "He's scared her for the last time."

"He won't be scaring her or any other woman for the next thirty or forty years by the time we get through with him," Sam assured him confidently as he stepped to his side and took the gun while two of the uniformed officers jerked Vanderbilt to his feet and slapped handcuffs on him. Glancing around while the old man was read his rights, he frowned. "Where's Sabrina?"

Blake started toward the thick stand of mountain laurels where he'd seen Sabrina dive for cover. "Hiding over here in the bushes unless she ran to get help. I distracted Vanderbilt long enough for her to get away, and that's the last I've seen of her."

Half expecting her to come bursting out of the undergrowth and throw herself into his arms any second, he pushed his way through the bushes. "Sabrina? Honey? It's okay, you can come out now," he called, but his only answer was the whisper of the wind through the leaves. Uneasiness curled into his stomach like a damp fog. "Sabrina?"

He heard it then, a soft moan that could have been his imagination...except that Kelly heard it, too. He saw the other man stiffen, then they were both fighting through the bushes, searching. Ten minutes later, Blake found her. Sitting on the ground, her back propped up against a tree, she was as pale as death and covered in her own blood. She'd been shot.

Later, Blake didn't remember Kelly calling for an ambulance. All he saw was Sabrina's bloodless face, the total lack of color in her cheeks, the pain that darkened her eyes. She stirred at his hoarse cry, a weak smile pushing up one corner of her mouth as he whipped off his shirt and dropped down beside her to press the cloth to the ugly exit wound in her left shoulder. "I-I'm all r-right," she whispered.

"Shut up." Rage tearing at him, his fingers shaking with fear, all he could think of was that the son of a bitch had shot her in the back. In the back, goddammit! And so close to her heart that if he'd hit her two inches lower, he would have killed her instantly. And she hadn't said a word. While he'd been fighting the bastard for the gun, she'd been quietly bleeding to death. Dammit to hell, hadn't anyone thought to call for an ambulance?

"Blake, the ambulance is here," Kelly said grimly, touching him on the shoulder. "You've got to let the paramedics take over from here."

Another voice, a woman's, said firmly, "You've done all you can for her, sir. Let us do our jobs and she's got a good chance of pulling through this."

He didn't want to step back, to trust her care to anyone but himself, but suddenly, there were hands to take over for him and keep pressure on the wound, and he was in the way. He stumbled back, his eyes burning with emotion as he watched the paramedics work over her with sure, skilled hands. He couldn't lose her, he thought fiercely. But God, how could she lose so much blood and still live?

"Come on," Sam told him as Sabrina was loaded onto a stretcher and quickly transported to the waiting ambulance. "I'll give you a ride to the hospital. You're in no shape to drive."

He would have preferred to ride in the ambulance, but there was no room, and time was at a premium. Nodding, he said tersely, "Let's go."

With sirens blaring and lights flashing, they went

through every light with the ambulance. His face haggard, his gaze locked on the window in the back door of the ambulance, where he could see the paramedics working fiercely over Sabrina, Blake never heard Sam speak to him or try to assure him that Sabrina was in good hands. Numb, fear gripping his heart and squeezing painfully, he prayed like he had never prayed in his life.

They reached the hospital in record time, but it seemed to take forever. Then Sabrina was whisked away from him, upstairs to surgery, and all he could do was wait. It wasn't something he was particularly good at. Kelly had to leave and get back to the station, but he promised to return when he could. Pacing restlessly, unable even to think about striking up a conversation with the three other occupants of the waiting area, he watched every tick of the clock and never felt so alone in his life. What was taking so long?

"Blake? Are you doing okay, son? I got here as soon as I heard."

Glancing up at the familiar sound of his grandfather's voice, he blinked as if coming out of a daze. "Pop! What are you doing here?"

"Detective Kelly called me," he said gruffly. "I figured you needed me."

He had, and he hadn't even known it. Emotion clogging his throat, he hugged the old man tight. "I can't lose her, Pop. I love her."

"Well, of course you do," his grandfather murmured affectionately, returning his hug. "You just now figuring that out?"

Blake gave a choked chuckle and blinked back the sting of unexpected tears as he drew back. "Yeah, I guess I am. I don't even know how it happened. I certainly wasn't looking to get involved with anyone so soon, especially after Trina."

With a click of his tongue and wave of his bony hand, the old man dismissed his ex-girlfriend as easily as if she'd been nothing more than a piece of fluff. "I never met the woman, but I could have told you she wasn't the gal for you. Not after you went with her for four years without even giving her a ring or anything. A man doesn't need that kind of time to decide if he's found the right woman— not if he really cares about her. Why, with your grandmother, I knew in the first week. For the next fifty-three years I never looked at another woman."

"Those were different times, Pop."

"Hogwash," he snorted. "Love was love, and it hasn't changed. Your grandmother didn't just fall into my lap, you know. She had plans and was all set to go to some fancy college in New York when we met. And let me tell you, it took some pretty fast talking on my part to convince her that she didn't want to go anywhere without me. But I knew as soon as I saw her that she was what I wanted when I hadn't even known I was looking. Anyone with eyes can see you feel the same way about Sabrina. When it's right, you just know."

Blake couldn't argue with that. He'd come to San Antonio with a bruised heart and ego, determined not to look twice at anything in a skirt. So much for his fine resolve, he thought ruefully. One look at Sabrina, and he'd gone down for the count like a boxer with a glass jaw. No one, not even Trina, had ever dominated his thoughts the way she had, distracting him at the damndest times.

And then when he'd seen her in Louis's clutches and realized that he could lose her before he ever had a chance to tell her what she meant to him, he'd wanted to kill Vanderbilt with his bare hands. The strength of his rage still stunned him. Because of his job, he saw violence and its aftermath every day of the week; he would have sworn he just wasn't capable of that kind of fury. He'd been wrong.

God, he loved her. So much that it scared him. He wanted to spend the rest of his life making her laugh, loving her, going to bed beside her and waking up with her in his arms. But even if she was able to pull through the surgery and make it, he might not get the chance.

Sinking into a nearby chair, he said, "Try telling Sabrina that. Even if I can get her to admit that she loves me, she's got this thing about marriage. Her mother and grandmother have walked down the aisle more times than Elizabeth Taylor, and she's convinced she just doesn't have what it takes to make a marriage work."

"So change her mind," his grandfather said simply. "If she loves you, she trusts you. And that's what marriage is all about, son. Love and trust. Not even the strongest attraction can work without that."

He made it sound so easy. But as an hour passed, then another, and people in the waiting room came and went and he and his grandfather still waited, he couldn't worry about the future when he didn't even know if Sabrina was going to make it through the rest of the day. What was taking so long? Unable to just sit there, he prowled around the Spartan room, watching minutes turn to hours, and had to fight the need to throw something.

Finally, three hours after Sabrina was rushed upstairs to surgery, her doctor, still in his green scrubs, stepped into the doorway of the waiting room. "Mr. Nickels?" he said as Blake turned toward him expectantly. "I'm Dr. Richardson. I understand you're Sabrina Jones's fiancé?"

Blake nodded, promising himself that the small lie would be the truth before too much longer. "How is she? What took so long? Is she conscious? When can I see her?"

He threw questions at the doctor like darts, not giving him time to answer one before he thought of another. Laughing, Richardson held up a hand in protest. "Hold it! Let me tell you what I know, then you can ask any questions you want." His twinkling eyes turning serious, he said, "Sabrina's a lucky young woman, though I doubt she'll feel like one for the next couple of days. That bullet came awfully close to her heart.''

Blake paled. ''But she's going to make it?''

''Oh, yes. She lost a lot of blood, and she's going to have to take it easy for a while, but she's young and strong. Barring any unexpected complications, I don't see any reason why she shouldn't live to see her great-grandchildren.''

Deep inside, the knot that had tied itself around his heart loosened. She was going to be okay. He felt his grandfather's hand on his shoulder and laughed shakily. ''Did you hear that, Pop? She's going to make it.''

''I never doubted it,'' the old man said, squeezing his shoulder reassuringly. ''She may not be big as a minute, but she's tough. I knew it the second I laid eyes on her.''

''When can I see her?'' Blake asked the doctor. ''I won't stay long,'' he assured him when the other man hesitated. ''I just need to see her, touch her. Two minutes, tops. I promise.''

''She's still in recovery. She won't even know you're there.''

''That's okay. *I* will. C'mon, doctor. If she won't know I'm there, what harm can it do?''

''All right,'' he said reluctantly. ''But only *one* minute, and not a second over. Ms. Jones might be tough, but a gunshot wound isn't something you bounce back from the next day. Once you've seen for yourself that she's really still breathing, I want you out of here for the rest of the day. Got it?''

Blake nodded. ''One minute, no longer. Scout's honor.''

He would have agreed to just about anything short of murder to get within touching distance of her, but once he was in the recovery room, standing at Sabrina's bedside, he didn't know how he was ever going to leave her. God, she was pale! And so still. The sheet covering her barely moved as she breathed. His throat tight, he reached out and closed his fingers around her limp ones. She never moved.

"Hang in there, sweetheart," he whispered roughly. "You hear me? You're going to be all right."

"You have to leave now, Mr. Nickels," the recovery-room nurse said quietly from behind him. "Dr. Richardson said one minute."

"I know. I know. I'm going."

But he didn't. Not for another thirty seconds. Not until he took one last long look at her, committing every inch of her to memory. It was all he would have of her for the next fifteen or twenty hours. God, how was he going to stand it?

Turning away, he growled, "I'll be back," then walked out the door. It was the hardest thing he'd ever done.

Sabrina shifted slightly in her hospital bed, only to suck in a sharp breath as her shoulder seemed to burn. The doctor had given her something for the pain, but it only made it bearable as long as she was relatively still. Whenever she inadvertently moved the wrong way, she paid for it.

Sweat breaking out on her brow, she squeezed her eyes shut and waited for the throbbing to ease, silently cursing her own weakness. She didn't have time to be laid up, she told herself. Not now. Not when the biggest story of the decade was wrapping up and she had the inside scoop. She had to get out of here and over to the *Daily Record.* Nearly twenty-four hours had already passed since Louis had deliberately shot her in the back, and if she didn't get her version of the story out soon, it was going to be old news and worthless.

Fighting pain and exhaustion, she'd read both papers from front to back page, cursing what she was missing. After Louis's arrest, the police had searched his house, where a diary was found hidden under the mattress of his bed. In it, he'd described how he'd met his victims at the bookstore and grocery store, even the flower shop and a singles' club, then proceeded to make friends with each of them. And when they didn't fall in love with him, he killed them.

With her out of commission, Fitz had assigned someone to follow up the story—a cub who had done a decent enough job and who would, with time, develop his own style and ask all the right questions. But for now, he'd missed more than a few pertinent details, which made Sabrina itch to get out of bed and reclaim her rightful spot in the pecking order. He didn't do the job like she did and wasn't even in the same ballpark, let alone the same league, with Blake.

Her heart constricting just at the thought of him, she felt stupid tears well in her eyes and quickly blinked them away. She would not, she told herself fiercely, cry over the man. Just because he was too busy writing up the rest of the news about Louis to come and see her didn't mean she was going to get all watery-eyed. He'd get around to visiting her eventually. And when he did, she'd tell him what she thought of a man who took advantage of a woman with a bullet in her shoulder just to win a bet.

It wasn't as if she cared about him, she thought as a hurt ten times more powerful than the one in her shoulder lodged in her heart. Okay, so maybe she had let him get to her just a bit. She wasn't made of stone. The man was damn attractive and the kind of lover that most women would sell their soul for. If her heart wanted more from him than a few nights, a few weeks, in his bed, then no one would ever know that but her.

Staring blindly out the window as the day began to fade, she swallowed the lump in her throat. She wanted to go home. She knew it was too soon—she couldn't possibly take care of herself yet—but she needed some time to herself. She had a private room, but people still came and went at their own discretion, often without bothering to knock. If she could get home, at least she could cry in peace without anyone walking in on her.

As if on cue, the door opened behind her, but she didn't spare so much as a glance for her visitor. Meals were delivered like clockwork, and she'd heard the familiar squeaky wheels of the food cart as it was pushed down the hall ten minutes ago.

"You can just put it on the table," she said quietly. "I'm not very hungry. Maybe I'll eat it later."

"You sure?" a teasing male voice asked from the doorway. "I went all the way downtown to get you a George's special, and even had the nurse heat it up in the microwave in the staff break room. It'd be a shame to waste it."

"Blake!" Startled, she turned too quickly, only to groan as her wound clenched like a sprung trap. "Oh, God!"

Cursing himself, Blake swore and hurried to her side. "I'm sorry! Dammit, I should have said something, but I wanted to surprise you. I guess I did." Tossing the foam container of Mexican food on the bedside table, he leaned over her worriedly and gently brushed her hair back from her face. "Are you okay? Damn, you're as white as the sheets. Maybe I should call the nurse."

"No!" She didn't want the nurse. She didn't want anyone but him and it scared her silly. Her shoulder was on fire, the pain raw and biting, but all she could think about was leaning into his strong, sure hand and letting him make everything feel all better. But she couldn't do that. Her emotions were too volatile, her need for him too strong. And there would come a day in the not too distant future when he wouldn't be there for her. As much as she wanted to, she couldn't let herself depend on him.

Blinking back foolish tears, she had to force herself to pull back slightly. "I'm fine," she said thickly. "Really. Just a little sore. The doctor warned me I should move in slow motion for a while. I just forgot."

Not sure he believed her, Blake stared down at her searchingly. The last twenty or so hours had been the longest of his life. He'd lost track of the number of times he'd started for the hospital, his only thought to see her, when he'd suddenly remembered that she needed to rest, to recoup her strength. So he'd stayed away and filled the time haunting the police station and writing stories that only made sense by the grace of God, unable to concentrate on much of anything but Sabrina.

She was okay. He could see that now for himself, but it was going to be months, maybe years, before he'd be able to push the image from his mind of her lying in the bushes, covered in her own blood. Just barely resisting the urge to snatch her close, he had to content himself with taking her hand instead.

"You, slow down?" he teased. "Because of a bullet? I would have sworn that it would take nothing less than getting run over by a freight train to take the starch out of you, Jones. In fact, I expected to come in here and find you pounding out the story on a laptop."

"Don't think I haven't thought about it," she retorted sassily. "I saw your byline—it was good. But my version will be better, so don't go making the mistake of thinking I'm out of the running to win our bet, Nickels. This is just a temporary setback." Glancing down at their joined hands, she frowned in bemusement. "What are you doing?"

He grinned and tightened his fingers around hers. "Holding your hand. You got a problem with that, Jones? Because if you do, you'd better speak up. From now on, I plan to touch you every chance I get."

Her eyes widened at that, but she quickly recovered. "I might have something to say about that, Nickels."

"You're damn right you've got something to say about it. I'm hoping it's 'yes.'" His smile fading, he said gruffly, "I thought I'd lost you, sweetheart. Dr. Richardson assured me after the operation that you were going to be fine, but you'd lost so much blood—''

"You were here?"

"Hell, yes, I was here!" he said, surprised. "Where else would I have been? Over at the *Times* writing up the story while you were fighting for your life?"

"I don't know. I didn't know—"

"Because you were still out cold when they let me in to see you," he said. "Richardson gave me one minute with you, then threw me out of here. Honey, I've talked to your nurses at least six times today. I couldn't come visit you until Richardson gave me the okay."

"Oh. I thought…" She swallowed, shaking her head as foolish tears stung her eyes. Obviously what she'd thought didn't need to be repeated. Of course he would check on her and make sure she was all right. He was a caring man—she'd seen the way he looked out for his grandfather and knew from firsthand experience just how gentle he could be. He wouldn't dump a wounded woman on the hospital steps, then head for work as if nothing had happened. "Forget I said anything. I guess I was just feeling sorry for myself."

"Considering what you've been through, I'd say you were entitled," he replied. "I guess you heard Vanderbilt confessed."

"No! When?"

"After his diary was found. He won't ever hurt you again, honey," he assured her quietly. "In fact, Kelly said the D.A. is going to make sure he spends the rest of his life behind bars."

Relief coursed through her, but the news brought her little joy. The women Louis killed weren't the only ones who lost their lives—he'd lost his, too, and she couldn't help but feel sorry for him.

"I'm just glad it's over." She sighed. "Maybe now life can get back to normal."

"Actually, I was thinking you should take a vacation when you get out of here and just forget all this for a while. It'll do you good to get away."

Surprised, she smiled faintly. "There's the small matter of my job, Nickels. If I left now, you'd steal all my readers while I was gone, then I wouldn't have a job to come back to."

"Then I guess I'll just have to go with you. Tell me where you want to go and I'll take care of the reservations."

Stunned, Sabrina just stared at him, sure he was teasing. But his eyes were dark with an emotion that set her heart tripping, and she'd never seen him more serious. Suddenly breathless, she said huskily, "You want to tell me what's going on here, Blake? I think I missed something."

For an answer, he drew her hand to his chest and pressed it to his heart. "You didn't miss anything, sweetheart. I just never asked a woman to marry me before and I'm not doing a very good job of it."

Sabrina couldn't have been more stunned if he'd asked her to do a striptease in front of the Alamo. He wanted to marry her. Her heart turned over at the thought, joy flooding her. Then she remembered, and the smile blooming on her face vanished.

"Blake, you know how I feel about marriage—"

He cut her off with a kiss, stealing her protests and her thoughts before she had a chance to put up her guard. Softly, sweetly wooing, his mouth played with hers, gentling her, seducing her until her head fell weakly back against her pillow and her blood hummed in her veins. And when he finally let her up for air, it was to discover that he'd stretched out with her on the bed on her good side, uncaring who might walk in.

"Blake, please..."

"Oh, I plan to, Jones," he groaned, nuzzling her ear. "Just as soon as you're strong enough, I plan to please you until neither one of us can move.'' Lifting his head, he gazed down into her eyes. ''I love you, sweetheart. You've got to know that.''

She did. Somewhere deep inside, she'd known it the first time they'd made love. She'd felt it in his touch, his kiss, seen it in the heat of his eyes and recognized the same feelings in herself.

The truth hit her from the blind side, shaking her to the core. No, she thought, swallowing a sob. She couldn't love him. She could care for him, want him, need him more than she needed her next breath, but she wouldn't, couldn't let herself love him. Pain squeezing her heart, she pressed trembling fingers to his mouth. ''Please, don't say that,'' she whispered in a voice that had a tendency to crack. ''It can't change anything.''

''Honey, it changes everything if you love me, too,'' he argued earnestly. ''If you don't, tell me now. I won't bother you anymore.''

One word, a simple no, from her and he would walk out, just like that. He wouldn't pressure her, not if she didn't love him. He'd laid his heart on the line, and the next move was hers. If she couldn't return his feelings, he'd wish her a nice life and that would be it. They would be finished.

It would come to that eventually when he found out he couldn't change her mind about marriage, but she wasn't ready to say goodbye to him. Please, dear God, not yet. And what would it hurt to tell him, anyway? she reasoned. It wouldn't change anything, not in the long run.

''It isn't that I don't love you—''

''Then you do?''

''Yes, but—''

''I don't care about the buts,'' he said quickly, kissing her fiercely. His grin broad, he cupped her face in his hands and kissed her again. ''You're not your mother or your grandmother. Just because they made mistakes doesn't mean you will.''

''I already have,'' she reminded him. ''Or have you forgotten Jeff?''

He dismissed that with a flick of his hand. ''Harper's not even worth bringing up. You married a man you didn't have a damn thing in common with. The two of you together were doomed from the start, and I certainly don't blame you for having the good sense to quit beating a dead horse. I am not Harper.''

She had to laugh at that. ''No, you're certainly not.'' He was as different from Jeff as West Texas was from the Gulf Coast. ''But there was a time I thought I loved Jeff, too.''

''As much as you love me?''

Caught in the trap of his eyes, she couldn't deny him the truth. ''No,'' she said huskily. ''I never loved anyone as much as I love you.''

''Then listen to your heart, honey. We were made for each other—you know we were. We think alike, work alike at the same jobs, we even like the same restaurants. We respect each other and love each other. With so much going for us, how can we fail?''

She wanted to believe him, God knew she did. And her heart was on his side—it had been for weeks now. She only had to look into his eyes and feel his hands on her to know that if there was one man on this earth she could spend the rest of her life with, it was Blake Nickels.

Knowing she was going down for the count, she grasped at one last feeble straw. ''What about your family? Your parents are expecting you to eventually come to your senses and go into politics, and I just don't think I'm cut out for that kind of life. I would ask too many questions of the wrong people or say the wrong thing and embarrass the country—''

Stunned, he eased her back into his arms, chuckling

softly. "Sweetheart, I've found my niche in life, and it's right here. My parents know and accept that. And my grandfather adores you. If he were twenty years younger and you were thirty years older, I'd have some real competition on my hands."

He'd shot down her last argument, and they both knew it. Dragging her hand to his heart, he asked solemnly, "Will you marry me, Sabrina Jones? I'm crazy about you and want to spend the rest of my life with you."

Tears spilling over her lashes, all her doubts swept away by a tide of love so strong that it seemed to steal her breath along with her heart, she grinned up at him. "I think I should warn you that I intend to keep working for the *Record.* Do you think you can handle competition from your wife?"

His eyes flaring with heat, he chuckled. "Jones, haven't you figured it out yet? I can handle anything you can dish out."

"We'll see about that, Nickels," she retorted. Sliding her arm around his neck, she pressed a teasing kiss to his mouth. "If I remember correctly, we still have a little matter of a bet to settle. Just because we're getting married doesn't mean I'm going to let you off the hook. I plan to beat you soundly."

He laughed, delighted with her, and pulled her close for a deeper, hotter kiss. He could see already that the next forty or fifty years were going to be very interesting. He could hardly wait.

*   *   *   *   *

Silhouette's newest series

YOURS TRULY

Love when you least expect it.

Where the written word plays a vital role in uniting couples—you're guaranteed a fun and exciting read every time!

Look for Marie Ferrarella's upcoming Yours Truly, *Traci on the Spot*, in March 1997.

Here's a special sneak preview....

COMING NEXT MONTH

#769 RENEGADE'S REDEMPTION—Lindsay Longford
Royal Gaines was on the edge. Why else would he agree to track down some lowlife's ex-wife and kid...for a price? But when he located innocent Elly Malloy and her adorable son, he realized they'd all been had. Now he would do anything to protect them...and redeem himself in their eyes.

#770 SURRENDER IN SILK—Susan Mallery
Seven years ago Zach Jones trained Jamie Sanders to survive in a man's world. And she'd learned well, becoming the best spy in the business. Now she wanted a normal life, wanted to feel like a *real* woman. But could the only man she'd ever loved see her as wife material?

#771 BRIDE OF THE SHEIKH—Alexandra Sellers
Minutes from becoming a newlywed, Alinor Brooke was kidnapped from the altar—by her *ex*-husband! Sheikh Kavian Durran claimed they were still married, that Alinor had ruthlessly deserted *him* years ago. But Alinor remembered differently, despite Kavian's claims. And then the truth became startlingly clear....

#772 FRAMED—Karen Leabo
Detective Kyle Branson was playing with fire. He'd grown too close to suspected murderess Jess Robinson, and now his job—his very life—was on the line. Because though he believed in Jess's innocence, he couldn't deny that her closely guarded secrets threatened them both.

#773 A CHILD OF HIS OWN—Nancy Morse
Though Dory McBride was wary of rugged drifter Ben Stone, she hired him as her handyman. There was something about his soulful expression that had her aching to heal his lonely heart. But the closer he grew to Dory and her young son, the more she suspected Ben's true motives for entering her life.

#774 DARE TO REMEMBER—Debra Cowan
Devon Landry thought she'd put her dad's death—and a broken engagement—behind her. Until she learned the images stirring in her mind were actual *memories*...of her father's murder! Lead investigator Mace Garrett knew he had his work cut out for him—especially when he learned the star witness was the woman who'd thrown him over!